## Praise for Shanora Williams

### *Beautiful Broken Love*

"Williams shows herself to be deft at narrating . . . with fully fleshed-out characters whose anxieties and actions feel true to life. She alternates teary moments, which might evoke Emily Henry, with sizzling sex scenes and charming dates. A sports romance that captures the highs and lows of the game of love."

—*Kirkus Reviews* (starred review)

"An impressively well written, authentically original, emotionally engaging read from cover to cover . . . Author Shanora Williams once again demonstrates her extraordinary talents as a storyteller."

—*Midwest Book Review*

### *Wanting Mr. Cane*

"A smoldering love story that will melt the screen right off your phone! Five forbidden stars!"

—Sierra Simone, *USA Today* bestselling author

"A scrumptious morsel of forbidden love dusted in sugary, sexy urgency. This story had me hungry for more, long after I turned the last page."

—Dylan Allen, *USA Today* bestselling author

### *The Perfect Ruin*

"A shocking, sensual thriller."

—Tarryn Fisher, *New York Times* bestselling author

"Twisty and impossible to put down! 10/10, would recommend."

—Claire Contreras, *New York Times* bestselling author

"I was hooked from the very first twist."

—Alessandra Torre, *New York Times* bestselling author of *Every Last Secret*

"With diabolical turns and surprises at every corner, it's an ideal summer read."

—*Booklist* (starred review)

"Williams is an award-winning author of romance and suspense novels; her tale of revenge will find an easy spot in fiction collections. Tailored for book clubs and for those who like to read about the sleazy side of rich elites."

—*Library Journal*

## *The Other Mistress*

"Fans of *The Wife Between Us*, by Greer Hendricks and Sarah Pekkanen, won't be able to put this one down."

—*Booklist*

"A fast-paced psychological trip with a climax that will shock the most voracious readers. Recommended for fans of Alyssa Cole, Liv Constantine, and Megan Goldin."

—*Library Journal*

# SWEET LITTLE HEARTS

# OTHER TITLES BY SHANORA WILLIAMS

## Ward Duet

*The Man I Can't Have*

*The Man I Need*

## Cane Series

*Wanting Mr. Cane*

*Breaking Mr. Cane*

*Loving Mr. Cane*

*Being Mrs. Cane*

## Nora Heat Collection

*Dirty Little Secret*

*Caress*

*Crave*

*My Professor*

## Stand-Alones

*Bad for Me*

*Coach Me*

*Temporary Boyfriend*

*My Fiancé's Brother*

*Doomsday Love*

*Until the Last Breath*

*Beautiful Broken Love*

## Series

*Mr. Black Duet*

*FireNine Series*

*Ace Crow Duet*

*Venom Trilogy*

## Thrillers

*The Perfect Ruin*

*The Wife Before*

*The Other Mistress*

*The Bitter Truth*

*Whispers of the Lake*

*Most of these titles are available in Kindle Unlimited.*

*Visit http://www.shanorawilliams.com for more information.*

# SWEET LITTLE HEARTS

SHANORA WILLIAMS

This is a work of fiction. Names, characters, organizations, places, events, and incidents are either products of the author's imagination or are used fictitiously. Otherwise, any resemblance to actual persons, living or dead, is purely coincidental.

Text copyright © 2025 by Shanora Williams
All rights reserved.

No part of this book may be reproduced, or stored in a retrieval system, or transmitted in any form or by any means, electronic, mechanical, photocopying, recording, or otherwise, without express written permission of the publisher.

Published by Montlake, Seattle
www.apub.com

Amazon, the Amazon logo, and Montlake are trademarks of Amazon.com, Inc., or its affiliates.

EU product safety contact:
Amazon Media EU S. à r.l.
38, avenue John F. Kennedy, L-1855 Luxembourg
amazonpublishing-gpsr@amazon.com

ISBN-13: 9781662533242 (paperback)
ISBN-13: 9781662533235 (digital)

Cover design by Hang Le
Cover image: © Crissy1982 / Getty; © Kisialiou Yury, © Vilor, © KresnaBaron, © Michael Kraus, © MeSamong / Shutterstock

Printed in the United States of America

*To anyone learning how to be vulnerable and soft after years of hardness . . .*
*you deserve to be loved.*

# AUTHOR'S NOTE

Dear Reader,

Seeing as *Sweet Little Hearts* is the title for this novel, I have to let you in on a little secret: *Not everything that happens in this book is sweet.*

Though this is a story about a struggling single father / widower, a nanny, and an adorable four-year-old overcoming life's obstacles, there may be a few triggers involved, so I feel ever so inclined to give you a heads-up. Possible triggers include grief, discussions about a deceased loved one, stalking, harassment, and verbal/physical abuse (not from our hero).

I'm all about protecting mental health, so if any of the above trigger you in any way, please take caution. If you choose to proceed, I hope you enjoy Javier and Octavia's story!

*Sweet Little Hearts* is a spin-off novel that can be read on its own. If you'd like a better understanding of the characters and want to learn more about how their story began, I highly encourage you to meet them in *Beautiful Broken Love.*

# ONE

## OCTAVIA

When I was little, I was a firm believer that love expressed in any form was amazing . . . until I was introduced to the toxic side of it.

At first, you don't even realize the harm. You ignore the red flags and the subtle twists in the pit of your stomach warning you that something isn't quite right. Then the person claiming to love you does something unforgivable, and you're left with no choice but to walk away from it.

It's heartbreaking when all you've ever wanted is to love and be loved.

To feel safe and cared for.

I couldn't help thinking, after all I'd endured, is it even worth it to be in a committed relationship? Is it worth putting trust into more people, just to either lose them or be hurt by them?

In the end, I came to my own conclusion: Falling in *love* had to be a joke. Because if love was serious, it wouldn't have done me so dirty.

# TWO

## OCTAVIA

"Are you nervous?" Davina's voice poured out of my car's speakers as I gave my steering wheel a right turn.

"Nervous? Why would I be nervous?" I asked, driving along a single-lane road. I'd gotten off the highway about twenty minutes ago. Atlanta traffic was a pain in the ass, so it was a relief to be on a quieter, emptier street.

"Because, as much as I like Javier as a person," my sister said, "he doesn't mess around when it comes to Aleesa."

"Um, yeah. I gathered that when he freaked out about me tickling her chin in Miami. But no, I'm not nervous. I'm seeing this opportunity like all the others. He's just a parent who needs assistance."

"Okay. Well, just do me a favor, Tavia, and *don't* piss him off, please."

"What?" I shrieked, feigning innocence. "How could I ever piss anyone off?"

"You'd piss him off because you love to make fun of people." She laughed. "To us, it's all harmless jokes. We're used to teasing each other, but Javier didn't grow up the way we did. If you embarrass him in his own home, he'll probably fire you for it."

"Fine. I promise to be on my best behavior." I sighed. "Especially with Mama needing more money for Abe's therapy."

Our baby brother, Abraham, was autistic, and after years of trial and error, we'd found the perfect clinic for him. His new therapist was patient, kind, and thorough but insanely expensive. Ever since starting there, though, Abe had built more confidence in himself, was a bit more eager to try new things, *and* was becoming better at communicating with us. The communication part was important. In my opinion, the therapy was worth every penny. Unfortunately, to keep this good thing going for him, I needed to keep raking in *more* pennies.

"Don't worry about money, sis," Davina said. "I told you I'm helping them. His therapy payments will be taken care of."

"Yeah, but if I'm going to be away from home for who knows how long, I need to contribute something. I feel guilty every single time for just packing up and leaving when I get a new job. And with Mama's fragrance shop going downhill . . ." I blew out an exasperated breath. "I just want to support them where I can. If Abe loses his spot at the clinic, they won't take it well."

"Everything will be fine," my sister cooed. "I would never let them sink. They'll be okay, Octavia. Besides, Mama has dealt with much worse. You are trying to get back on your feet, so just focus on this new job. Everything will work out."

I released a frustrated breath. I had driven four hours to Atlanta so I could be interviewed by Javier Valdez, an NBA player and the starting center for the Atlanta Ravens. He wasn't as famous as my sister's fiancé, Deke Bishop, but people loved him nearly just as much. He was thirty-four years old (four years my senior), and I'd have found him extremely irresistible . . . if he wasn't such a grumpy asshole 70 percent of the time.

The 30 percent when he *wasn't* a Scrooge was when he interacted with his daughter. She was the only person I saw him being genuinely nice to. Well, her and his best friend, Deke.

To many, getting the chance to work with a man who played professional basketball (and who was sexy as hell, might I add) would've been a dream.

Javier Valdez was a six-foot-five Argentinean giant with *insane* attitude. It could've been a dream for me for sure . . . if he didn't loathe me. I was surprised he'd given me a call a week ago and asked if I could meet him at his house, or that he wanted me anywhere near his precious baby girl.

I believe during my brief trip to Miami with Davina a few months ago, he realized I was a good fit for Aleesa. Davina flew out to meet one of her investors, Chester, for lunch, and afterward he invited us to a penthouse party he was hosting. I joined her because I had never been to Miami and it had felt like the perfect opportunity. That's when I met Javier and Aleesa.

Though uptight and standoffish, Javier had witnessed firsthand how great I was with his daughter. Aleesa and I got along well.

Listen, I had even played tag with her in the hallway on Chester's floor . . . while wearing a short, skintight dress. By the end of our game, she was worn out and ready to go to sleep, which Javier had been trying to get her to do for hours. I didn't like to brag, but I was damn good at this nannying thing.

My navigation system showed that I was two minutes away from my destination.

"I'm about to pull up to his house," I told my sister. "I'll let you know how it goes . . . and if I need you to send Deke over to cuss him out."

Vina snorted a laugh. "I highly doubt Deke will be doing that."

"I bet he would for me."

"You know what? I bet he would too." She laughed again. "I love you, sis. Call me if you need me."

"I love you too. Bye."

Not long after, I spotted a black wrought iron gate. At the call box, I typed in the code, and the gates began to separate.

As I drove, I drank in the details of his towering two-story home, with an ivory stucco exterior and a Spanish tile roof. Palm trees with bold green leaves danced with the wind in front of the house. The driveway looped in a circle, and a fountain spurting water stood boldly in the center of it, surrounded by fresh florals.

It reminded me a lot of a coastal vacation home. A beautiful mansion, but also a very simple-looking place . . . which fit Javier completely.

Beautiful, simple . . . and *mean*.

After parking, I climbed out of my Honda, and my feet landed on granite cobblestones. I made my way to the front door, which was tucked away through a heightened arch. A chandelier dangled from the roof, and eight shallow steps led to a porch.

I gave the doorbell a ring. It took close to a minute for the door to open.

Javier stood on the other side, wearing a white T-shirt, black basketball shorts, and Nike socks. A pair of black slides were on his feet as well. His shirt had his team's name on it and the number eight below, at the center—his jersey number.

Oh, and let me not forget to mention the pink unicorn headband on his head. I tried not to laugh as I observed him, and it didn't help that he wore this serious scowl, trying to seem all macho while looking me up and down.

"You are kind of early," he said in that thick Argentinean accent. His brows dipped as he scanned me up and down. "Did you press the buzzer at the gate?"

"Uh . . . no, I didn't. In your text, you said to just type the code and come in."

He looked away and blinked, as if trying to remember that.

"Um . . ." I checked my phone for the time. "Should I wait six more minutes and come back to the door, or . . . ?"

"No. It is fine. I was just in the middle of doing something with Aleesa." Just as he said that, I heard a squeal and footsteps padding on the floor. A small hand wrapped around the door below him, and Aleesa yanked it open wider.

Aleesa was absolutely adorable, with sandy-brown hair that fell in loose curls and the prettiest sage green eyes. Her skin was a shade or two lighter than Javier's warm beige.

When she saw me, she gasped and placed both hands on her cheeks, as if to say *Oh my gosh! It's her!*

She squealed as she rushed to me, then threw both arms around one of my legs and hugged me tight.

I laughed, bending over to hug her back. "Hi, sweet girl! My goodness, that's a big hug. How are you?"

"I good. You wan' play wif me?" she asked, peering up at me.

"Well, that's up to your dad." I stood straight again and eyed him. "Don't want to break any rules too soon."

He sighed and stepped back. "Come in."

Aleesa released my leg, but only to grab my hand and drag me into the house. She led the way through the foyer, lined with polished marble floors, passing off-white walls with several portraits tacked to them.

One of the photos caught my eye, of a woman in a white wedding dress, standing next to Javier, who wore a suit. I didn't get a chance to really observe it, though, because Aleesa was now taking me to the center of their living room and showing me a dollhouse and collection of mermaids.

She went into great detail about them, and I nodded, taking note of which was her favorite. Through the corner of my eye, I spotted Javier near the kitchen, watching us. The kitchen was absolutely incredible, by the way. All stainless steel, with a massive white-quartz island and dark-gray cabinets that had silver handles and knobs.

"Aleesa, how about a Popsicle and ten minutes of TV, princesa?" he asked, already opening the freezer.

"Yes! I wan' watch *Bluey*!"

Javier nodded, carrying the Popsicle with him to the living room. He spread out a blanket for her to sit on, then opened the wrapper and offered the lime-green Popsicle. He turned on the massive TV with the remote, went to *Bluey*, and placed a kiss on her forehead, smiling down at her.

While the theme song played and Aleesa licked away at her cold treat, he finally faced me. He didn't smile. I'd have been slightly intimidated, but it was hard to take him seriously with that unicorn horn still on his head.

“We can sit here.” He gestured to the nearest table, a wooden six-top table with black Scandinavian-style chairs.

Sitting opposite me, he immediately folded his arms. “So, I have simple questions first,” he said.

“Okay.” I placed my forearms on the table and interlaced my fingers.

“When would you be able to start?”

“I could literally start today if you wanted me to.”

He was quiet for a moment, taking in that knowledge. “You understand that this is a long-term commitment, right? Not something that you can do for a couple of weeks just to make your résumé look better.”

“Yes, I understand. You’re a busy man and a pro athlete. I get it.” I could tell he was trying to test me, work me up a bit, because that last part was definitely a dickish thing for him to say.

His lips twisted as he regarded me. “And you are CPR certified?”

“I sure am. I have the certificate in my car if you want to see—”

“Why do you really want to do this?” he asked, cutting me off.

“Do what? Take care of your daughter?”

“Yes. I look at you, and I do not see a woman who wants to be stuck somewhere for months, taking care of another person’s child. I have had many people want this job, only to be in it for something.”

“Well, I can guarantee you, I’m not in this for anything other than to take care of her and get paid,” I assured him, huffing a laugh.

Bluey squealed in the background as we held a staring match.

He blinked first.

“I would not want any images of her being taken,” he went on. “I would need someone who respects her privacy and mine. Someone we can trust.”

“Understandable. I’ve signed NDAs before. If you need me to do that for you, I’m more than okay with it.”

He narrowed his eyes, assessing me further. What? Was he annoyed that I was okay with everything? Homeboy could take his best shots. I’d heard it all.

He leaned forward, resting his forearms on the table. "My issue with you is that you seem to not take anything seriously in life. It seems to all be some sort of game to you, as if you can just laugh your way through every problem and make them go away."

I frowned at his statement. Fucking *ouch*.

"My daughter's care is important," he pressed on. "I travel a lot, so I cannot be here to hold your hand. That means I need someone responsible and dependable . . . and a part of me is not sure I can fully depend on a person like *you*."

"A person like *me*? Not to be rude, but you don't even know me."

"Exactly. All I know is that you are my best friend's fiancée's sister."

"And all I know is that you are my sister's fiancé's best friend. You could be a serial killer, for all I know, but I took the risk anyway by showing up."

He scowled. "I am not a serial killer."

I smirked. "Prove it."

His scowl deepened. "How the hell does someone even prove that? What am I supposed to do, dig up holes and show you that I do not have bodies in the ground?"

I shrugged.

"How would I even have time to do any of tha—you know what? Never mind." He flicked his hand, as if dismissing it all, but I didn't miss the way his cheeks reddened.

Davina was right. He was easy to embarrass. Almost too easy, really.

"Would you be one hundred percent committed to the position?" he asked, sounding entirely fed up. "That means traveling when necessary, taking Aleesa to her classes and appointments, making sure her meals are healthy, and making sure she gets enough exercise daily."

"I'm one hundred percent committed."

"Good." The word was cut and dried. "Because I expect and want the very best for her."

"Yes, I can tell by that unicorn headband you're wearing. Only the best of dads would willingly wear that."

Confusion contorted his face, but when what I said registered, he reached up and snatched the headband off.

I suppressed another laugh.

"See, this is what I mean," he exclaimed, but not too loudly for Aleesa to hear. "Nothing is taken seriously by you."

"If that's how you feel, why did you have me come all this way to be interviewed?"

"Because I wanted to know my options . . . and see who I was really dealing with. So far, I am not impressed and am regretting that I ever asked. I do not have time for these mind games."

*Oh, boy.* I leaned back in my chair just as Aleesa shot up with her Popsicle stick.

"I done!" she yelled. She rushed to the trash can and threw the stick into the bin, then she scurried my way and tugged on my N.W.A T-shirt.

"What's your name?" she asked.

"Octavia," I answered with a smile.

"Octava," she said.

I laughed. Most kids her age struggled with my name. "How about you just call me Tavia?"

"Tava," she said, trying to repeat.

"That works too." I gave her a wink, and she grinned before wrapping her arms around me as best she could. Then she peered up and, once again, asked, "Can you play wif me?"

"What about *Bluey*, Leesa?" Javier asked, pointing over his shoulder at the TV. He gave her a sweet smile.

"No. I wan' play wif Tava."

Javier looked from his daughter to me, trying his best to suppress another scowl.

I shrugged. "Kids really love me."

With an irritated sigh, he sat up taller in his chair. "Fine. I will take you on, but *only* because my schedule is about to get busier and I need someone to look after her right away. But if you mess up even once,

Octavia, you are gone." He raised a stern finger. "*One strike* is all you will get from me. Is that clear?"

"Sir, yes sir," I answered, giving him a mock salute.

He growled something in Spanish as he pushed out of his chair. "I leave for Boston Monday night. Since you say you can start as soon as possible, I will want you here on Sunday so that we can go over contracts and agreements. Can you do that?"

"Sure."

"Good." He cut a glance at Aleesa, who had managed to climb onto my lap and started playing with my locs.

"I love you hair, Tava," she cooed, running her fingers over one of the gold jewels.

"Thank you, angel."

"Where will you sleep?" he asked.

"Oh, I'll probably just book a hotel for the night."

He shook his head. "Do not waste your money on a hotel. I have a guesthouse you can use. I will show it to you after you finish playing with Aleesa."

"Aww." I smiled at him. "See, I knew I could unthaw that heart of yours a little bit. Thank you, Javier."

He rolled his eyes. "Thirty minutes to play with her, then you go." He walked to the living room and slumped down on one of the sofas.

"Noted," I mumbled.

Yay! At least I had the job. Still, I had to be careful. I had no doubt he would fire me in a heartbeat if I so much as coughed near Aleesa. He was a hard-ass, but it was fine. I'd dealt with my fair share of assholes. It helped that he would be traveling often, so I wouldn't have to see him so much or be in the midst of his grouchiness.

Aleesa watched him for a few seconds, then she turned her gaze to mine and grinned. "Daddy's mad," she whispered.

That statement pulled a quiet giggle out of me.

Yeah. I was *definitely* going to have some fun with this little girl.

# THREE

## OCTAVIA

***OVER SIX MONTHS LATER***

Yogurt was in my Barbie doll's hair again.

A shrill giggle split the air, and I gave Aleesa a sideways glance. This little girl was going to be the end of me, I swear. How could someone so tiny create *so much* mess?

On this particular morning, there had been an orange juice spill, oatmeal smeared on the table, and now yogurt in my Black Barbie's silky dark hair. All this had been done, and it was only nine o'clock in the morning.

"Today is going to be a long day with you, isn't it?" I got up to collect the pack of baby wipes from the counter. Plucking one out, I wiped as much of the yogurt out of my doll's hair as possible.

Technically, this was Aleesa's Barbie, but she had about fifty of them in her playroom and she'd given this one to me as a gift. She specifically chose this one because it *looked like me*.

"Sowwy, Tava." Aleesa grinned when I glanced over my shoulder, then stuffed a strawberry into her mouth.

"That's all right, angel." I sighed. "What's not all right, though, is that you're getting oatmeal in your beautiful tresses. Let's not rub our hands in our hair, okay? Would you like a wipe?"

"Yes, pwease."

See? How could anyone be upset with her when she had such a cute voice?

I helped her clean up just as I heard footsteps thumping through one of the hallways.

*Oh shit.* This was not the time for *him* to come to the kitchen.

I'd hoped he would sleep in a little longer so I could give Aleesa a bath and get her out of her pajamas. He wasn't particularly fond of Aleesa's messes, and he *definitely* wasn't fond of her still wearing pajamas during breakfast.

He griped about teaching her how to be clean and tidy, while I countered it with letting her explore and be a three-year-old. And, in my opinion, washing up after breakfast seemed much more logical for a child who loved smashing food into her hair. It didn't matter to him, though. He still wanted her prepared before starting the day.

"Quick," I whispered, wiping her mouth. "GG is coming. Be good and don't tell Daddy about the yogurt."

Right after saying that, Javier stepped around the corner and entered the kitchen, wearing his usual getup—basketball shorts, a solid-colored T-shirt, and Nike running shoes. I swear this man's wardrobe had no variety. Today, his T-shirt was gray . . . and he was sweating. Must've woken up early to hit the home gym. He normally didn't do that after a home game.

"Morning, Leesa." He leaned down to kiss his daughter on the cheek.

"Morneen, GG," she sang.

I stifled a laugh.

"Why does she keep calling me that?" He swung his eyes to me.

I put on a straight face and shrugged. "I'm not sure."

Actually, I *was* sure.

*GG* stood for *Grumpy Giant*. Which Javier Valdez was. Six feet and five inches of tan, grumpy, muscled man.

The man was a pure grouch. He had a heart in there, but it was damn near impossible to get a laugh out of him unless you were family or one of his closest teammates.

I'd tried many times to make him smile, but he never, ever gave me the satisfaction. Over six months, and the most I'd get was a quirked brow if I tried to make a joke. And if that famous brow didn't shoot up, he always said "I do not understand your sense of humor."

"She is still in pajamas?" he asked.

"I was just getting ready to take her upstairs for a bath," I said.

"That should have been done a little earlier, no?"

It was his passive aggressiveness that bugged me most. Not even that deep, sexy accent could disguise it.

"You're right," I said, swallowing my pride. "I'm sorry. She kept saying she was hungry, so I decided to feed her first."

He said nothing in response. Instead, he scooped Aleesa out of her booster chair.

She ran her sticky hands over the scruff on his jaw. "Scratchy Daddy." She giggled.

"Sí." The skin around his eyes creased, and his mouth curved upward. That smile of his was so rare. *Beautiful* and rare. "I should shave, yeah?"

*Absolutely not,* I wanted to say. I rather liked his beard . . . but who cared what I thought? He most certainly didn't.

"What all did you eat for breakfast?" he asked her. He always did this, just to hear her recount everything . . . and probably to make sure I was giving her a well-rounded meal.

"Um, I had o'meal, milk, strawbebbies, yogurr, and candy."

"No, you did not have candy!" Javier exclaimed, laughing.

Aleesa giggled herself, then blushed.

"Sos muy graciosa, mi amor."

He told her that often. After a quick Google search, I found out it meant "You are funny, my love."

He was such a bittersweet man. Only ever sweet for Aleesa, of course.

After planting a kiss on her chubby cheek, he placed Aleesa on her feet before looking at me again. "Will you bathe her and get her ready, please? She has ballet class an hour early today, remember?"

I took her hand with a nod. "I remember."

"And do not forget to brush her hair with the pomegranate gel. It stays put longer when you use that."

"You got it."

"You'll have to leave on time if you want to find parking," he went on.

"Javier, would you rather be the one to take Aleesa to ballet today?"

He gave me a puzzled stare. "You know I cannot do that. The team has to watch film in two hours."

"Right."

"But it is not that I do not *want* to take her," he added quickly. "I just cannot today."

"Yep. I get it."

He frowned at me, probably trying to find more ways to defend himself. "I really hate when you do that."

"Do what?"

"Make me feel . . . *stupid*. Always messing with my head."

I threw a hand in the air, feigning innocence. "Javier, all I asked was if you wanted to take her today. You seem like you really want to, and I wanted to give you the option. I'm not trying to make you feel stupid."

He folded his arms. "But you are messing with my head."

"I think you're messing with your own head by worrying about all the things I know how to take care of. I've been doing this for months now. I can handle it."

His jaw steeled as he looked away. "Fine."

"Are we good?" I asked, trying to catch his eyes again.

"Yes. We are good. Just get her ready, please."

"'Kay." To spare us both the awkwardness, I picked Aleesa up and settled her on my hip. "Come on, big girl. Let's get you cleaned up."

I walked around the table and left the kitchen, but not without looking over my shoulder at Javier. He watched us go with a slight dip between his brows.

He didn't look away until we disappeared around the corner.

When Leesa and I made it upstairs, I looked at her with a smile and said, "I was messing with him just a little bit."

# FOUR

## JAVIER

Sometimes I asked myself what I was thinking by hiring Octavia Klein.

That feisty, slightly obnoxious, hardheaded woman was not my usual hire, but she was *great* with Aleesa.

She taught my daughter manners. Read to her two to three times a day. Made every single one of Aleesa's appointments and classes on time. She even cooked healthy homemade meals for her, and that was extremely important to me.

It did not help that she was all my daughter talked about. Nonstop. For over half a year. Aleesa was at the point of refusing my bedtime stories completely because she wanted her *Tava* to read them to her.

All that was wonderful. Seriously. I was happy that my baby girl was happy, but I had to say I was surprised Octavia was still around. She really worked my nerves and was always finding ways to get under my skin.

I was not sure why I still allowed her to irritate me after so many months. She knew just how to scrape my nerves too. Never too much to anger me, but just enough to get inside my head and make me second-guess everything.

Most of the nannies I had hired had bailed after three or four months. Octavia was coming up on *seven* months and hadn't shown any signs of wanting to quit. I was not sure if that was a good sign for me.

Most could not keep up with my demands; however, Octavia would take them like they were no big deal to her—as if having issues thrown her way could never set her back. I guess I should have expected that from a woman as carefree as she was. She had a strong spirit, one that reminded me a lot of Eloise. Was that why she got under my skin?

I shifted in my chair with a sigh as my deceased wife crossed my mind, watching the film run as Coach Harrison rambled about certain plays.

"You good?" a deep voice asked beside me.

I turned my attention to Deke Bishop, one of my best friends on and off the court, and the most famous of us in the room. He gave me a curious once-over, his eyes gleaming under the projector light.

"I am fine," I answered.

"I'm just asking." He threw two innocent hands into the air. "You've been huffing and puffing ever since you got here."

That was because it bugged me that Octavia had asked if I wanted to take Aleesa to ballet. She knew I would if I could, but there was always shit interfering with my bonding time with Aleesa, like watching films and going to meetings, practices, and games.

Do not get me wrong; I love what I do. I love my career, and I love basketball. It is my heart and it is part of what centers me, but nothing centers me more than my family. I do everything for Aleesa so she can live a good life—one far better than mine was growing up.

I was not going to tell Deke all this, though. It was bad enough that he kept heckling me about Octavia. He said that I talked about her a lot. He assumed I was into her. But what else was I supposed to talk about when she worked for me and spent more time with my daughter than I did?

He claimed I never talked about my previous nannies as much as I did her. I called bullshit on that.

Some days, Octavia was amazing. On other days, she was a handful and I wanted to fire her simply because she agitated me. It was her mouth, really. So sarcastic and witty . . .

It had been a long time since I came across a woman with such a solid spine. A woman who was respectable and understanding but also took no shit from anyone, not even her own boss.

Perhaps that was why I found myself constantly talking about her around Deke. She was not afraid of me like the others were. Like *many people* were, actually. Almost like she could see right through me, down to my soul.

Once the film was wrapped up, I walked with Deke to the parking deck so we could get to our cars.

"Davina's got some meeting in LA. Everyone's all over her lately. She says being engaged to me is a gift and a curse." He laughed.

"How so?" I fidgeted with my car key as we stopped in front of my Mercedes G-Class.

"A gift because she's getting hella opportunities for Golden Oil." Deke plucked his keys out of his pocket. "A curse because she's busier than ever and her sleep has been shitty. And, trust me, that woman *needs* her sleep. She's like a grizzly bear when she doesn't get enough."

"Do you think she has also not slept well because of the wedding?"

"Possibly. Her and Tisha have been planning in between working. I keep telling her to take it easy, but you know how she is." He shrugged. "Always wanting to keep herself busy."

"Well, the wedding is in four months. It is coming down to the wire, and all those little details matter."

"Well, that's why we hired a wedding planner—so she wouldn't have to worry about all those little details. My girl has some control issues she has to work on." He paused and looked around. "Don't tell her I said that."

I laughed. "Tell Davina I said hello. I should get home and check in with Aleesa."

"Tell little Leese I said 'What's up.' Octavia still giving you hell?" He grinned, like he wanted to laugh. Deke always got a kick out of hearing my stories about Octavia. He liked that there was someone giving me a taste of my own medicine, as he called it.

"She has Aleesa calling me GG now." I scratched my head. "No idea what that means, but Aleesa giggles every time and Octavia thinks I do not notice when she tries not to laugh."

"GG?" Deke mulled it over, tugging on his bottom lip. "Yeah, no idea what that stands for. I bet D knows."

"Yeah, I am sure she does. Those two talk on the phone almost every day."

"Y'all coming to the party tonight, right?" EJ's voice echoed through the parking deck. I looked over my shoulder and spotted our starting point guard jogging toward us with a brown sweat suit and backpack on.

"Hell, no." Deke walked to the driver's side of his Ferrari.

"Count me out," I muttered. "I told you I hate your parties, EJ."

"Oh, come on. Y'all haven't been to one in months!" EJ frowned as he looked between us. "It's because both of y'all are pussy whipped now! Deke and his fiancée and Javier with that fine-ass nanny."

I smacked the back of his head.

Deke busted out laughing.

"Bruh, y'all are gonna get enough of smacking me on the head." EJ puffed out his chest. "Can't be mad at me for speaking the truth. What's her name again?"

"Octavia," Deke filled in when I refused to answer. Then he smirked. I wanted to smack him too.

"Well, shit. If you don't want her, I'll take her from you, Valdez." EJ did some weird thing with his face, biting his bottom lip and narrowing his eyes while running a hand over the top of his head.

"You are not taking anything," I grumbled. "She would not even want you."

"Damn. Watch out, EJ," Deke called before settling into the driver's seat of his car. "Javier might fight you over that, seeing as he secretly wants her to himself."

"I do not." At least, I didn't think so . . .

Yes, Octavia was beautiful. Only a fool would deny that. I loved her hair—locs, as she called them—and how she styled them in a different hairdo every other week. And I would never admit this, but I looked forward to seeing which style she wore next.

There was something fascinating about it, especially when she put those little hair jewels on them. Some days the jewels were gold. Other days they were silver. Either one made her brown skin pop. Made her seem ethereal, angelic. *Untouchable.*

Yes, untouchable.

Because she *was* untouchable.

She was my daughter's nanny. There was no crossing that line. Ever.

Deke closed his door, then started the ignition of his Ferrari, causing it to growl to life. He crept forward in it, rolling his window down and looking between me and EJ. "I'll see y'all later."

"At the party, right?" EJ asked.

"No!" Deke said, then he peeled off and left the parking deck.

EJ twisted around. "Javier, my boy. Come to the party. Just this once. I promise it'll be worth it."

"Goodbye, EJ." I gripped the handle of my car door. "I will catch you later."

"Y'all never have any fun, man." EJ scoffed and walked away.

I'd have felt bad for him, but nothing seemed to bother that guy. And it didn't matter, because he spotted the next targets to harass about his party, our teammates Jacobi and Brantley.

As I drove out of the parking deck, my phone chimed in my pocket. I dug it out at a stoplight and saw a text from Octavia.

Octavia: Aleesa bumped heads with a classmate during dance. Big knot. Icing it now. She's still a little upset.

*"What?"* I hissed.

Below her text, an image appeared of Aleesa's forehead, with a raised red bump on the center. My heart dropped.

I dropped my phone into the cupholder and pressed my foot on the gas, hurrying home.

# FIVE

## OCTAVIA

"Does it still hurt?" I removed the ice pack from Aleesa's forehead, and she looked up at me with big green eyes.

She was in the process of eating a Popsicle, which was the only thing that had calmed her down when we made it home. She smiled up at me, licking away, and you'd think the accident had never happened.

When it did, though, my heart had sunk like a rock to my stomach. I saw it coming from a mile away but figured their instructor would catch the girls before they clashed. Unfortunately, this was one of those incidents where you can see something happening but by the time you react, it's too late to prevent it.

"Not hurting." Aleesa licked the Popsicle.

"Good. I'm just going to keep ice on it for now. Okay? You finish your Popsicle."

"'Kay."

I sat on one of the barstools as Aleesa remained perched on the island counter, still dressed in her white tights and black leotard. She looked so cute . . . minus the knot.

Moments later, I heard the door to the garage open and then slam shut. Javier's footsteps were heavy as he stepped around the corner, eyes wide and swimming with concern.

"Hey," I said, but he ignored me, going straight to Aleesa and picking her up to inspect her head.

"Hey, Daddy." Aleesa's voice was bright and bubbly.

"How did this happen, again?" he asked, studying her head a few seconds longer.

"She and another girl named Rosie bumped into each other while dancing. Both girls were already sort of teetering while trying to hold a pose. Both tipped to the side and came head-to-head."

The kitchen fell silent as he continued staring at the knot.

The silence was thick, and slightly uncomfortable, so I climbed off the stool and continued with "She's fine now. I wouldn't worry."

"What if she has a concussion?" he asked, snapping his gaze to me.

"Uh . . . I don't think she does. The run-in wasn't *that* hard. They aren't football players, Javier. They're three- and four-year-old girls."

"Octavia, this is not the time for you to get smart with me," he said in a near growl. "You brought my daughter home with a knot the size of Pluto on her head. She is hurt. This is *not* a joke."

"I know it's not a joke." I frowned as he placed Aleesa back on the counter and ran a thumb over her forehead. "I was just as concerned as you are right now, but as you can see, she's okay. She wasn't disoriented, and she didn't pass out or anything. I truly don't believe she has a concussion, but if you want me to take her to urgent care, I can."

"Where were you when this happened?" he asked. More like demanded.

"I was sitting on the bench with all the parents."

"Are you sure you weren't outside of the room? Or texting? Could this not have been prevented?"

I scoffed. What was with him? "I don't understand why you're interrogating me about this. Children have accidents all the time."

Javier shook his head and removed Aleesa from the counter to place her feet on the floor. "I do not want this to happen again."

"Okay. But I can't prevent every accident she has, and neither can you."

"Well, I can try."

"Look," I said with a sigh. "I'm very sorry that it happened. I wish you could be a little more reasonable about this."

"Reasonable?" he asked through gritted teeth. "Oh, I am being unreasonable?"

"Yes." I folded my arms. *"Unreasonable."*

"No, what is *unreasonable* is you acting like every serious situation is no big deal, Octavia!"

"Oh, you mean because I don't coddle her the way you do? Sorry to tell you this, my friend, but I don't have the helicopter gene in me. I don't hover over her or try and dictate her every move! Kids have to explore! They have to learn!"

"You know what?" Javier cut a hand through the air. "I'm the parent. I should not be arguing with you about this. We do not see eye to eye. Clearly I was wrong to hire you."

I blinked at him, stunned. His words were sharp and seemed to cut through me like a dozen knives. I hated that they felt so powerful, and I wasn't sure why, out of everything he'd said to me during all these months, those words bothered me most.

Maybe because I thought I was doing right by Aleesa.

Maybe because I cared about her and liked seeing her explore and try new things.

Maybe because it was true that we didn't see eye to eye, but I'd hoped he would eventually look past our differences and realize that, no matter what, Aleesa was okay. She was protected and she was happy with me.

I only ever had her best interests in mind.

But I suppose he couldn't see that.

I smashed my lips together, fighting the sting in my eyes by lowering my gaze to Aleesa. She'd finished her Popsicle and was looking between us, confused and upset too.

"You know what? You're right." I threw my hands into the air, as if throwing in the towel. "You're her father, and you know what's best for her. I overstepped. Maybe you're better off finding someone else to look after her since I'm so terrible at my job."

"I never said—"

"I was going to wash her up and make her some dinner, but I'll leave you to it. See you in the morning."

"Octavia, wait," Javier called as I walked toward the patio doors. "I didn't mean it that way; I just—"

"No, I think you meant exactly what you said, Javier." I twisted around to glare at him. "It's been over half a year, and you still don't seem happy with *anything* that I do. I'm trying my hardest to make this work—to spread just a teensy bit of excitement around here for her—but you hate it. I don't want to make this about me, but it's like no matter what I do or how hard I try, it's never good enough for you." I drew in a deep breath, still fighting my tears. "So maybe it's like you said. I'm just not the right fit for you and Aleesa."

"Tava?" Aleesa called.

I lowered my gaze. She was pouting, and seeing her that way hurt me even more. I looked away before my bottom lip could tremble. Then I walked out of the house and shuffled across the lawn until I reached the guesthouse. The tears finally blurred my vision as soon as I walked inside.

I adored Aleesa. I loved that little girl so much, to the point I'd have done *anything* for her. But Javier . . . God, he was not making this job easy for me. I'd dealt with my fair share of difficult parents. I understood that most only wanted the best for their children, so I often took their harsh criticisms with a grain of salt.

I'd dealt with sticklers; passive aggressiveness; and sugar-free, gluten-free, dye-free parents. But I'd *never* dealt with someone who so clearly *loathed* having me around. I figured by now he'd have softened up. I couldn't have been that bad to be around, right?

All his loathing reminded me of one thing. One *person*, really. My ex.

Fucking Luther Hall. That manipulative, selfish, lying piece of shit.

I had sworn on my life that I would never again put up with a man who didn't appreciate me, or didn't accept me for who I was. I would never keel over for someone who didn't respect me. It didn't matter how much Javier paid me. I had value, and he wasn't about to shred it. It was better to move on than sit and take the punches.

Maybe Javier was right, though. Maybe he never should've hired me.

If he hadn't, then I wouldn't have felt like my mental health was slipping day by day. I had pretended some of his words and actions didn't bother me all that much, but deep down they did. Why? Because I had a problem with wanting *everyone* to like me, and I couldn't understand why he hated me.

I had felt like I needed to go over the top to impress him with my cooking, my baking, and even tending to his daughter just to feel accepted by him. Though I hated admitting it, I would go over the top when he was around just to see if I could get a teensy bit of a smile out of him. It never worked. And relying on someone else to make me feel worthy was a terrible habit.

Davina always said this was something I needed to work on.

I cared too much about what other people thought about me. I'd been that way since I was a child. Always wanting approval. Always wanting to be the good girl. Always the one holding back my feelings and emotions just to spare someone else's. Always putting others before myself.

I had thought, surely, I was making progress with all of that. After years of therapy, I had felt confident enough in myself to give this world another shot.

But if things continued on this track, I wasn't sure how much longer I could be a nanny for Javier. I had never quit a job . . . but this would be the first time in history that I did.

All because of a grumpy single father with a chip on his shoulder.

# SIX

## JAVIER

Octavia did not speak much the day after Aleesa's accident. It was the strangest thing, seeing her cooking in the kitchen without talking, breaking out in some random dance, or even trying to get a rise out of me.

She stuck to her work. She knew my schedule and that I had a game to travel for, so she came to the house at six in the morning, sat in the living room while Aleesa continued sleeping, and basically ignored me as I carried my suitcase with me out of the house.

I felt like shit for what I had said to her.

The truth was, I had not liked to see my daughter hurt. No good parent wants to see that, and we always look for someone or something to blame. I did not like to know there were tears in Aleesa's eyes that were caused by pain.

And the biggest truth? I did not like that I was *not there* to pick her up in that moment. I thought about that a lot—how Aleesa probably looked for me when she was hurt or scared or lonely. It caused so much guilt to eat at my heart and soul because all I ever wanted was to be there for her.

Maybe it would not have felt this bad if her mother was still in the picture. But now that my wife had passed away and it was just the two of us, that meant I was responsible for *everything* regarding Aleesa, including her happiness.

Our game that night was against Chicago. I did not play my best. Deke and EJ noticed, and on the flight back to Atlanta, they asked what was up. I could not tell them what was really on my mind—not because I did not trust them but because I did not think they would fully understand.

I was a full-time single father *and* an NBA player. Those two things simply did not mix. I knew many guys in the league who had kids, but a lot of them had wives or partners who held down their houses. Some of my teammates joked with me about how I needed to find a new woman to date that I could eventually turn into a wife, but I was not that guy.

I was not looking to fall in love again.

I could not even imagine moving on with anyone else. Who was worth trusting? Who was worth my time? And, most importantly, who would embrace Aleesa and love her like their own?

The whole idea of that seemed wrong because I had done it before. I put years into a relationship—one I never expected to be cut short. I never thought the woman I married would be taken away from me just like that.

In a snap.

A blink of the eye.

Just *gone*.

~

I was relieved to finally make it home again. It was close to two in the morning when I walked through the door. The living room was vacant, as well as the kitchen. Both were spotless.

That was one of the great things about having Octavia. She *loved* cleaning. My house was never out of order or filthy—not that it had been before she was hired. I had a cleaner who took care of my house.

But ever since Octavia was hired, my pantry had been organized with fancy containers and baskets, Aleesa's toys were always put away at night, and even the throw blankets would be folded neatly and placed in their designated baskets.

Making my way upstairs, I rounded the banister and walked through the hallway, stopping at Aleesa's door. It was cracked open, and from there I could see her night-light glowing, illuminating the pink butterflies painted on the walls.

I pushed the door open wider with my fingertips, and my heart pumped faster. An unfamiliar warmth coursed through my veins when I saw the perfect moment before me.

Aleesa was lying in her bed, but she was not alone. Octavia lay right next to her, with Aleesa settled close. Both were asleep.

Octavia had a hand wrapped around my daughter, as if she would never let her go. Seeing that made me feel even worse for what I had said the night before. She really was a good caretaker. And she really did care about my baby girl. I could tell none of this was pretend for her. It was genuine and honest.

Knowing she was probably exhausted, I walked to the side of the bed and tapped her on the shoulder. She startled awake, clinging to Aleesa, eyes wide, as if an intruder were breaking in to rob her.

I noticed she did that a lot. Startled easily. Jumped or tensed whenever I caught her off guard. Granted, many people would be startled if caught off guard, but with Octavia, there was always a hint of fear in her eyes . . . almost like she thought she was being attacked.

"It is just me," I whispered, holding a hand up.

"Oh." She blinked a few times. "God, you scared me."

"I apologize."

Her head dropped so she could look at Aleesa. Then she kissed her forehead before pulling her arm from beneath her and gently situating her on the pillows.

"She was good today," Octavia whispered when she stood up. She avoided my eyes as she walked past me and left the room.

I placed a kiss on Aleesa's temple, pulled the blanket over her, and left the room as well. I normally stuck around, lying with her a bit to make up for lost time, but there was something I had to say to Octavia first. I caught her near the mudroom, stuffing her feet into a pair of sneakers.

"There's leftover wild rice and chicken soup in the fridge if you want some," she said, standing upright once she was situated. "I also ordered pizza for lunch earlier, so there are still a few slices in the fridge as well."

"Ah." I scratched my brow with my thumbnail. "Thanks." I did not like how serious and to the point she was being. No jokes? No sarcasm? Nothing? I must have really hurt her feelings, which I did not think was possible.

She forced a smile at me, then turned for the patio doors in the kitchen like she always did when she was ready to go to the guesthouse.

I could still remember offering her the guesthouse as an option when she first moved here, but I had made it clear that she did not have to stay in it. I had three other bedrooms she could use, so I did not want her to think I did not want her in my house.

She had insisted on being in the guesthouse, though; said it would do her some good to have a place to go to *outside* of the one she theoretically worked at but still be close enough that she could pop in when needed.

"Hey, Octavia," I called as she gripped the door handle.

She paused before peeking over her shoulder.

I stepped closer, and she turned fully to face me. As she did, I tried not to focus on her flat belly below the white crop top, or the way her black leggings hugged her thick hips and thighs. Or her hair, which was simple today. Down and swimming around her shoulders. No jewels. I wondered if the lack was to match her mood.

Yeah, I had really fucked up.

"Look," I said, sighing. "I am really, really sorry for what I said to you yesterday."

"Oh, it's okay." She waved a hand, like it didn't matter. Like she wasn't bothered at all. But I knew she was. "Don't worry about it."

"No, I have worried about it." I took another step closer. "I was just . . . well, I do not like to see Aleesa hurt. I freak out and have the tendency to lose my temper, but I should not have taken it out on you. I just wished that I was there for her in that moment." I paused so I could gather my thoughts. "Sometimes I . . . well, I just get upset because life can be so unfair. All I want is to be there for her, but I know that I cannot always be, because I have to work to provide for her, and this career is so consuming, so . . ."

Ah. This was hitting a little too close to home. Being this honest. Being this open.

She was quiet for a moment. "I understand," she murmured, nodding. "And I apologize for not taking matters around here more seriously. I'll try to limit that and promise not to get on your nerves as much."

"So you have been purposely trying to annoy me?"

She lifted a hand, bringing her thumb and forefinger close together. "Just a teensy bit." She half smiled, eyes glimmering. It was nice to see some of her light return.

"Of course you were."

"No, but seriously, it's okay. You don't have to explain anything to me if you don't want to. You are her dad, and I need to just shut my mouth sometimes. But you should know that I'd never let any harm come to Aleesa. I love that little girl. She stole my heart the moment I met her and still has it."

I smiled. That, I believed. Her actions proved it daily. This wasn't just a job to Octavia. This was her passion. She devoted herself to taking care of *my* kid. She made sure Aleesa was fed, clean, happy. That was all I wanted for her, really. Someone to care about her and to love her.

"Thank you for all that you do for her."

She nodded. "Of course."

Our eyes lingered several seconds longer than usual. Then she jerked her gaze away.

"Anyway, I should get some sleep," she said. "No games or practice tomorrow, right?"

"Practice tomorrow night, but I'm free in the morning and early afternoon. I would actually like to discuss Leesa's birthday party with you, if that is okay? She will be turning four at the end of June, and I would like to throw a party to celebrate."

"Oh, I *love* parties," she cooed.

I could not help my smile. "You seem like the type to love parties."

"What's that supposed to mean?" she asked, a sassy hand going to her hip. She was smiling, though. Her playfulness had returned. Why did I feel so relieved about that?

"I just mean you seem like you like to have fun."

"Hmm. Suppose I do. And I gotta say, you seem to enjoy the opposite of fun."

Ah. Yes. It was definitely back. The jokes entwined with sarcasm were the Octavia Klein signature.

I huffed a laugh. "Good one."

She patted herself on the shoulder with a lazy smile. "I'll be here in the morning so we can chat about plans."

"Great. Thank you."

"Oh—did you have a good game? You guys won, right?"

"We did. It was not my best game, I won't lie," I said, scratching the back of my head. "But that is only because I felt very guilty today for being that rude to you. I took it too far."

"Javier, seriously. It's okay. Don't feel guilty anymore. All is forgiven."

"Are you sure?"

Her smile was warm, infectious. "I'm positive."

"Okay. Only if you mean it."

She hesitated, as if she wanted to say something in response but was not sure if she should.

Then she sighed and turned away. "Well . . . have a good night, Javier."

"Good night, Octavia." I almost wished she would say more . . . just for the hell of it.

Instead, I watched her walk out the door and shut it behind her. There seemed like so much more I could have said or done, but I was not sure what else to add. I figured perhaps it would come to me the next day, when I had some rest and a clearer head.

My stomach rumbled, reminding me that I had not eaten a proper meal in nearly eight hours, so I walked to the kitchen, opened the fridge, and grabbed the Tupperware filled with soup.

I heated it up in the microwave, sat at the table, and dug right in.

Then I let out a satisfied groan because *damn.*

I did not care how much Octavia got under my skin if it meant I could keep eating meals as delicious as these.

# SEVEN

## OCTAVIA

I loved the guesthouse.

It was about the size of a studio apartment and had just enough space for me.

When I first saw it, it reminded me of one of those tiny homes on HGTV. I'd always wanted to stay in a tiny home, so I fell in love at first sight.

The exterior was made of stucco, with dark-green shutters. Two windows on the face of the house revealed the front lawn and a distant view of Javier's whopper of a home. A three-step stoop led to a small porch that paved the way to a dark-green door.

The interior was what sold me. I didn't expect there to be two levels inside the guesthouse, so the first thing to catch my eye was the loft area on the second floor, where a full-size bed was set up, along with a mounted TV and a dresser. A round window was built into the wall next to the bed, providing a view of leafy treetops.

On the first floor, the kitchen had a sink, a fridge, an oven, and a row of cabinets for storage. A black love seat was placed against the windowless wall, and a beautiful rug matching the black, sienna, and beige color scheme was spread on the middle of the floor.

The two-person dining table was set up in front of one of the windows, with a perfect view of the lawn. I sipped so many cups of coffee there. This place had a cozy, industrial vibe, and I loved it.

Apparently, Javier's mother had decorated the place when he first moved in. The guesthouse was meant for her, but she realized quickly that she didn't like being alone, so it kind of just sat for years.

I'd never had a real place of my own. I think that was why I cherished it so much. If I wasn't staying with Mama, I was living with whichever kid I nannied.

I'd spent a few months in an apartment with my high school bestie, Naomi, when I was twenty-two, but that didn't last long because Naomi's job let her go and she couldn't afford to pay rent anymore, which resulted in me not being able to afford the full amount of rent and us having to break our lease and move out.

Now I had a place—at least for now—and it was marvelous.

I thought about all those things as I sat at the table, sipping my coffee and watching the sun rise. We were coming close to summer, which meant Javier would be home more since this basketball season would be over.

I wasn't quite sure how I felt about that yet—him being home more, that is. I felt like I finally had a good routine with Aleesa, but with him hovering around, things would definitely shift.

But that was okay.

I was good at adapting.

It was coming close to six in the morning, so I finished my coffee, washed the cup, then left the guesthouse to walk across the yard. Normally, I could sleep in another hour or so when Javier was home, but figured I would get a head start on the day.

Once I reached the back door, I took out my key and unlocked it to get inside. I flipped on the light switch to illuminate the kitchen and sighed.

I was in such a funky mood the day prior, but I didn't feel so awful anymore. Javier had apologized, and I truly appreciated that. Most people weren't mature enough to own up to their mistakes, but he had.

To show my appreciation, I whipped up some French toast, eggs, and bacon. I was just about to cut some fruit when I heard a high-pitched voice yell *"Tava!"*

"Right on time." I laughed to myself as I dried off my hands and hurried up the stairs.

Aleesa was in her bathroom, sitting on the toilet, a big grin on her face. "I'm done pooping."

"Good morning to you, too, little one." I helped her get situated, then we went to her bedroom to find an outfit for the day.

I let her pick out a shirt, found some cute polka-dot leggings and socks, gave her a quick bath, got her dressed, and then worked on her hair. As I brushed it into two pigtails, I noticed a looming silhouette in my periphery.

I gasped and paused, only to realize it was Javier.

"I could have gotten her," he said, rubbing his sleepy eyes.

"Oh, I got it. Don't worry." I forced a smile to calm my racing heart. "You were sleeping. Looks like you could use a little more of it."

He walked into the bathroom and bent over to place a kiss on Aleesa's cheek. "I will be okay."

I side-eyed his reflection in the mirror, finishing up Aleesa's hair. "I made breakfast."

"Yes. I could smell it in my dreams."

I laughed.

"Come on, amor." He said something else in Spanish to Aleesa before scooping her up and carrying her out of the bathroom. He began making playful growling noises as he nuzzled her cheek and nibbled at her nose.

"Scratchy Daddy!" Aleesa squealed.

"¿Sí?" he asked, looking into her eyes with a lazy smile.

"Sí." She giggled, running her hands over his shadow of a beard.

"Okay, okay. No more of scratchy Daddy."

I couldn't help smiling at their interaction.

I followed him downstairs, and once I made it to the kitchen, I reheated the food before plating it.

"You know I am capable of preparing my own food, right?" he asked in a light tone.

"I know. But I don't mind." I really didn't. It made me feel good to feed others. To know they enjoyed the food I made. Especially him. I placed his plate down on the table in front of him. "Apple or orange juice?"

"There are options?" he asked, and he was so serious that it was kind of cute. Almost like he never had the chance to choose between things as simple as juice flavors in his own home.

"I like having a variety," I told him.

"Apple, then, please."

I poured him a cup of apple juice, filled a small cup for Aleesa, and worked on the fruit again. Aleesa *loved* fruit.

Javier dug right into his French toast, taking massive bites. Aleesa kicked her feet as she nibbled on a slice of kiwi. I made a plate for myself before sitting in the chair next to Aleesa's and right across from Javier.

"So for the party," I started, cutting into my syrupy bread. "What theme are you thinking?"

"Oh—right," he garbled around a mouthful of eggs. He chewed a bit before swallowing. "I asked her a few days ago what she would want, and she told me 'mermaids.'"

I nodded. "That will be really pretty."

Aleesa watched the live-action trailer for *The Little Mermaid* almost every day. I knew the melodies and every word of them by heart now. How could anyone not sing along with an angelic voice like Halle Bailey's? It was going to be a delight to take her to a movie theater and watch the actual film. I could already imagine the stars in her eyes as she gazed at the big screen, hands clasped together, eager for it all.

"Yes. It will be good." He picked up his glass of apple juice. "My mother is working on invitations, and I am looking into a party planner right now, since it is a little over a month away. I wanted to speak to you about it because I may need more help than usual with Aleesa so that I can prepare."

"I'll be here to assist," I assured him.

He seemed almost relieved to hear that. "Okay. Good."

"But you know you don't have to hire a party planner, right?" I eyed him as he guzzled down some juice. "I love planning parties, especially for kids."

"No, Octavia. Absolutely not. That would be asking *way* too much of you." He sliced a hand through the air, as if that were final. "Handling Aleesa is a lot already."

"Aleesa is an angel. I don't mind at all. Really. Just tell me all the things you want, and I can figure it out."

"No. I could not put you through that."

"Javier." My eyes locked on his. "If I didn't want to, I wouldn't have offered my help."

He sighed, training those dark-brown irises on mine for several seconds. "Fine. Okay."

"Yay!" I did a tiny clap with my fingertips.

"Well, if we are doing mermaids, I was hoping to have an undersea theme. I would like there to be activities to keep the kids busy, and to have food catered. I would also like there to be a few games."

"That all sounds doable."

"And of course I would give you the money to arrange all of this." He raised a hand, as if to pause the entire situation and make that abundantly clear. "You would not have to come out of pocket for a single thing."

I fought a smile. "Okay."

"You can use the credit card I gave you for whatever is needed."

I blinked, a little surprised by that. "Are you sure?" The most he ever let me use the credit card for was groceries, gas, and miscellaneous needs for Aleesa. Each month had a budget, and he had made it very clear when I first started that he did not want me going over it.

"Yes."

"Um . . . okay. Sounds good. What's my budget for the party?"

"There is no budget," he answered with finality. "Just make it a wonderful day for her."

*Holy shit.*

"What?" Javier's shoulders slumped. "Your eyes are very big. Do you think that I should have a budget?"

"I can't tell you what to do with your money, but I will tell you that you don't have to break the bank to throw an enjoyable birthday party. Sometimes the simpler things are, the better. Kids don't care as long as they're having fun. And, like you said, I seem like the type to have fun. Let me put that quality to good use."

He cracked a smile. I was proud of myself for getting that out of him, even if it didn't fully spread across his face.

"Okay, sure. I will trust you with this." He studied me briefly, as if seeing me for the first time. "Thank you, Octavia."

"Of course. We have to make sure our girl has the best day ever, right?" I squeezed Aleesa's chin, and she scrunched her nose and laughed.

She was such a happy child. It surprised me sometimes how completely opposite she was to her father.

It made me wonder how her mother was. Was she just as bright and bubbly? Was she sweet? Did she love to cook? Dance? Sew? Sing?

There were pictures of her in the foyer and in Aleesa's bedroom. She was a gorgeous woman, and in all of them, she seemed happy.

But I of all people know smiles can be misleading.

Javier placed his fork down with a light clatter, then yawned. His plate was clean—hardly a scrap left.

"You should go lie back down and get some more sleep," I suggested. "At least another hour or so."

"I should be up for Aleesa. She will not see me tomorrow."

"Another hour won't hurt." I winked.

He looked deep into my eyes. "You make me feel useless, you know?" He said this in a semi-playful tone. He was teasing . . . and it was the dryest tease I'd ever heard, I kid you not. Did this man even know how to make a joke?

"I'm just here to help. Now *go*." I grabbed his plate. "I've got this."

He pressed his lips, slowly rising to a stand. Swinging his gaze to Aleesa, he sighed and blinked a few times. Then he walked over and kissed the top of her head.

"By the way, I don't think you should call yourself useless," I said before he left the kitchen. He paused and gazed over his shoulder at me. "Having a helping hand doesn't make you useless. It makes you smart. We're only human, Javier. No one is expecting you to be perfect." I pointed at Aleesa just as she leaned down and stuck her tongue out to lick syrup off her plate like she was a puppy. "*Especially* not her. As long as she knows you're there for her, she'll be happy no matter what. I know I was when my dad was around."

He stood there for a beat, seeming to process my words.

Then he nodded, held my gaze for a split second, and left the kitchen.

A hot wave ran over me.

There was something in his eyes right before he walked away. Something about the way he looked at me made me feel warm and a little fuzzy inside.

After cleaning the table and giving Aleesa a puzzle to do at her kid-size Hello Kitty table, I realized what it was that I saw.

Appreciation.

That was *genuine* appreciation.

Now we were getting somewhere.

# EIGHT

## OCTAVIA

"Why did you agree to this again?" my sister asked, laughing.

"Because he needs help, Vina." I wedged my phone between my shoulder and ear so I could finish scrambling eggs. "And because maybe he'll stop being so much of a dick toward me if he sees I can hold my weight around here. I thought he was going to fire me. At least now I know my paychecks are safe until her birthday."

"Please. He's not going to fire you," Davina muttered.

"How would you know, *know-it-all*?" I placed the bowl of eggs down and grabbed the phone again to hear what she so confidently had to say.

"I just know. With the way he talks about you to Deke . . . let's just say Javier doesn't seem like the kind of guy who brags, yet he's always talking about how patient you are with Aleesa—and don't even get me started on your cooking. Deke says Javier won't shut up about the meals you make. It's gotten to a point where he doesn't even think Javier realizes he's talking about you or the things you do."

My heart fluttered, hearing that.

No, wait. *Stop fluttering, heart. We don't flutter for men anymore.*

"And even though all of your views don't align with his regarding Aleesa," she went on, "he's told Deke you're doing a really good job with her."

"Really?" I huffed a laugh. "I wish he'd tell me that himself."

"You know how Javier is. He probably has to unthaw. I'm sure he'll get there with you one day."

"No, see, that's the thing. I *don't* know how he is. I mean, other than the fact that he's a basketball player, has a daughter, and was previously married, I barely know the man. I don't expect to know his deepest darkest secret, but he doesn't talk about himself much. He hardly even talks about his mom or sister, yet I hear him on the phone with them all the time. He's like a vault." I bit into a strip of turkey bacon. "Can't get a morsel out of that man."

"Yeah, well, just try and cut him a little slack," Davina said. "He's been parenting alone, and his schedule is insanely busy, I'm sure. He probably needs a break from the hustle and bustle. Deke is glad the summer is approaching."

"Why? 'Cause he'll get to dip his *thing* in your *thang* nonstop?"

"Tavia, please." She tried to use her serious big sister voice, but I could tell she was stifling a laugh. "I want to see you soon. My schedule is pretty clear for the first time in a while next week. I can come see you at Javier's."

"Ugh. I would love that," I sighed.

"I bet. Let me know what day. We'll figure it out."

"Okay."

"Love you, Poop-Butt."

"I love you, too, Stinky V."

I placed my phone on the counter after the call ended, then got back to my eggs. After scrambling them and making a quick breakfast wrap, I searched for my shoes.

It was when I had both shoes on that I heard my phone vibrate on the counter. I headed back to the kitchen and collected it from the counter, seeing an email with the subject line O, we should try again.

I figured it was spam, but I gave it a tap anyway.

Then my heart dropped as I read it.

What's up O,
It's been a while since we last spoke. Just wanted to tell you that I got a new job in Atlanta. I work for a tech company.
I saw you on TV sitting front and center during one of the Ravens' basketball games. You were holding one of the player's kids and the camera panned to you. You nanny for him now? The Javier Valdez dude? Your sister's engagement was all over the place, so I assume that's how you got that job, connected with the team somehow? That's cool. I know you wanted to be a nanny so I'm happy for you.
Let me know when you're free. I've been trying to make myself a better man. I miss you and would love the chance to see you.
With love,
Luther

My mouth became sour, while my throat thickened. How the hell did he even find my email address? I didn't care that he saw me on TV, but contacting me personally? I'd blocked *all* contact from him years ago . . . yet he'd found me.

Hands shaking, I collected my breakfast wrap and hustled out the door of the guesthouse. My legs could hardly carry me with how shaky they were, but I eventually made it to Javier's mansion.

Before I could unlock the back door, I heard someone wailing. My heart dropped and all thoughts of Luther vanished when I recognized the cry. I burst into the house, and the cries became twice as loud.

From the kitchen, I spotted Javier standing in the living room with Aleesa in his arms. He walked back and forth with her, shushing her, trying to calm her. His hair was tousled, his face tired, and when his eyes found mine, I saw the stress wearing around them.

"What happened?" I asked, rushing through the kitchen to meet him.

"She woke up crying. When I went to her room, she was holding her stomach. She says it hurts."

"Like a stomachache?" I asked, rubbing circles on Aleesa's back.

"Possibly."

"Aww. It's okay," I murmured to Aleesa. She reached for me, and Javier willingly handed her over, relief immediately sinking into his body.

"Why didn't you call me? I could've come over when she woke up."

"I did not want to interrupt your morning. She woke up around five, and we have agreed you officially start at seven on the days I am here. That would have been a breach of your contract, no?"

"Thoughtful," I said as I rocked Aleesa, "but I'm happy to get up for emergencies. I don't consider those breaches."

"Okay. I just did not want to cross boundaries."

"I understand." I offered him a smile, hoping it would calm some of his nerves. "I'm here to help take some of the burden off of you, Javier. I'm here for Aleesa, yes, but I'm here to help you too. Always remember that. Okay?"

He nodded, then sat on the edge of one of the sofas, elbows landing on his thighs and his face dropping into his palms. Pushing his hands upward, he raked his fingers through his full head of dark hair.

"I am sorry," he said. "I am just . . . *so tired*. Last night's game went into overtime, and I had to speak to the media. It is very hard some days . . ."

Aleesa had calmed down, her head now resting on my shoulder as she sniffled and shuddered.

"It *is* hard. I get it." I watched him a moment as he stared at the floor. He looked so sad, so . . . lonely. My heart hurt seeing him this way. I hoped he realized he wasn't alone. "Have you given her any medicine for the stomachache?"

"Not yet."

"Okay. No worries. I'll take care of it. And listen, don't be too hard on yourself. This is a regular thing for toddlers," I assured him. "Could be that she's constipated and can't poop, or maybe she found an old Fruit Snack under her bed and ate it. You really never know with kids, so don't stress too much about it. And if it feels like too much for you, just call me next time. I mean it when I say I'm here to help."

He pressed his lips, giving a quick nod.

I turned away with Aleesa to go to the pantry for the medicine basket. There were all kinds of things stored inside it. TYLENOL, BENADRYL, MOTRIN, cough syrups, gas tablets, vitamins. I came across the tummy-ache-relief medicine and grabbed it. I carried her to the island counter, placing her on top of it so I could open the box.

She stared at me, lips pouty and eyes damp.

"No feel good, Tava," she said in a fragile voice.

That little voice broke my heart.

"I know, angel. It's okay." I rinsed out the measuring cup. "We're going to take this"—I poured medicine into the cup—"so it will make you feel better. It tastes like grapes. You like grapes, right?"

She wiped her eyes. "Yes."

"Good." I gave her the cup, and she brought it to her lips and drank it down. I took it away, rinsed it out, and replaced the medicine in the basket. It was still a bit early in the morning, and I could sense she was tired. Aleesa wasn't an early riser, so she could use another hour or two of sleep, I was sure.

I scooped her off the counter, carried her to the sofa, and laid her down. She wasn't having that, though. She crawled onto her dad's lap and snuggled into his chest instead.

He held her close, and I offered him a blanket.

He covered her delicately, as if she were a newborn, tucking the blanket between her chin and shoulder, then making sure her bare feet were covered.

I went to the kitchen and fiddled around, unsure what to do now. This was the first time Aleesa had been sick since I had been hired. She'd had a couple of accidents here and there and the sniffles, but nothing that had made her feel like she felt today.

Most Saturday mornings I spent time getting ready for the day, doing her hair, taking her for walks or to the park, going grocery shopping, or letting her ride her tricycle in the courtyard.

It didn't help that my mind was still racing from that email from Luther. Aleesa would have been a welcome distraction from his bullshit. I could feel myself getting worked up about it again and my anxiety spiking, so with my back to Javier, I closed my eyes and took several deep breaths while counting to ten.

"Are you okay?" Javier asked.

I turned around. His head was slightly cocked, and the skin between his brows was pinched.

"Yeah." My response was breathy, rushed. "I'm okay. Just hoping Leesa feels better soon."

Javier seemed to buy my excuse, because he looked from me to Aleesa again as she rested on his chest. "I hope so too."

It didn't take long for her to fall asleep. Javier leaned back with a relieved exhale, stretching his long legs and resting the back of his head on the top of the sofa.

"You think I am a failure," he muttered.

"What?" My eyes widened. "No. Why would you say that?"

"I cannot even calm my own daughter enough to give her medicine."

"That's not true." I entered the living room again, dropping down on the recliner across the room from him. "You're both tired. And I'm sure you were about to handle it just fine."

"Sure . . . but you are much better at this than I am."

I smiled a little. "I'm just used to working with kids. I actually want to finish school so I can get a degree in children's psychology."

"You do?" he asked, truly surprised.

"Yes. I love kids. I love how innocent their minds are yet how big their imaginations can be. Things that are so small to us are significant to them. It's not hard for them to appreciate the world."

"That is an interesting take."

"Besides, it's different when you're a parent. It's kind of your job to freak out and stress over them."

He laughed at that. Actually laughed. With teeth showing.

Then he dropped his head to study his daughter. "I worry for her so much."

"About what?"

He was quiet a beat, head shaking as he stroked her cheek with his thumb. She let out another long breath after a deep inhale. "Because her life will always seem a bit broken without her mother in it. I wish sometimes that it was me who was taken, not Eloise."

*Oh.*

"It is hard to raise a child through grief," he continued. "People expect me to be this happy man, one who should be grateful that I am still alive and that my daughter is too. And trust me, I *am* glad that I have Aleesa. I am glad that she is here and that she is healthy, but there is not a single day where I do not feel like I do not belong here. Not one day where I do not know Aleesa would be better off if she had her mother instead of me."

"Javier, I—"

"I am sorry." When he looked up, his eyes were glistening. "I have shared too much. As I told you, I am just *really* exhausted." He tried laughing it off.

"No—don't apologize. Trust me, I get it." I threw up a hand, hoping he wouldn't rile himself up too much. "I've lost a father and a brother-in-law. And I know those two are not the same as losing a spouse, but I understand grief. My dad was the best man I ever knew." I had to pause and look away to bite back tears. "I . . . um . . . I can still remember the things he did for me and Davina. He was seriously the best." I tugged at one of my locs, eyes still wandering. "And Davina's first husband, Lew, he was a *really* great guy. He loved her and truly felt like a brother to me." My eyes flicked to Javier's again. "So believe me, I get it. I'm not judging you for what you think or how you feel. Yes, girls need their moms, but they also need their dads. You're doing fine."

He kept his eyes on me the entire time. His gaze fell to my nose, then my mouth. I stared at his lips for a bit . . . until I realized we were looking at each other a few seconds longer than necessary. He seemed to realize, too, and tore his eyes away.

"I, um . . . I can go lie her down if you want me to," I offered, gesturing to Leesa.

"That is okay." He rose with her. "I can at least handle that."

A soft laugh escaped me. "Okay."

I watched him round the corner and disappear. When I heard his heavy steps lumbering up the stairs, I slouched back on the recliner and replayed our conversation in my head.

He was finally opening up to me.

This was a good thing . . . but also triggering.

I missed my dad *so much*. I'd have done anything just to speak to him again, at least one more time. And Lew . . . man, that was a tough loss too.

Lew was so young, and Davina was so in love with him. Every Christmas, he'd give me these silly gifts. Socks with butts on them, shirts with sayings on them like *Thou shall not try me* or *Sarcasm is my second language*. And with those silly gifts, he'd add in a romance book or a bookstore gift card.

I understood why it was so hard for Davina to move on from him. And I could understand why Javier always had his guard up. He had lost so much of his peace. He had lost a *wife*, but he couldn't do what Davina was able to do.

He couldn't stay in his house or in his bed and cry the days away. He couldn't hide from the world and shut everyone and everything out for weeks. He had a child that depended on him, which meant he had to wake up *every single day* and find just enough strength within himself to keep going for her.

I couldn't imagine how hard that was to do—not taking the time to be selfish or to wallow, all because someone quite literally *needs* you to survive. With the sacrifices he had made for Aleesa . . . I could only imagine how he truly felt inside after doing this alone.

So focused on my own feelings, I hadn't really thought of it that way until now.

I realized my sister was right. I needed to take it easy on him because he wasn't grumpy and standoffish for no reason.

He was just a man trying his best while coping with grief.

# NINE

## JAVIER

Right after putting Aleesa down for a nap, I went to my bed, only to have a familiar nightmare. One that always happened around the time of year Eloise had died.

Eloise sat on a bed with a light shining down on her. Her silky dark-brown hair swam to her shoulders, and she wore the pink nightgown that was her favorite. She looked really beautiful that day.

I realized after a while that she was in our bed, sitting right in the middle, with her back against the headboard. She held a baby swaddled in pink. I approached the bed, and she looked up at me, smiled, then offered me the baby.

"She's all yours," Eloise said.

I studied my baby's face. My beautiful baby girl with the button nose and sandy curls. Her green eyes were just like Eloise's.

I looked at Eloise again, but people were now surrounding her. Blood poured from between her legs, and when she saw this, she screamed. Someone took the baby from me, and I was torn between going to Eloise or making sure my baby was okay.

But Eloise made the decision for me. She pointed at our daughter, demanding that I go. Then she continued screaming.

Some time passed. I did not know where I went, only that I was taking care of our baby. Finally, I returned to the room to check on her, but Eloise and every single stranger was gone.

The only trace that my wife had ever been there was the massive bloodstain in the middle of the bed.

# TEN

## JAVIER

I probably should not have revealed so much to Octavia.

After that conversation with her during Aleesa's stomachache, she looked at me with way too much sympathy in her eyes.

Or maybe it was pity.

I did not expect sympathy from anyone. I believed that life was just . . . well, *life*. Shit happened, sometimes it was unfair, and there was nothing anyone could do about it. That did not mean you had to be content with the cards life dealt, though.

So many people say that as time passes, life gets easier after losing someone you love. That was not the case for me.

I was a solo father trying to raise a girl who would eventually become a young woman, and then an adult woman. I wanted her to become a person who was smart in her choices, strong, cautious, and resilient. But I was afraid that in doing so, I would strip away some of her softness.

Octavia said girls need their father, and I believed that, but in my opinion, they need their birthing parent most.

Why? Because they spend months growing inside their womb.

They are fed with nutrients from their bodies.

They are birthed by that parent through that odd combination of pain and love.

They are literally attached to that parent until the cord is cut.

Regarding Aleesa, my mother and my sister, Catalina, were around and helped me as much as they could, but my mother spent most of her time with my grandparents in Argentina, and my sister was a pretty popular painter in New York.

I appreciated both of them when they visited and took Aleesa under their wings. They taught Aleesa things I could not . . . and so did Octavia. That was why I could not be fully irritated by her pity.

Still, I felt stupid for spilling my guts like that. It was unlike me and troubled me so much that my game was off in our second semifinal.

"You've got bags under your eyes, man," Deke said during halftime.

"I'm fine," I lied, waving him off. I lifted the hem of my jersey, using it to wipe away some of the sweat above my brow. The whistle blew when Vonny, one of our shooting guards and the team captain, fouled one of our opponents.

"Oh, come on," Jacobi yelled, sitting left of me. "That's bullshit and they know it."

"Straight-up bullshit," Deke grumbled. "Swear they're out to get us this year."

"Bishop!" Coach Harrison called. "Get in there. Vonny, sit for a sec! Cool off."

Vonny jogged toward the bench as Deke took his place on the court. The foul that'd disrupted the stadium meant nothing when EJ slid a nice pass to Deke and Deke rose to the tips of his toes to sink a three.

"Let's go!" Jacobi hollered, clapping his hands. He swatted his towel at the court, then shook my shoulder. "Come on, Valdez! Cheer up! Where ya head at?"

*Not here.*

I was relieved when the final buzzer went off. But, of course, it was my turn to deal with the media again, which meant I had to answer stupid questions about how off my game was on the panel.

I do not think the media realizes that it is not intentional for any athlete to have bad games. Honestly, I don't believe they see us as human at all. We are merely entertainment to them.

"Can you tell us what was going through your mind when you played today, Javier?" one of the journalists asked.

"Life" was all I said.

"Of course. Could you elaborate?"

"I do not think there is much more to elaborate on."

"Is it because the anniversary of your wife's passing is approaching?" another journalist asked—without waiting his fucking turn, I should add.

I clenched my jaw.

Deke shifted in the chair next to me. "Easy, big dog," he murmured to me with his mouth away from the mic. Then he leaned forward and said, "I feel Javier on this life thing. It gets crazy. Sometimes when we're in the game, some of us have personal things going on outside of it, which makes it hard to concentrate on the court. For example, my fiancée has been sending me color samples for our wedding place mats. Hard not to think about whether we should choose burnt orange, sage green, or burgundy. Picking colors has to be more important than playing basketball, right? I mean, these are real problems we gotta figure out."

Everyone laughed, and the next questions were directed at Deke and my other teammates, Vonny and Pavlo.

Once we wrapped up, I rode in an SUV with Deke, EJ, and Jacobi to our hotel.

"Thanks for stepping in like that." I eyed Deke, who sat next to me on the second row of the SUV. Jacobi was up front and EJ on the third row.

"Don't sweat it," he said. "You know I got your back."

I appreciated that more than he knew.

Once we'd arrived at the hotel, Jacobi and EJ took off in separate directions, leaving me and Deke standing in the lobby. A few fans from the bar spotted us and approached, begging for autographs. Deke, of course, was happy to oblige. He loved the attention and ate it up like candy.

I was the complete opposite of him. I did not care for all the attention, but I did not like to be rude to my fans, so I signed their items.

"What's going on with you anyway?" Deke asked as we took a private elevator to our rooms.

I rubbed my forehead with a sigh. "I had that dream again . . . about Eloise."

"Oh. Shit."

"Yeah. *Shit.*"

"I'm sorry, man. I know that's tough. Especially with it being so close to the date you lost her and all."

"I just do not understand why I keep having it. It keeps haunting me every single year, and it's becoming more and more vivid."

Deke shrugged. "Maybe it's trying to tell you something."

"Tell me what?" I snapped. "That my wife bled out and there was nothing I could do to save her?"

Deke stared at me. If he were anyone else, he would have been intimidated. But this was Deke. He knew me well.

"You need someone to listen, or someone to give advice?" he asked in a calm voice.

"I . . . I don't know." I closed my eyes, trying hard to fight the wave of emotion ready to drown me. "I just do not understand why shitty things like that happen. I was so worried about Aleesa, but Eloise clearly was not well, and maybe if I had paid closer attention . . ." The sentence fell off. I released a defeated sigh, knowing it was pointless to even voice this. Eloise was gone. She could not come back, no matter how much I wished she could.

The elevator swelled with silence until the bell chimed and the doors split apart. We had made it to our floor.

Deke gestured out the doors, insisting that I go first. I did, and he followed right after.

I stood in front of my door, ready to just forget this day, shower, and go to sleep. I could FaceTime Aleesa in the morning, before the next game. I wanted to tonight, but it was too late to call. Seeing her would have made me feel better, though, that was for sure.

"If you're looking for advice . . ." Deke trained his eyes on me. They were mildly intense but soft around the edges. "I think you need to stop blaming yourself and start *forgiving* yourself."

# ELEVEN

## OCTAVIA

I took Aleesa to the next semifinal home game. It was the last home game of the season, and she missed her daddy.

Luckily, Davina was able to join us. We sat on the second row, swarmed by fans in red or black uniforms, face paint, or curly wigs.

"How ihh eheryin wit wurr?"

I looked at my sister, who had a mouth full of hot dog. "What?" I laughed.

She chewed some more before swallowing. "I said 'How is everything with work?'"

"Oh. It's fine. But stop talking with your mouth full. You know it grosses me out."

She rolled her eyes, taking another bite of hot dog. After chugging down some Diet Coke, she said, "I really need to lay off the carbs. How am I going to fit into my dress if I'm eating stadium food?"

"Didn't you say you hadn't eaten all day?"

"I didn't," she confirmed. "I was rushing back from that meeting in Denver so I could make this game. Deke really wanted me to come."

"Well, if you ask me, stadium food is better than no food." My sister had a bad habit of skipping meals if she got too consumed with work. "I'm surprised Tish let you go all day without eating."

"Tish wasn't with me for that meeting," Davina told me. "She's on a little getaway with her man."

"Ah."

"But seriously. Work is good? No issues?" She eyed Aleesa, who sat in the seat between us and was staring up at the massive jumbotron.

"No, not really. I mean, Grumpy Giant is still a *little* closed off, but his attitude toward me is a lot better."

"Is it?" Her brown eyes expanded as she tucked a curl behind her ear. "In what way?"

I hesitated and she noticed. Her head cocked, and her eyes narrowed.

"Did something happen?" she asked with a whisper of a smile.

"No, no." I waved a dismissive hand, shaking my head. I wasn't even sure why I was hesitating. I told Davina *everything*. But . . . this felt like something I didn't need to share. Javier had confided in me, and I respected that. It felt wrong to repeat any of what he'd said the day Aleesa had a stomachache.

"Tavia?" Davina called in her big sister voice.

I looked into her curious eyes before glancing down at Aleesa. She clapped and squealed as the Raven's mascot ran onto the court, flapping its big black wings.

"Okay. Don't tell Deke, because I don't know if I should even be sharing this, but he talked a little about his wife for the first time a few days ago."

"Oh." My sister shifted in her seat, causing her gold bangles to rattle. "What did he say about her?"

"To sum it up? Basically, he wishes she were here taking care of his baby girl instead of him. He said it was hard to parent through grief. And I can tell he feels so much pressure and everyone has all these expectations of him. But . . . I don't know, Vina. It seems to really be weighing him down. I've never seen him like he was that morning. He looked so . . . broken and sad."

"Because he is." My sister sat back in her chair with a sigh. "That's why I told you to take it easy on him. He's pretending to get by with his grumpy ways, but . . . I know a broken person when I see one."

She paused, and we both took the opportunity to look at the court, where a woman was doing some kind of bird dance with the mascot. This, of course, made Aleesa giggle.

"I think you just have to get to know him a bit more, and vice versa," Vina said. "This summer will probably help with that since he'll be home more."

"Yeah," I murmured. "Maybe."

An announcer's voice broke through the speakers of the arena, and Aleesa jolted in her chair.

"Ah! Tava, it's loud!" she yelled, covering her ears. She was hit or miss about the noise. During some games, she was tolerant of the booming voice flowing through the arena. Other times, like now, it was too loud and startled her.

I dug into her backpack, rooting around for her noise-canceling headphones. After placing them over her ears, I picked her up from her chair and placed her on my lap. Now content, she kicked her feet because she knew what was coming next.

After the dancers did their thing, the arena darkened, minus the spotlight revealing the player tunnel. The announcer raved about the Ravens before calling each one onto the floor.

When number eight was announced and the name Javier Valdez echoed around us, Aleesa clapped, and I stood with her in my arms so we could cheer.

The first thing he always did when running out was turn his head to look for his daughter.

"That's Daddy!" she squealed. "Hi, Daddy!"

Her squeal was adorable, and her joy was infectious. I smiled and waved with her as Javier blew a kiss. He always did this—blew her a kiss, then smiled as he jogged toward the lineup—but there was something about it today that caught me off guard.

Maybe because right after doing it, he looked me in the eyes with that same smile and bobbed his head.

Or maybe my mind was playing tricks on me.

I tore my eyes away when Deke Bishop was called to the floor and the arena burst into an uproar. That was the thing about my future brother-in-law. Everyone loved him. I was positive that 90 percent of the audience were specifically here to see him.

Deke jogged out with that cocky smile of his, waved at the crowd, and then looked our way. He pressed two fingers to his lips, kissed them, and threw them in the air, eyes locked on Davina.

She kissed her fingers to return his love.

"Ugh," I groaned. "Y'all are so in love. It makes me sick."

She bumped me with her shoulder, blushing. "Don't be a hater."

~

"I need to tell you something." I glanced at Davina after pulling my gaze from the jumbotron.

She turned her head, finding my eyes. "What's up?"

"Luther emailed me."

Her face immediately twisted into a frown. "And said *what*?"

"He said he moved to Atlanta and has a job with some tech company. He also said he saw me in the crowd during one of the games, with Aleesa, so he assumes I'm in Atlanta, too, and wants to meet up. He claims he's changing his ways." I rolled my eyes.

Davina gave me a careful once-over. "You're not considering it, are you?"

"No—girl, hell no!" I practically shrieked and was glad Aleesa was tuned out, too busy watching the players run back and forth on the court.

Vina's shoulders slumped with relief. "Good. 'Cause he doesn't deserve any of your time anymore. He lost that privilege the moment he disrespected you."

"I just don't get how he found my new email address," I said, watching one of the Ravens miss a layup. The crowd groaned in unison.

"Did he say what kind of tech company he's working for?"

"No . . . but I do remember him always talking about hacking and how easy it was to find someone's information." I shuddered at the idea of him digging deep into the web just to find an email address for me. "I should've known better."

When I left Luther, I had changed my phone number and abandoned my email address to make a new one that didn't have my first or last name, and I had been glad that I'd never given him Mama's address.

Mama had met him once during a dinner at Luther's and my place and had told me the next day that she didn't like him. That was in the beginning of our relationship. I remember being so upset with her for being judgmental and not accepting him, but now I could see why she'd said it.

She'd seen something in him that I couldn't see. Something . . . *dangerous*. Davina said something when she met him, too—that there was something off about him. But my sister, though fiercely protective, knew when to back off. She told me I would see the truth eventually.

Luther would tell me that my family was crazy for thinking so badly about him, and I let him manipulate me into thinking my family actually *were* the crazy ones.

"If I were you, I would delete his email and act like you never saw it. Your life is way better without him in it, sis."

"Yeah." I sighed. "You're right." I whipped out my phone, went to my emails, and surfed until I found it. "Deleted," I said after hitting the trash icon. I don't know why I hadn't done that sooner. That action alone brought me so much relief.

But that same night, while alone in the guesthouse, hearing crickets chirp and the wind rustle, I took it upon myself to search for Luther on Instagram.

I hadn't done this in years, but there was something niggling at my brain, begging to see if he had changed. His Instagram handle was the same. *LuthTooReal.*

"Stupid username," I mumbled.

His most recent image was of him posing with a group of men. They all wore the same pastel-blue shirts with a logo on the chest.

CordTech.

The next image showed him dressed in a suit, standing in front of a church, with the caption Praise God and the prayer-hands emoji.

Last I checked, Luther had too much of a god complex to consider religion.

Another image showed him sitting on the beach with the caption trying to let go of regrets.

That's when I closed the app.

My heart was much too soft to go through his pictures, reminiscing about certain things, like how well kept his beard was or the dark waves in his hair. That light-brown skin, the crooked smile, and those ocher eyes.

Luther was attractive, but his looks were deceptive. Maybe he had changed. Maybe he hadn't.

But for what it was worth, I really hoped he was a better man. If he truly had altered his ways, I wished him all the luck in finding someone who found him worthy.

# TWELVE

## OCTAVIA

The Ravens won the semifinals and were headed to the conference finals.

Javier had to leave early to fly to Houston, which meant I was up an hour prior to his leaving to shower and get dressed so I could make it to the mansion.

As I walked in through the back door, I spotted him sitting on one of the barstools in the kitchen, scrolling through his phone. He heard the door and lifted his head. Wisps of his hair fell into his eyes as he did that. He was going to need a haircut soon.

"Good morning," I murmured.

"Morning." He slid off the barstool, pushing his hands into his front pockets when he stood. "I am just waiting for Jackson to get here with the car." Jackson was his driver.

"Gotcha. No issues with Leesa this morning?"

"None at all. Last I checked, she was drooling all over her pillow."

I laughed. "Good."

His eyes lingered on mine for several seconds before he straightened up and said, "Oh—before I leave. I meant to give you something last night after the game but forgot."

He made his way toward his bag on the floor in the foyer. After digging through one of the larger pockets, he pulled something out and twisted around to face me again.

"For you," he said, handing a book to me.

*Parable of the Sower* by Octavia E. Butler.

I ran my fingers along the cover, smiling so hard I felt like my face was going to break. I looked back up at him.

"Are you serious?" My voice came out softer than expected. "You got this for me?"

"I did. I . . . well, there was a bookstore in the hotel we stayed in, and I saw this book on display. It had your name on it, which I thought was interesting at the time—and I always see you reading during your downtime, so I figured you would like it . . ." He scratched the back of his head with a wry smile.

My heart pumped faster, and I couldn't help shaking my head.

"If you do not like it, I can always donate it or—"

"No—Javier, I love it," I said, meeting his eyes again. "I love it. Thank you."

"So why did you shake your head?" he asked.

"Because there is a funny story behind this author's name and mine. It's not a coincidence that I have her name, you know?"

"No?"

"No. My mom named me after her, and it was *this* exact book that made her want to. It's one of her favorites and the reason why she became a fan." I huffed a laugh. "Apparently when I was born, I cried so hard she thought I could feel her pain, just like the heroine in the book."

"Oh, wow." He chuckled. "That is very interesting."

"Wait until I tell her and Davina about this." I giggled. "They are going to lose it. You know, this is sort of kismet. You had no clue that I was named after this author, but you got me her book."

"*Kismet*? I have not heard that word before. You will have to forgive me. English is not my first language."

"That's okay. It just means *fate* or *destiny*. Maybe I was meant to work for you after all. And maybe you were meant to give me this book so it could all come full circle somehow."

"Ah. I see." He nodded, head lowering.

*Wait.* What was that? A blush? Wow. Javier Valdez was actually blushing.

"This is a really sweet gift, Javier. Thank you again."

"You are welcome, Octavia."

His phone chimed in his pocket, and he dug it out. "Jackson is here." The phone went back into his pocket, and he released a long exhale. His cheeks were still tinged pink. "If there is anything you need, do not hesitate to reach out to me."

"Okay."

"And if Aleesa does not feel well, you can always—"

"Call Dr. Navarra. I know, I know."

He forced a smile. "I will just give her one last kiss before I go."

I nodded. That warm and fuzzy feeling was hitting me again. I cleared my throat as he left the kitchen to jog up the stairs, then made my way to the sofa with the book. I studied the cover with a goofy smile. I don't even know why I was smiling. It was just a novel. I always received books as gifts . . .

But Javier had thought of *me* when he bought it.

He thought about me . . . even when I wasn't around.

I didn't know what that meant exactly, but knowing so caused constant flutters in my stomach.

# THIRTEEN

## JAVIER

The Ravens, unfortunately, did not make it to the NBA Finals.

Los Angeles and Houston did.

It sucked that we didn't. Our team had worked harder than ever, some of us clocking in early and late hours at the gym just to better our game. We had a good season, despite not making it, and truthfully, I was relieved it was done for now.

It was never the game that I grew weary of. It was all the traveling and missing out on time with my family. Going from state to state, jumping on and off charter planes, waking up in different hotels with different views. Sometimes jet lagged, sometimes not. It was completely exhausting.

Now that the season was officially over and summer had peaked, it meant I could focus more on Aleesa. We were one week away from her birthday party. My mother was flying in from Argentina and would be staying with us for a few weeks, and my sister, Catalina, was flying in from New York.

Octavia, as promised, had taken care of everything for the party.

And I mean *everything*.

Every decoration, party bag, table setting, and food choice and even the custom cake. She'd even hired someone to come and set up a large glass tank so an actress could use it and pretend to be a mermaid. This was per my request. I wanted Aleesa to have something she could remember. Perhaps it was too much, but there was no such thing in my mind when it came to her.

The morning of the party, Octavia was there bright and early, helping my mother and sister get Aleesa ready. Octavia took care of bathing her and styling her hair, while my mother and sister helped her get dressed before taking about a million photos of her.

I handled the caterers and determined how the backyard would be set up, and about an hour before the party, my mermaid princess waltzed out the back door, calling my name.

"Oh, mi princesa! Look at you!" I lowered to a squat and held my arms open as she ran toward me in a shimmery blue dress and a matching tiara. Her sandy hair was in two curly pigtails, and she had blush on her cheeks.

I frowned.

"Catalina, I told you no makeup." I stood up with Aleesa in my arms, locking eyes on my younger sister. "She's four, not four*teen*."

"It was just a teensy bit," my sister said, waving a hand at me. "It's her birthday. Let her look pretty."

Catalina was forever the rebel. A lot of our facial features were similar, especially our eyes, brown and framed with thick, long lashes. When you saw her dark-brown hair that cascaded into a fierce ombre of red orange to her shoulder blades, you knew to expect some sort of trouble from her.

I prayed for the man who would one day take my sister's hand in marriage and have to deal with her for the rest of his life. She was a free spirit, never one to be shackled by life. If you did not support that, she would happily shove her middle finger in your face.

"Oh, please," my mother said, approaching us, ready to squeeze Aleesa's cheeks. "Mi niña is *always* pretty. Muy, muy bonita." She made kissing noises, and Aleesa giggled. My mother was no taller than five feet, with wavy deep-brown hair that reached the middle of her back.

Her skin was slightly darker—more a rich beige—most likely from a recent tan on one of the beaches of Argentina.

That was one thing about my mother. If she was not in the United States with us or checking in with my grandfather in his retirement home in Argentina, she was soaking up sun at one of the nearby beaches.

My daughter left my arms, and when my mother had her, she carried her toward the empty water tank, where the mermaid actress would be soon.

I carried my line of sight to Octavia, who was wearing a one-piece black bathing suit under jean shorts. She had piled all her hair into a ponytail on top of her head, so her locs went in all sorts of directions. Messy and cute. She straightened up one of the snack tables, then flipped her wrist to check her Apple Watch.

Catching where my attention had gone, Catalina brushed against my side and said, "You look at her in a very familiar way."

I dropped my gaze to hers. "What are you talking about?"

"In that *familiar* way, you know?"

"No, I do not know, because you are not making sense."

"Yes, you do." She grinned, then strolled away, heading in Octavia's direction. She plucked a cherry from under the plastic wrap covering a fruit tray while saying something to Octavia. Octavia turned her head and locked eyes on me.

Then they both laughed.

What the hell did my sister say to her?

I shook my head, focusing on the DJ instead, who was connecting his speakers.

Within the next twenty-five minutes, I spotted two familiar faces walking through the backyard hand in hand. Deke and Davina. I could not help but smile as I watched them.

Deke carried a present wrapped in pink gift wrap under his free arm but gazed down at Davina as she talked. It seemed he wasn't listening at all, by the way he stared at her as if she were a meal. But I knew he was. He was always listening to her.

It was nice seeing them together. Seeing him happy. And her . . . especially after all she'd been through. Because of it, it seemed Davina and I understood one another on a different level. We were sort of like the people in a grief support group who like to be present but not say much. Just nod in agreement and accept life for what it is.

Davina spotted me and waved, causing the glittery gold bangles on her wrist to sparkle under the sun. She released her fiancé's hand to meet up with me.

"Hi, Javier. How are you?" she asked, grabbing both of my hands and squeezing them.

"I am doing good. And you?"

"I'm great. I know we're a little early—sorry. Deke said he wanted to be the first one to give Aleesa a gift." She rolled her eyes in that *he's so extra but I love him for it* way.

I turned my eyes to Deke as Davina released my hands. Deke simply smiled and shrugged. "What can I say? I'm her favorite person." Our hands connected in a clap followed by a brief brotherly hug. "What's up, Valdez?"

"Not much. I thought you had to meet Arnold today?"

"I do, but I pushed the time back. He can wait. I wasn't missing out on my little homey's day. Where's the birthday girl anyway?"

"She was with my mom near the snack table." I peered around until I spotted them near the mermaid tank, where toy fish were now scuttling inside. "Well . . . now they're by the tank again."

When I pointed, Deke nodded and took off. He jogged across the backyard, toting the present, but as soon as he'd gotten closer to Aleesa, he set the present down to scoop her up from behind.

Caught off guard, Aleesa squealed loudly as he twirled her around in his arms.

My mother laughed, placing a hand on her hip.

When Deke set my daughter back down, he reached for the present while saying something to her. A laugh came from my right, and I glanced at Davina. She watched Deke's interaction with Aleesa thoroughly, with soft eyes and a warm smile.

"Do you think you two will ever have kids?" I asked.

"Oh, um . . ." She bobbed her head, eyes lingering on Deke a moment longer before they swiveled up to mine. "I think so. I mean, we've talked about wanting kids in the future. We have to get through this wedding first, though."

"That is true. Is all of the planning stressing you out?"

"You know, it's not so much the planning that's stressing me. It's trying to balance work *while* planning a wedding. It's hard to be fully present sometimes with the wedding planner when I'm being called to the warehouse for an emergency or someone has sent an urgent email." She shrugged, as if it were no big deal. "But I can handle it."

"I am sure you can. You are a strong person."

She smiled. "Thank you, Javier."

"Javi!" I turned to the sound of my mother's voice. She was standing in the middle of the yard, her phone raised in the air. "It is your abuelo! He wants to speak to you and wish Aleesa a happy birthday!"

"Be right there, Mamá." I looked at Davina again. "Duty calls. Can I get you anything to drink?"

"I'm okay. You go take care of business."

Davina gave me a pat on the arm before walking away to meet Octavia, who was chatting with the mermaid actress. Fortunately, Deke was making his way toward us with Aleesa on his shoulders. In her hands were two brand new baby dolls . . . and a pack of STARBURSTs.

"Candy? *Really?*" I pressed my lips as he removed Aleesa from his shoulders.

"I couldn't help myself, man. She loves them."

"You are lucky it is her birthday." I lowered my eyes to my daughter, who was trying her hardest to open the sleeve of candy. "Come, Leesa. Abuelo Pedro wants to speak to you."

~

An hour later, the backyard was swarming with bodies.

Children from Aleesa's ballet class or former playgroups, as well as some of my teammates' kids, ran across the grass, full of laughter and squeals. Most slid belly down on the waterslide, while others blew bubbles or jumped around the sprinklers.

Aleesa, now standing in a pink bathing suit with holographic mermaid scales, was decorating a mermaid craft at the activity table. I stood several feet behind her, keeping a close eye on how she handled the glue stick (she loved trying to smear it on her palms), but it was hard concentrating with some of the parents chatting me up.

This was the one thing I could not stand about parties. The socializing.

Because I played for a professional sports organization, everyone always asked me questions or looked at me to carry conversations. My teammates that were around did not seem to care for it, either, so they either stuck with their kids or made themselves look busy.

Anyone who really knew me could have told you I was not good at carrying conversations. I did not mind silence. In fact, silence was a delicacy I thoroughly enjoyed. But since I was technically the host, they looked to me.

Do not get me wrong, I was thankful for Deke and Davina being there. They, along with my family and Octavia, were the only people I could tolerate, because they treated me like a normal person.

But Deke and Davina were sitting beneath the shade of the patio deck, eating slices of pizza, while my mother and sister were going between the snack tables and the house for replacements and refills. Octavia was on the other side of the table, directly across from Aleesa, coloring a unicorn mermaid.

"It was a close one, though," one of the fathers said, nudging me with an elbow. I was pretty sure he was a dad of one of the friends from Aleesa's first playgroup.

How had he even gotten an invite? She had not attended that playgroup in almost a year. My mother had sent out all the invitations. I guess I really needed to clean up my contact list.

"I tell you, that Bishop has great aim," the man went on, gesturing with a hand to Deke. "He hardly ever misses, does he?"

"He does not," I said.

"You think he'll want to talk about the games?" the man asked, eyeing Deke again. A starstruck fan.

I looked Deke's way. He had his chin tipped up and a smirk on his lips as he waved his hands, insisting Davina do something. She laughed as she raised a napkin and wiped his chin with it.

"Yeah, I do not think he wants to be bothered right now."

"Right, yeah." The man sipped his drink.

"Your defense was great," one of the mothers said.

"Thank you, uh . . ." What was her name again? I swear all these moms looked and acted alike.

"Gianna," she said, doing her best not to frown.

I heard Octavia snort a laugh. I glanced at her. She shrugged.

"Right. Thank you, Gianna. I am so sorry," I apologized. "It has been such a long day already."

"Of course. I can only imagine how exhausted you are, taking care of Aleesa on your own," Gianna said with sympathetic eyes. "That's why I believe kids need *both* parents. Much easier to share the load." Gianna sipped her drink while I held back a grimace.

What the hell was she saying? She acted like I *chose* to have a motherless daughter.

I folded my arms, clinging to restraint. I was not about to curse this woman out at my daughter's party. She probably did not even mean it in a bad way. Still, she could have chosen better words.

"That's why he has help," Octavia said, lumping herself into the group.

Gianna looked Octavia up and down, her fingers curling around her sparkly plastic cup full of lemonade. "Right. The new nanny."

"That's me."

"Oh, boy." Her laugh was snarky as she looked at the man beside me.

Okay. I was wrong. Gianna was a rude, inconsiderate woman.

"Yeah. Anyway, I just wanted to let you know that your daughter is eating grass." Octavia's mouth twisted into a faux smile as she focused on Gianna, who stared at her for a brief moment before twisting her neck and searching for her daughter.

And sure enough, there was her child next to the mermaid tank, on all fours, face down as she munched on grass like a calf.

"My God! Penelope!" Gianna crowed, rushing away from us.

I suppressed a laugh, but the man next to me did not. He busted out laughing before guzzling down the rest of his lemonade. "Gonna get a refill. Maybe I'll get a chance to chat with Deke Bishop."

When he walked away, I looked for Octavia again, but she was back with Aleesa, helping her apply glue to one of her pom-poms.

"You did not have to do that," I said, smirking. "But thank you."

"Yes, I did. She's a b-word."

"B-word?" Aleesa questioned.

"Don't worry about it, angel." Octavia smoothed some of Aleesa's frizzy hair down with the palm of her hand. She then stood as Aleesa reached for a container of purple beads. "Anyway, I can't stand that woman. She's always shooting me ugly looks at ballet. Her daughter's adorable, though. Hope she doesn't get sick from all that grass."

"Yes, well, typically I ignore women like Gianna."

"Must suck being rich."

"Only when dealing with the uppity rich types like her."

She bit back a smile.

I do not know why my eyes lingered on her mouth or the way she caged her plump bottom lip between her teeth.

I cleared my throat and took a step back, pulling my eyes away. "I should see about the cake."

"Oh, I can do it," she offered.

"No, no. That is okay. You stay with Aleesa. I will be right back."

I marched away before I could look at her again.

Because I was doing a lot of that lately. Looking at her. Studying all her details. *Admiring* her.

# FOURTEEN

## OCTAVIA

The cake was massive and shaped like a mermaid's fin. I was glad the baker I found had made it stand out so well.

It'd received so many compliments, and it got to a point where everyone thought it shouldn't be cut because it was too beautiful to eat. But, of course, we cut it. And that moist vanilla and ombre purple frosting was delicious.

The party wrapped up within two hours. I gave Deke and Davina big hugs before they took off. Deke had to go early to meet his manager, then had a flight the following morning to Seattle. Davina wanted to stay a bit longer, but Deke wasn't having that.

I swear it seemed like he could never get enough of her. Such lovebirds. I had to admit, though . . . I was a little envious of their love. It was so real and beautiful. They cared about each other so much, and it showed in the way they looked at each other, spoke to one another, and spoke *about* each other.

Maybe if I'd had a love like that instead of what I had with Luther, I wouldn't be so opposed to commitment.

The kids, after running through sprinklers, doing crafts, playing games, and spending some time in the pool, were beat by the time the party was over. Aleesa as well. I remember thinking she was going to sleep so well that night.

After having dinner a few hours later, I gave her another bath and got her ready for bed. She was yawning and rubbing her eyes during her bedtime story, and as soon as I lay her down, her eyes closed and she drifted off.

After dropping a kiss on her forehead, I stepped out of the room and headed down the stairs. That's when I heard faint murmurs a short distance away.

I rounded the corner, realizing the voices belonged to Javier's mother and sister, Paola and Catalina.

They were nice women. Well, more so Catalina than Paola. Catalina was a sweetheart, and we pretty much had the same sense of humor. Paola, however, gave me the occasional side-eye, probably because she didn't trust me. I could understand that, especially if Javier had a hard time sticking to one nanny for long.

"He hasn't spoken about her all day," I heard Paola say. "I am worried about him."

"You don't need to worry, Mamá. He's fine. Okay? You know Javier doesn't like when you get worked up. Especially around this time of year." Catalina, I'd noticed, didn't have much of an accent, unlike her mother and brother. But I think that was due to the fact that she'd spent more time in the United States growing up than Javier.

He was six years her senior, and their mother had sent them to live with their aunt in the United States for a better education. Catalina had liked learning in the United States and had flourished. Javier hadn't, and because of that, he'd only spent two years in the United States as a kid before returning to Argentina and completing his education there.

According to Paola, she was upset with him for not making the United States work, because she'd spent a lot of money to make it happen. But since he'd received lots of attention for his basketball skills in his home country (and become a rich NBA player, I'm sure), she'd let it go.

"Sí, sí, pero . . ." Paola let out an exasperated sigh. "I just want him to . . . oh, what is the word? To . . . to *acknowledge* how painful this is. I showed a picture of Eloise on my phone to Aleesa, and he walked away. He could not even face it."

"He's just not in the mood to talk about her, and that is fine. Just let it go. When he's ready to talk about it, he will."

A faint thump sounded behind me, and I turned around. At the end of the hallway that led to the pool, the blinds on one of the windows were still drawn. Javier sat outside in a chair that faced the pool, the blue glow illuminating his features as he stared at the water.

I walked down the hallway and opened the door to walk out. The sun had fallen beneath the horizon, but there were still streaks of orange lingering in the sky. The backyard was clear, minus a few streamers and runaway confetti.

Javier heard me coming and lifted his head, eyes glistening like he was on the verge of tears. My chest felt tight and heavy, seeing him this way. I almost paused and thought to go back into the house, or even to the guesthouse, for that matter, just to give him some space, but it seemed too late now. It would have been not only rude to duck off, but awkward too.

He sat up and cleared his throat, blinking several times to dry his eyes. "Aleesa go down okay?" he asked.

"Yep. She's good," I answered. "Went out like a light."

His lips tilted upward on one side, a weak attempt at a smile. Silence ticked by for about five seconds before he said, "I know they are talking about me."

I blinked at him before turning my attention to the house. From here, I could see Paola folding blankets in the living room and Catalina storing things away in the kitchen. Both of their mouths were still moving, and Paola seemed worked up as she snatched up another blanket and folded it. She was probably speaking fully in Spanish now.

"I think so, yeah."

"Every year," he sighed.

I kept quiet as he leaned forward, resting his elbows on the tops of his legs and threading his fingers together. Walking closer to him, I grabbed one of the chairs from the table and brought it near him, but not too close, in case he still needed some space.

"I know everyone is always asking about Aleesa," I said in a quiet voice, "but what about you? Are *you* okay?"

He pursed his lips, still staring at the rippling water. "I am not sure how to answer that."

"What's the first word that comes to mind?"

"No."

"No, you're not okay?"

"No. I am not okay."

"Okay. That's okay."

"Great. Now can we please stop saying the word *okay*?"

"Well, you said it this time, so . . ." I raised my hands and shrugged.

He shook his head, but I didn't miss the faint smirk riding his lips. At least that one was closer to a real smile.

"Hey, um . . . thank you for everything you did to make today happen," he said. "Everyone had a great time, and I cannot remember the last time I saw Aleesa so happy."

It was stupid of me to blush, but I did as I adjusted myself in my chair. "Of course. It was no hassle at all."

"I'm sure it was a bit of a hassle," he said, calling my bluff.

"Okay, fine. Sort of, but only because finding a pretend mermaid to be in that tank for two hours was near impossible."

He chuckled, teeth glinting in the light.

"But it's fine," I said. "I love planning parties and would do it again in a heartbeat."

He nodded appreciatively. Then his smile slipped away, and he sighed again.

"Listen . . ." I leaned forward, finding his eyes. "I know I'm just the nanny, but if you *ever* need to talk about anything, I'm happy to listen."

His head turned so his deep-brown eyes could connect with mine. "I appreciate that, Octavia. There is not much to talk about, though."

"I don't believe that."

"No?"

"No. You lost a spouse. And I don't want to cross lines or anything, but I know you lost her around this time of the year. It's not only Aleesa's birthday but the anniversary of your wife's passing too."

His head turned left, then right in defeat. "I hate that they call it an *anniversary*. Like a person's death is something that should be celebrated. *Life* should be celebrated. Not death."

"Well, you technically did celebrate a life today."

He contemplated that, lips twisting. "A life for a life, it seems," he muttered.

Silence greeted us again.

"Your mom seems really worried about you."

He made a noise between a scoff and a snort. "She always is."

I paused before saying "*I'm* worried about you, Javier."

"You should not worry about me, Octavia. I will be fine."

"I used to tell myself the same thing until one day I woke up crying hysterically from a bad dream and didn't stop crying the whole day. It's like it all hit me at once."

"Your father?"

I nodded. "Nothing could console me. I lost him and had to finally accept that he wasn't coming back. That day I just let it all out."

"I see."

I studied his profile, his sharp jaw and full lips. "Can I ask you something?"

He seemed to hesitate. "Sure."

"Why don't you ever talk about her?"

I watched his Adam's apple bob as he allowed the question to marinate. His eyes lowered to his lap. "It is . . . complicated."

Oh. That wasn't what I expected to hear.

I wanted to ask him what made it so complicated, but this was not the time to overstep. If there was one thing I didn't mess around with, it was grief. Especially someone else's.

"I'll accept that." I smirked. "For now."

"Oh, for now?" he asked, laughing.

"Yes, for now. Hopefully one day you feel comfortable enough to talk about her."

"I would not be surprised if that happened soon. You are very easy to talk to when you're not being sarcastic, and for some reason I find that incredibly annoying." One of his half smiles appeared and caused the center of his cheek to sink in, making it look like he had a dimple.

I busted out in a laugh. "I get that a lot."

"Octavia," he said, turning in his chair to face me a bit more. I perked up, fully alert. "If my . . . *moods* are too much for you, I will understand if you do not want to work here anymore. I know that I am not an easy person to deal with. It is why a lot of the prior nannies either quit or were let go." He scratched his chin. "I do not mean to come across as angry or irritable all of the time. It is just . . . well, some days I think about my past and it weighs on me, and I handle things the wrong way. But I am working on it."

"Well, if you're working on it," I said, "that's all that matters. I wouldn't worry about how anyone else perceives me if I were in your shoes." I leaned forward even more, catching his eyes. "But I have to let you know something, Valdez. I'm not going anywhere. I've dealt with humans that could make you look a saint. Trust me. It's all good over here."

A smile swept across his lips as he sat back in his chair with a nod and a breath of relief. "Glad to hear you will stay, *Tava*."

I grinned.

I wanted to talk more. Ask more. But I didn't want to pry too much or come across as desperate for company . . . even though I was starting to appreciate Javier's.

It didn't help that he looked into my eyes like he, too, wanted to ask me a million questions. Like he'd rather spend time getting to know me than doing anything else. And not in the surface-level way, but on a deeper level. A level that not many people reached unless they'd already formed a solid connection.

But that could never happen.

Why would we *ever* let that happen? For Aleesa's sake, I wouldn't.

Yes, Javier was sexy as hell. Yes, I'd have pounced right on him and climbed him like a tree . . . but he was my boss. I was his child's caretaker. And I had a very strict rule about not sleeping with anyone I worked for. I liked maintaining a professional image and wasn't going to let a bout of lust for an NBA player destroy that.

As if he was thinking something along the same lines, Javier cleared his throat and shifted his gaze as he gripped the arms of his chair.

"You should go and get some rest," he said. "It was a long day for you too. I will head into the lion's den and deal with my family."

A laugh escaped me as I watched him stand. "Okay. Good night, Javier. Try not to bring their claws out."

Chuckling, he rounded the pool, then started walking toward the back door. "Good night, Octavia." He looked back at me, his hand lingering on the door handle, almost as if he was torn between staying outside with me or going in and escaping whatever this humming electricity was between us.

With a small, warm smile, he entered the house. I found it hard to stop thinking about that smile for the rest of the night.

# FIFTEEN

## JAVIER

I could tell Octavia was glad the summer had come and my schedule was freer, because she was eager to request days off. This was a part of our contract: During the summer, she was allowed to have two days of the week off if she desired. And desired she did.

Octavia's first day off was on a Tuesday. I wondered what she did when she wasn't with us, so much so that I took it upon myself to let Aleesa run in the backyard, just so I could get a better view of the guesthouse.

Not that I could see much inside it.

And not that it was any of my business.

I saw her, though, lying on a towel on the grass outside, sunglasses covering her face, her golden-brown skin glistening, probably from sunscreen. A book was in one of her hands, the other tucked beneath her head.

She wore nothing but a yellow two-piece bikini. I remember thinking yellow paired *really* well with her skin. I wanted to see her in more yellow.

"Tava!" Aleesa started running toward the guesthouse, but I caught her and tossed her over my shoulder like a bag of potatoes.

Absolutely not.

I was hardly the type of man to wander around outside unless it was to use the pool, sauna, or hot tub. And we weren't dressed in swimming attire, so . . . how was I going to explain myself to Octavia if she caught us?

"Just mind your own business," I muttered to myself as I carried a whining Aleesa into the house.

~

There was something that was really getting to me.

Now that I was home more, I noticed that whenever Aleesa was napping and Octavia was waiting for her to wake up, she was on her phone a lot more instead of reading. Reading was her go-to thing. Every break she had, I had caught her reading.

But not lately.

She was either texting or scrolling through *BOBBLE*—a useless app that loved reporting the latest celebrity drama—or another app. And call me whatever name you want for being so nosy, but I recognized the name of the other app she was using.

*Spark.*

Spark was a dating app. And I only knew that because my sister, Catalina, talked about it all the time. Apparently, it was great for matching people for perfect ongoing hookups . . . or one-night stands.

Something about Octavia having that app bothered me more than it should have. Was she looking for something ongoing . . . or a one-night thing? Was she currently talking to someone?

The next day Octavia took off was on a Thursday. I noticed her leaving when I looked out the window of Aleesa's playroom. It faced the front yard and cobblestone driveway. Octavia kept her car parked there, but on this particular night she was taking an Uber.

She wore a skintight red dress and high heels. Her hair was pinned up, a few locs hanging around her heart-shaped face. And she had those jewels in her hair again, the ones that made her appear ethereal, like a woman from another planet, too beautiful to belong in a simple place like this.

She was already beautiful, but there was something about the twinkling of those jewels, or the shells or the beads, that did something to me. I wanted to touch them. Tug on them. Feel her hair run through my fingers and . . .

*No.*

Not the nanny.

I watched her climb into the back seat of the Uber and leave. Afterward, I felt a little annoyed. Probably because I knew she was going on a date.

A date with some guy she had met on Spark.

And that she would most likely be drinking if she needed an Uber.

And that if she was drinking, she was expecting something to happen with whoever this guy was.

But again, her personal life was none of my business.

# SIXTEEN

## OCTAVIA

I know, I know.

It was stupid to arrange a date while being a full-time caretaker for an NBA star. Javier didn't like to see himself as a star, but he was.

Most if not all of my time was spent taking care of Aleesa. Javier was busy about 85 percent of the year, with back-to-back games every week during the season and practices in between. The NBA season lasted far too long, if you asked me, but who was I to say anything.

With a schedule like his, there was no room for me to have a deep, personal life, and that was fine because I wasn't looking for anything long term. I'd gotten out of a serious three-year relationship. I'd almost married the guy . . . until I stumbled into a rude awakening.

This was why I always told Davina that I didn't care about dating again. I didn't really trust men anymore, and if anything, they were only good for one thing . . .

*Dick.*

"You have really pretty eyes, you know that?" my date said after sipping from his tumbler of scotch. His name was Terry. We'd been chatting on Spark for four weeks before officially setting up a date. "They remind me of Cleo's."

My brows dipped, and I blinked with confusion. "Who?"

"Oh—nobody. Just the mama of my oldest kid." He waved a hand, half laughing.

I refrained from rolling my eyes.

Unfortunately, Terry was not living up to the flirty text messages we'd shared before our first face-to-face meet.

Don't get me wrong, Terry was handsome, with deep-brown skin and dark waves in his hair that melted into a fade. One diamond earring pierced each of his ears, and he had really nice lips that I knew would be good for . . . *certain* sexual favors. But what he'd failed to mention was that he was a father of three children, all under the age of ten, and that all those kids had different mothers.

This I found out when his phone rang and one of his kids' mothers interrupted our conversation to ask if he could send money for formula. He apologized once he was off the call, then proceeded to tell me about his children. He then went on about how his last relationship hadn't worked out but they were trying to coparent for the baby's sake.

Three different mothers to his kids. It took everything in me not to get up from that table and walk out of the restaurant. The *only* reason I didn't was because a part of me was considering sticking it out just to satisfy my hankering for sex.

I'd make sure he put on a condom, and it helped that I was on birth control, so I wouldn't be one of his baby mama victims.

I squirmed in my chair, battling my sexual frustrations. It'd been so long since the last time I had sex. My vibrator, Rosie, had become my best friend, but I could go only so long without the real deal.

The one good thing about Terry was that he didn't secretly want a serious relationship. Maybe that was because he was too busy popping his seed into every woman he met. That or he had too much on his plate already on top of a massive fear of commitment.

Regardless, it was good that he wasn't seeking something deeper. No relationship business, no expectations, no attempts to be tied down. At least we agreed there.

Both Terry and I mentioned in our bios something along the lines of wanting a hookup with a person who isn't full of expectations but likes having a good time. He probably should have added that he had a weak pull-out game to his as well. Thank God for birth control.

"I'm glad we're finally getting a chance to hang out."

"Yeah. This is nice," I said, gesturing to the restaurant, feigning enthusiasm. At least he had good taste. "You chose well."

He smirked. "Only wanted the best for a beautiful woman like you."

I tried not to cringe as I wondered how many women he'd fed that same corny line to.

He'd made a reservation for dinner at a downtown steak house called Portman's. It was a bitch trying to reach the parking lot with all the construction going on. The Uber driver had to go a different route and dropped me off half a block away. I had to walk a good three minutes just to get to the front door, which caused me to show up ten minutes late.

Terry had thought I was ghosting him. I was starting to regret that I hadn't.

Our food arrived, and Terry cut into his steak while I dug into my honey-glazed chicken. He spoke about his job being a local barber and how he had a good clientele. But as he chatted about opening his own shop and I sipped my tequila and lime, I heard a bubbly, familiar voice.

The voice of a child.

The voice of a child *I nannied.*

Giving my head a turn, I spotted Javier standing at the hostess stand with Aleesa behind him. She had one of her hands pressed to the glass of the fish tank, giggling as she tugged at the hem of her daddy's shirt with the other.

"Oh shit," I hissed. If I could have sunk and melted into the booth, I would have. It was one thing seeing him at his house, but for your boss to see you on a *date* . . . well, that seemed odd.

*Please don't look this way.*

*Please don't look this way.*

*Please don't look this w—*

"You okay?" Terry's voice cut through my thoughts. He looked me over with a mildly confused expression. "Is the food not good?"

"No, the food is good. Sorry, I just . . . I thought I saw someone I knew."

With a dip between his brows, Terry peered over his shoulder to look around, as if he'd know the person I was talking about. As he performed his scan, I did too.

Javier was still there . . . and he was now eyeing both of us.

"Oh, God." I planted an elbow on the table and used my hand to cover the side of my face.

"What is it?" Terry asked.

I shouldn't have cared that Javier saw us. Honestly, it was just a date, and my personal life had nothing to do with my job. But I *did* care because he was now walking through the restaurant with the straps of a to-go bag in one hand and his daughter's hand clasped in the other.

He came straight for our table, eyes dark and hard, a giant among mortals. Everyone stared at him in awe, some whispering and gasping, others snapping pictures on their phones. As always, he wore basketball shorts and a T-shirt. That day, the shorts were navy blue and his white shirt hugged his biceps.

Then Javier did something I did not expect.

He put on a charismatic smile as he approached the table.

"Hi, Octavia." He looked from Terry to me. "I was not expecting to see you here. Everything okay?"

"Hold on." Terry cocked a brow, looking from Javier to me. "Who the hell are you?" Before either of us could answer, Terry proceeded with "Are you in a relationship?"

"No, I—"

"No, we are just really good friends," Javier said, glancing at Terry. Then he focused on me again. "Leesa wanted to come over and say hello. How is your night going so far?"

I dropped my gaze to Aleesa, who slipped her hand out of her father's so she could hug me. I hugged her back, of course, but it wasn't my strongest. I was so confused.

"Javier, what are you doing?" I asked through a forced smile.

"Just checking in. That is all," he answered.

"Wait, Javier *Valdez*?" Terry was no longer confused and annoyed but starstruck now. "Oh shit, man. I knew you looked familiar! Look, I didn't know anything about . . . whatever might be happening between y'all, man. She said she was single."

"I am single!" I countered.

Javier held up a patient hand. "There is no need to apologize. We are not dating. I just wanted to check in and see if she was okay."

"Hmm. That sounds real intimate for a couple of friends," Terry said with a frown.

"Trust me, it's not what you're thinking," I assured him.

But Terry wasn't having it. He gave me a look, as if he didn't believe a single word coming out of my mouth. He then shook his head, guzzled down the rest of his scotch, and peeled out of his chair.

"Look, I don't know what's going on between y'all, but I don't have time for complicated-relationship shit."

Um . . . that was hypocritical of him to say, considering the three women and children he was neglecting right now.

Terry started to walk off but caught himself and snatched his phone out of his pocket. "Actually, before I go, can I get a pic with you?" he asked Javier.

"Sure." Javier crouched just a bit so Terry could snap a selfie.

Meanwhile, I was still in total disbelief. Was this *really* happening? No, it couldn't be happening. There was no way Javier just barged in like that to interrupt my date. Why didn't he just leave the restaurant? Why did he bother coming over to speak? Any other time in public he would have flat-out ignored me and acted like he never saw me.

If I told Davina or Deke this, they'd never believe me. Because it was totally *unlike* him.

"Bye," Aleesa sang, watching Terry go.

Terry left in a flash. It was now I realized he hadn't paid. *Great.*

"Would you like a ride home with us?" Javier asked, as if everything was perfectly normal.

"What?" I hissed. "No! Why would I want to go anywhere with you? You just ruined my date!"

"You did not want to spend another minute with that man, Octavia. I saw it all over your face."

Okay . . . that was partially true. Terry wasn't the man I expected, but Javier still had no right to interrupt us. Did he not realize how it looked having a sexy-as-hell professional basketball player approach our table just to see if I was okay? Terry probably felt intimidated. Had it been a woman coming up to Terry during the middle of our date, I would've assumed they had a thing going on too.

That was not the case between me and Javier, though, and never would be.

"You don't know what I like, Javier," I finally said after several seconds of stewing.

"Please, just come home with us," he insisted, reaching for my hand. "I know you do not have a ride back."

"Javier, I'm not going *anywhere* with you," I snapped in a whisper. "I'll catch an Uber."

"Octavia, I insist. *Please.*"

I blinked up at him as he kept his hand stuck out. Damn him and those sad eyes. Damn him for ruining my one shot at getting laid. He had no idea how much time I'd spent chatting with Terry, getting to know a few important facts about him so that our first hookup wouldn't be completely awkward. I mean, yes, Terry would've been a one-night stand situation, but I could've used him to satisfy myself for the night and then never bothered with him again.

Drawing in a breath, I pushed Javier's hand out of the way and stood up on my own.

"I'm only going because I don't want to wait for a ride," I grumbled. "Now excuse me. I have to pay the bill." I tried making my way around him, but he caught my arm with a delicate hand.

"I will take care of it," he said. "Will you go with Aleesa to the car?" He handed me the car key to his Mercedes. "I parked in the back."

I had the urge to tell him that it was my day off—that I didn't have to be a nanny at this particular time, per the contract. But one thing I didn't want was a bunch of media screaming about a certain basketball player's nanny causing a scene. And the last thing I wanted was to be fired over a shitty date.

So, I held Aleesa's hand, collected my purse, and exited the building.

"The nerve of your dad," I muttered when we reached the car. I clicked Aleesa's seat belt into place. She kicked her feet as I adjusted and tightened the straps, completely oblivious to what was going on between the adults. I envied her naivety.

Afterward, I sat in the passenger seat with my arms crossed tightly over my chest. When I spotted Javier coming toward the car, I pointed my knees to the passenger door and glared out of the window.

He climbed in, taking up way too much space for my liking. He smelled clean, like he'd recently showered and applied a light spritz of cedarwood-scented cologne afterward.

After placing the to-go bag on the floor of the back seat, he started the engine and rolled out of the parking lot. He turned on a KIDZ BOP soundtrack for Aleesa. She belted out "Calm Down" by Rema and Selena Gomez, and her cute singing voice was making it insanely hard to stay mad.

I cut a glance at Javier. He didn't say a word. And he looked angry, as if he had the *right* to be.

"Baby, com dan, com dan," Aleesa sang.

He had no right to be mad. He ruined my night. Now, I was going to have to use Rosie again.

I fished my phone out of my purse and fired up a text to send to Davina.

Me: you will not believe what Javier just did

She responded almost instantly. Which most likely meant she wasn't working.

Vina: What did he do?
Me: He just ruined a date I had!
Vina: A date? How are you even able to have one of those right now?
Me: That's not the point
Vina: Okay . . . how did he ruin it?
Me: It's one of my nights off and I was at a restaurant with a guy I met. Javier ended up at the same restaurant for a to-go order and saw us. Came to the table and interrupted the whole thing.
Vina: Stop lying. Javier wouldn't do that.
Me: I kid you not. He ruined the whole thing. On purpose. I'm pretty sure my date thought we were in some kind of complicated relationship. He didn't seem mad at Javier though, just me. Started obsessing over Valdez and everything. Fucker.
Vina: This is hilarious.

You wouldn't think so, with how blandly she texted. She never used emojis or symbols or anything. I sent her the middle finger emoji.

Vina: Sorry but that is so interesting. I can't even picture Javier doing something like that.
Me: Are you laughing about this? I can't tell. You're so dry when you text.
Vina: Yes, I'm laughing. And shut it.

Then she followed up her previous text with: Can I tell Deke?

Me: Please do. Maybe he'll talk some damn sense into his friend.
Vina: On it.

After texting her, I went to Naomi's name in my messages and sent her a text too:

Me: I hate men.

My other best friend was a slower texter. She worked the night shift as a labor-and-delivery nurse, so I didn't expect a reply from her for a few hours. But at least she had the notification.

When we pulled up to Javier's place, I climbed out first. I didn't have the heart to storm away. Because storming away would've meant not saying good night to Aleesa.

I helped her out of her car seat and carried her to the house while Javier collected the to-go bag. Once inside, I kicked out of my heels before making my way to the living room.

"Tava. Can you eat wif me?" she asked as Javier placed their food on the counter.

"Oh, honey, I don't think so. I already ate, so I'm a little full already."

"Please," she begged, clasping her hands and giving me puppy dog eyes. Guilt gnawed at me. This girl was too much. She knew exactly how to play her cards to win me over.

"How about I just sit with you?" I offered.

"Yay!" She ran to the table and climbed into her booster seat, ready for her meal. I sat in my designated chair, which was right next to hers, while Javier placed a plate on the table in front of her. I felt him looking at me. I didn't bother looking back.

This had to be a violation of my rights, right?

A breach of contract of some sort?

But then again, there was no clause stating that my boss couldn't interrupt my dates. There was, however, a clause stating that he could not terminate me due to anything pertaining to my personal life.

Aleesa dug into her food, and Javier did the same. He'd gotten the glazed chicken too. The few bites I'd had were delicious . . . but I wasn't about to agree on anything with him right now.

Aleesa made all kinds of noises while she ate, bobbing her head and kicking her feet. She tried offering me a broccoli floret, but I politely declined.

"Suit you'self," she quipped.

I fought a smile. She was making it *really* hard to stay serious. And it didn't help that she'd taken a page out of my book. Whenever she'd decline something healthy that I would offer, I'd say "suit yourself."

Once she'd finished eating, I helped her out of her chair. "Are we good now?"

"Can you read to me, Tava?"

*Oh my goodness.*

I side-eyed Javier, who was placing their plates in the sink. He could have intercepted her at any time and told her I had to go, redeemed some of my respect, but he hadn't. The prick. He still hadn't said a single word. And he still looked angry. The fuck was wrong with him?

"Just one story, then I *really* have to go, okay?"

"Okay." She grinned and tugged on my hand, leading me out of the kitchen. I followed her up the stairs and into her room. I never read her a story without putting her pajamas on first, so I changed her clothes, then helped her brush her teeth.

After detangling her hair, I put her cute little bonnet on. I'd bought the bonnet when I first started working with her. Why not? Her curls were too beautiful not to protect. And she loved it, said it made her feel like a princess.

I sat in the recliner in the corner, and she plucked a book from her shelf—one about a baby panda searching for his family.

Somehow, reading a story turned into her showing me the play food she'd made earlier—and a naked doll with crayon all over it that she said needed a bath—until eventually, she rubbed her eyes and told me she was ready for bed.

I laid her down and turned on the white noise machine.

Someone turned the big lights off, so the night-light took their place. I looked over my shoulder after tucking her in. Javier stood between the jambs of the door with a shoulder pressed to one.

At least he didn't look angry anymore.

"Good night, Leesa. I'll see you tomorrow." I planted a kiss on her forehead, then tugged my dress down by the hem before heading to the door.

"*Excuse* me," I grumbled through gritted teeth. Javier shifted sideways before making his way into the room to give Aleesa a kiss.

I drifted through the hallway, ready to take the stairs down and get the hell out of there, but Javier called my name.

I stopped in my tracks and twisted around as he left the door open just a crack. When he fully faced me, I got tired of bottling my anger.

"You embarrassed me tonight," I snapped. "I just . . . I'm still trying to wrap my head around it. Like, what were you even *thinking*? You had no business interrupting my date like that!"

He took a step closer but said nothing.

"Aren't you going to at least apologize?" I demanded, stepping closer too.

"No," he answered.

Anger bubbled in my veins. I wanted to yell. *Scream.* He was so lucky Aleesa was around.

"Why the hell not?" I demanded.

His eyes traveled from my head to my toes.

Then, in two long strides, he closed the gap between us, cupped the back of my head, and kissed me.

# SEVENTEEN

## OCTAVIA

I moaned as Javier took several steps forward, bumping me backward until my back pressed to the nearest wall and caused one of the portraits to shake.

He picked me up in his arms, and my dress rose higher up my thighs. One of his hands slid up the side of my leg while the other, which was on the back of my head, came around to grip my face between his long fingers.

The grip was possessive and powerful, and it definitely sent a message.

"I will not apologize for *wanting* you to myself," he growled on my mouth.

*Wanting me?*

I searched for words to say but hardly had enough time to catch my breath, because his mouth was crashing down on mine again. He removed his hand from my face and carried me through the hall to his bedroom.

I'd been in his bedroom only once, and that was to get the *Bluey* adhesive bandages. Aleesa loved them, but Javier hid them because she didn't use them for cuts or scrapes. She used them like decorative stickers. Other than that, I'd had no reason to go in there.

But now I did. And it was *with him.*

He didn't stop kissing me, even when my back landed on the plush king-size bed. I grabbed hold of his face and kissed him deeper, then our lips parted only briefly so he could lean up and remove his shirt.

Once it was gone, he dove in again, wedging his massive body between my legs. His erection rocked up and down, pressing on my pussy, making me wetter by the second. A quivering, desperate breath left my body. It'd been so long since I felt this. One shift of my panties, one tug of his shorts and boxers, and he would've been inside me.

Just like that.

He was a hell of a replacement for Terry. Javier was someone I could see myself sleeping with, but I could never go through with it—well, that's what I told myself.

No. Really. I had to be smart. I couldn't jeopardize my career for a man's penis. *Ever.* Even if there were no strings attached. Even if we were both willing to look the other way. It was unprofessional as hell and could get very ugly.

The thought of that slapped some sense into me. If things went awry after this, if we took it too far and *did* have sex, how would we feel tomorrow? Or better yet, how would *he* feel?

I had a good guess. He would regret it. One hundred percent.

"Wait." I pressed the palms of my hands on his chest, and he pulled away, lips swollen, eyes glazed with lust. He was unbelievably hard beneath those thin basketball shorts.

Moonlight bathed his bronze skin, highlighting dark-brown nipples on a beautifully sculpted chest. He had a drool-worthy six-pack, too, with deep cuts on either side that created a delicious V.

He was so sexy. *Too* sexy, really.

Seeing that tent in his pants stirred something up inside me. Made me riled up and eager, as if he were water and I was in a desert, parched and only wanting what he could bring. Yes, I was acting like a thirsty bitch.

He would have been perfect to have right now, just to satisfy me. Just to scratch that itch . . .

But, again, we couldn't. Damn it. Turning him away was going to ruin me.

"We shouldn't," I finally told him, coming to my senses.

He stared down at me and immediately started nodding, dark strands of hair tumbling onto his forehead. "Yes. You are right. I—sorry. You are right."

He climbed off the bed and combed his fingers through his hair.

"It's just Aleesa," I added as I sat up, hoping he would understand.

Fortunately, he did. He nodded again. "Yes, Aleesa. We cannot ruin this for her. She enjoys having you here way too much. And I do not want you to look at me differently."

"I wouldn't look at you differently," I murmured. "But I'm afraid *you* would. Or that if you met someone in the near future, you'd let me go as your nanny because of what we did. And . . . I really like my job." I shrugged innocently, hoping those reasons were enough.

His dark eyes landed on me. "I do not plan on meeting anyone in the future." His words were final. As if he knew what all his life had in store for him.

I huffed a laugh. "You don't know that."

"Yes, I do. I do not wish to meet anyone. I do not think I will ever marry again. It is all just too . . . complicated."

Hmm. I could relate. Still, I blinked at him, unsure what to say to that.

"But like I said, you are right. We should absolutely *not* do this," he said, more to himself than to me.

When he sat on the edge of the bed, I slid forward so I could climb off. The moment was over. The electricity was fizzling away. It was time for me to go.

I tugged my dress down before pushing loose strands of my locs over my shoulders.

We gazed at each other. The room fell to a calming silence.

A slice of moonlight took up half the room, bathing his broad shoulders, dark hair, and part of his firm jaw in silvery light.

I should've walked away.

Right out that door.

And it was like he was telling me to do it—to just go. Because if I didn't, something would happen that neither of us could control.

But then he stood up and inched closer, examining every detail of my face. He towered above, locking eyes with mine. Heat radiated off his body, warming me up, luring me in.

"Go, Octavia." He whispered it like it was a warning.

"Okay," I whispered back, even though everything in me was dying to stay.

But I had to go. *Right now.*

I turned around, ready to make my way to the door and escape all the heat and desire swelling in his room.

Before I could, though, Javier caught my wrist, twisted me around, and muttered, "Fuck it."

Then he kissed me again.

# EIGHTEEN

## JAVIER

I didn't know what the hell I was doing. She *needed* to go . . . but why couldn't I let her?

I had her in my hands now, her soft face clasped in mine, her supple golden-brown skin beneath the pads of my fingers. She tasted like remnants of tequila and lime, and I wanted to drink it all away.

I picked her up and held her in my arms again, kicking the door closed as quietly as possible. I could not risk Aleesa waking up and climbing out of her bed to find us tangled around each other.

I turned for the bed and laid Octavia down again. But this time, she didn't stop me. Even though, deep down, I wished she had. I wished she'd have told me to fuck off or told me that I was not important. Or even that she did not want me. Then I would have let her go. I would have accepted that.

But she didn't.

And it didn't help that through every parted kiss she looked into my eyes with stars in hers. Not the kind of stars that made her look starstruck like my fans. The kind that held burning adoration and desire. The kind that made me feel wanted. *Needed.*

"I cannot pull away from you," I breathed on her lips.

"Don't," she murmured. She sat up. "Unzip the back of my dress."

I nodded, and she wasted no time flipping over so she could perch on her knees. Her ass was perfect. I wanted to rub it, caress it, kiss it. But instead, I focused on her zipper, pulling it down until it stopped. I helped her take the dress off, and it slipped over the edge of the bed and hit the floor with a gentle *woosh*.

She turned back over and faced me in a red lace bra and matching panties. Her body was incredible, slender yet thick. Satiny brown skin that I wanted to kiss every inch of.

"*Fuck* . . ." I rasped, "sos muy hermosa, Octavia."

"What does that mean?" she breathed.

"You're so beautiful." I slid my palms up her thighs.

She grinned.

I could not believe she wore this on a date. Matching lingerie? She was expecting to have sex with that man. The sheer thought of that irritated me more than it should have. I did not want anyone to have her. I did not care if that made me selfish. She was mine now.

Where had these feelings even come from? Why was I suddenly so territorial over her?

"Why are you dating?" I asked after another kiss.

"I'm not," she answered.

"So who was that man?"

"Just a hookup that was supposed to lead to what we're doing now. Nothing deep."

I frowned as her mouth grazed my throat. She carried her kisses up, going over my jaw and then my cheek. Then she paused and looked into my eyes.

"What's wrong?" she asked, searching my face for answers of her own.

I shook my head. "It is nothing." I tried kissing her again, hoping to rinse away my stupid feelings, but she caught my face before I could place my lips on hers.

"Javier." She studied all the features of my face. "Are you jealous?"

"Yes," I growled. I saw no point in lying.

"Why?"

I balanced myself on my hands, studying the smoothness of her body, that flat belly and those thick thighs. "Because I did not want him to have you. I do not want *anyone* to have you but me."

I expected her to get upset about that. Honestly, I was upset with myself for cutting in on her date. But when I saw her, it was like my body wasn't connecting to my mind. My legs moved before I could think things through.

If only Aleesa had not pointed out that her Tava was sitting across the restaurant. I never would have noticed, and I would have gotten over it. Then again, if she had not done it, we would not have been where we were. In the same room. *My* room.

Touching.

Kissing.

Wanting.

"That isn't fair." She pushed my shorts and boxers down, then cupped my dick in her hand. I groaned as she stroked it, making me grow harder than I was before. Damn, her hands were so soft and perfect.

"I know," I mumbled on her lips.

"Prove it, then." She tipped her chin to thrust her tongue into my mouth and then broke the kiss. "Prove that you want me."

Her words were more than enough to fuel me.

I tucked my fingers under the straps of her panties and removed them. She slid to the top of the bed, resting on the pillows, and I climbed up, settling my face between her legs.

The heat of her pussy radiated on my face. She smelled good. Clean. *Fuck.* What was I getting myself into?

"Are you sure?"

"Javier," she pleaded. "I don't want to think about it right now. I just . . . I need it. I need *you. Please.*"

"Okay." I tucked my hands under her thighs and hauled her closer, hoisting her hips up as I rested on my knees.

She gasped, then sank her teeth into her bottom lip as she watched me with excited eyes.

I lowered my mouth and spread my lips to bury my tongue in her pussy.

Her next gasp was sharp, piercing straight through the air. Out of instinct, her body bucked from the shock, but I did not let go. I looked down at her as I feasted, lapping my tongue around her clit before plunging it inside her.

I wanted to taste her. *All of her.* I had been dying to for who knows how long now, and I knew it was wrong. I had been trying desperately hard to deny how much I wanted her, for the sake of her position and mine. But on this particular night, all those morals went out the window. I told myself it would be just for the night. Only tonight and never again.

"Oh my gosh, Javier," she panted, cupping her lace-clad tits as I swirled my tongue in loops.

I kissed her clit, suckled on it, staring into her eyes as she stared right back at me. Then I lapped my tongue faster over her swelling ball of nerves. It did not take long for those brown eyes of hers to roll to the back of her head and for a squeal to burst out of her.

I lowered her hips as she came, finishing her off with slow, tender licks. She panted raggedly, clutching a handful of my hair and grinding her pussy on my tongue to soak up every second of it.

Then, finally, she released me.

"Do I need to keep proving myself?" I asked.

"Yes, please." The words came out half in a moan. I climbed up her body and found her mouth, kissing her deeply. I gave her the chance to taste herself before snatching my mouth away and reaching into the nightstand for a condom.

The last time I had sex was nearly a year ago, and it was a complete accident that had happened on the road. To say I was horny as fuck now would have been an understatement. If there was a meter for my level of horniness, I'd have broken right through it. I was not about to let this night end without both of us being satisfied.

I rolled the condom on as she unclasped her bra from behind and removed it. Just as I thought, her breasts were perfect. Brown nipples at a delightful peak. Full enough to fill my hands. I leaned down to suck on them as I slowly stroked my dick.

"Damn, Octavia," I groaned around her nipple. "This is crazy."

"I know." She clutched my hips while tilting hers, eager for me to enter her.

Gripping the base of my dick, I pressed the head at her entrance. I could already feel her warmth and was so ready for it to suck me in and coat me.

She held on to my hips, guiding me deeper as she gazed into my eyes. She had no idea how much that action turned me on—proving that she wanted this just as much as I did. My dick spasmed in my palm as I thrust in another inch. And then another.

With each one, our mouths parted, as if this feeling were unreal. As if nothing could feel better than this. Another inch in, and that was half my dick. She moaned, sinking her teeth into her bottom lip. I could not hold back any longer. I pushed all the way in, and a massive groan left me as she cried out in bliss.

"Do you feel that?" My voice was a rumble in her ear. "You are *mine*, mi amor."

"Tell me in Spanish," she pleaded through quicker breaths.

"Sos *mía*, mi amor."

"Oh, God."

I pushed one of her thighs up, willing myself to go deeper. She whimpered.

"Fuck, Octavia." I groaned. "You feel so good."

"And you feel so big," she said.

I began to thrust, planting one elbow outside her head, then lowering my face to taste her lips again. She fed into each thrust, taking them as I delivered, matching my rhythm. My dick was so hard I could not think about anything else but coming.

Being inside her was nothing like I had imagined. This woman was consuming me in every way and causing me to lose control.

I managed to get on my knees and guided her legs up so her feet were on my shoulders. The side of her foot grazed my cheek, and I kissed it before lowering my mouth to her ankle.

She seemed to like that. She gazed at me, as if she wanted me to do it again. So I did. I kissed the side of her soft foot, the delicate ball of her ankle.

"You're too good at this," she sighed. Reaching up, she gripped my face in her hands and brought me down so we could kiss again.

A guttural groan filled my throat as she closed her legs around my waist, forcing me deeper.

"Aye." I dropped my head to kiss her throat, suck on the bend. My hand palmed one of her tits as I slammed into her. "You are everything."

"Oh," she moaned, back arching. I could feel my pelvis rubbing against her, building her up. "I'm gonna come again."

Seeing her become riled up, watching her chest rise and fall, and hearing her breaths grow labored as she neared climax made me swell inside her.

I cupped her mouth as she cried out in ecstasy.

"Shh, amor," I whispered, planting a kiss on the apple of her cheek.

She moaned behind my hand, nodding obediently. And I don't know . . . that did something to me. Made me want to hear her react uncontrollably again.

I continued triggering her G-spot, stroking exactly as I had before. Her eyes rolled back, and she clutched her breasts. She threw her head back as she came for the second time that night . . . and I could no longer hold back.

I was already on the brink, and when she let go, so did I. I slammed into her several times before a ferocious groan filled the hollow corners of my room.

So much for being quiet.

"Fuck, Octavia. *Fuck.*" Groaning, I clutched her upper arm and burrowed deeper, wanting to stay inside her warmth forever. My orgasm was strong enough to make me collapse on top of her and throb as I continued my release into the condom.

Buried deep inside her, with the side of my face resting between her breasts, I closed my eyes and caught my breath. I listened to her pounding heart, her erratic breaths coursing through her lungs.

"That was . . ." Her voice trailed off.

"Yeah." It was all I could muster.

Sluggishly, I pulled out of her, my condom heavy with come. I studied her a moment before getting off the bed and making my way to the bathroom to toss the condom into the trash bin and clean myself up. Then I grabbed a washcloth, ran it under warm water, and carried it to the room.

"Should I . . ." I hesitated as I held the washcloth, debating whether I should help her clean up or just leave her to it. "Would it be too intimate for you if I help?"

She smiled, eyes soft and understanding. "Javier, you just had your penis in my vagina. I don't think it gets more intimate than that."

Heat crawled from my neck to my face as a wave of embarrassment ran over me.

"Right." I huffed a laugh. "Okay."

I wiped the come away, being thorough and making sure I caught it all.

Once she was all clean, she smiled again and said, "Thank you."

I nodded, searching for my shorts while she climbed off the bed to look for her bra and panties. She put neither of them on, but she did slip back into her dress. She didn't bother zipping it, though. She held all her things close to her chest and said, "I should get to the guesthouse."

"Yes. Of course." I bobbed my head like an idiot. Because what else was I supposed to do? Ask her to stay? Ask for more?

No. I could not have more.

I'd already blurred the fucking lines. If word of this got out, no one would shut up. We both had clearly needed this, and it was done now. It was enough. It *had* to be enough.

She headed to the door and pulled it open with a soft creak.

"Octavia . . . you will not tell anyone about this . . . right?"

She looked me over as I stood half naked in the middle of the room. "No," she responded. "This stays between you and me."

"Okay," I whispered, relieved. "Well, good night."

"Good night." She took off, closing the door behind her. I waited until I could no longer hear her footsteps trailing down the staircase before I left the room and went to one of the guest bedrooms in the back of the house.

Through the window, I watched her walk across the lawn, still holding her bra and panties close to her chest with one hand while the other carried the straps of her heels.

As she went, there was pep in each step. She crossed one foot in front of the other, then threw her head back briefly to look at the sky. I was almost positive she was smiling.

I turned away from the window when she finally made it to the guesthouse. I did not know whether to smile like her or to feel disappointed in myself for caving to my desires.

# NINETEEN

## OCTAVIA

I woke up the following morning with way too much anxiety—well, a mixture of that and excitement.

I was anxious because I didn't know what the new day would bring. I'd just had sex with Javier Valdez . . . the man who paid me to take care of his daughter. There was no way this was going to end well.

Regardless, I'd gotten exactly what I'd wanted the night before, and *wow*. It was incredible. The things he did with his mouth and his dick . . . *whew*. I didn't have the words to describe it. One orgasm would have been more than enough, but getting two in one night? Hell, it was possible he'd just ruined me for any other man.

Not even my ex was that good. Luther was selfish in bed. He only cared about getting himself off. But not Javier. I told him to prove how much he wanted me, and he did that plus more.

I decided that in order to spare any awkwardness when I went to his house, I could make a couple of breakfast sandwiches. So, I popped some biscuits into the oven, then whipped up some eggs.

While heating the sausage, I read over Naomi's text again.

Naomi: Hello to you too. Why do we hate men?

Right. I'd told her the night before in my text that I hated men. I wasn't sure what to tell her now. I mean, technically, I still didn't care for the male mentality. Especially when men were full of toxic masculinity. But how could I despise a man like Javier? A man who'd just marvelously dicked me down less than twelve hours ago.

Me: I did something bad

Naomi responded in a matter of seconds.

Naomi: Oh lordy. What did you do girl?

Instead of texting it, I called her.

"You had to call me?" she answered. "This must really be bad."

I laughed. "I'm calling because I'm not leaving proof on my phone about this conversation."

"What happened? Come on, stop leaving me in suspense! You know I can't stand it."

"Well, I may *not* hate men as much as I thought . . . for now, at least."

"Oh. So the date went that good?"

"Oh, girl, no. The date was tragic," I told her, taking out the aluminum foil.

"Okay, you're losing me."

"The date was awful. The guy walked out on me, but only because someone I never expected showed up and interrupted it."

"I swear on all things holy, Octavia, if you don't spit that shit out, I'm gonna lose my shit." She really would too. She worked third shift, and this was the time she'd be well on her way to a shower and proper sleep.

"*Javier* showed up at the restaurant."

"Wait . . . basketball-player boss? That Javier?"

"Yes. He crashed my date. Came right over pretending we were a couple or something. I was so pissed off, but I didn't drive, and Terry left, and he had Aleesa there, so I was pretty much forced to ride back to his house with him. But when we put her to bed . . ." I sighed. "Naomi . . ."

"What?" she shrieked, fed up with my stalling.

"He told me he wasn't going to apologize for ruining my date because *he wanted me*. He didn't want anyone else to have me."

She gasped sharply.

"And then he just walked right up to me and kissed me in the hallway. Just like that. Picked me up and went to town, girl."

"Stop lying!"

"I'm so serious."

"So y'all *did it*, did it?"

"Yes. And it was so good. *Too* good, honestly." I bit my bottom lip, trying my best not to reminisce about the finer details.

That was hard to do, though. The man was *packing*. I mean, I figured by the size of his hands and his shoes that he might've had a big dick to go along with them, but he was hung, and girthy, and knew *exactly* how to use that thing. That was one hell of a combo.

Naomi squealed with delight, then cackled like this was the funniest news of the century.

"This isn't funny, Naomi! I'm over here all nervous now because I have to face him today, and I just have this feeling he's going to be all regretful about it."

"What if he isn't? What if he wants more of that kitty cat?"

I snorted a laugh. "Crazy thing is I told him we shouldn't do it for Aleesa's sake, but we both couldn't resist. It's like we didn't want anything more in that moment than each other." I shook my head, resting my lower back against the counter edge.

It still blew my mind that it'd happened.

Me and Javier.

In *his* bed.

I felt a clench between my thighs at another memory. Him buried between my legs, his mouth on my skin, his kisses passionate, hungry, and slightly possessive.

"What if he regrets it and fires me?" I wrapped the biscuits in foil before tucking them into a container.

"You think he would?"

"I don't know. He doesn't seem like the type to sleep with his nannies."

Wait. Had he slept with any of his nannies before? Because if he had, that changed things as well. I would surely get fired then, because that would mean nothing made me special or set me apart from the others.

No. He couldn't have. I truly couldn't see Javier fooling around with the people he hired. And he and I . . . we had a connection. Something deep and genuine. He couldn't have felt this with the others . . . *right?*

My stomach rumbled, but I wasn't sure if I was hungry or nervous.

"I have to go, but I'll call you when I get some free time."

"Okay, my love," Naomi sighed. "Keep me posted. And don't freak out on him. Just play it cool and pretend like it never happened. Get a good read on him first before saying anything."

"I'll try."

When the call ended, I collected the container and grabbed my tote bag. Slipping my phone into my back pocket, I left the guesthouse and made my way to Javier's back door.

I was relieved to see the kitchen was vacant; however, I heard heavy footsteps above, which meant Javier was awake. I placed the container on the countertop while wishing I wasn't such a neat freak.

Because of my good habits, the kitchen was spotless, the living room was organized, and not a single toy was on the floor. If it were a little messy, I could've cleaned to make myself look busy. Aleesa, I'm sure, was out cold and wouldn't be awake for at least another hour or so.

I removed one of the wrapped biscuits, grabbed my romance novel, which was on one of the shelves, and sat on the sofa. As I bit into my sandwich, that's when I heard footsteps coming down the stairs.

I chewed quickly and swallowed the bite as Javier rounded the corner. My breath nearly hitched at the sight of him.

Good Lord. The man looked like a snack.

Normally, he wore basketball shorts and solid tees. But right now, he was wearing jeans and a black button-up shirt with the sleeves rolled up to his elbows. His hair was combed back, with a few loose strands dangling on his forehead. A silver Versace watch was strapped around his wrist. From where I sat, I could smell his cologne drifting toward me, warm and spiced. Like sandalwood and dark musk.

When he spotted me, his eyes widened a bit and his lips parted. He'd shaved as well. He normally had stubble along his jawline and around his mouth, which gave him a rugged look. But today he was sharp. Clean.

My mind went to the calendar. I hadn't even checked today's events because I was too busy worrying about our reckless acts. What did he have planned?

"Hi," I said, swiping crumbs off my lap.

"Hey," he said back. He wore a pair of white Nikes, which seemed spot on for him. I couldn't picture him wearing designer dress shoes. Did they even make dress shoes in his size? Well . . . I was sure he could order a custom pair.

"I made breakfast sandwiches." I pushed to a stand to go to the kitchen. "I wasn't sure if you'd want one."

"Uh, sure. I can take it with me."

Damn it. Where was he going?

As if he could read my thoughts, Javier huffed a laugh and said, "You have no idea what is happening today, do you?"

Ashamed, I said, "Sorry. No. But I can check my phone." I started to dig into my hoodie pocket, but he shook his head and approached the bar counter. When he rounded it and came closer, my breathing shallowed.

He peered down at me, eyes soft. "There is a charity event at Element today. We reached one million dollars in donations, outside of my and Deke's contributions, and are celebrating."

"Oh!" I snapped my fingers. Right. Element was the recreational center and gym Javier and Deke owned in Atlanta. A lot of their money came in the form of memberships, and those dollars were used to help kids in need and to support the community. "Yes! You told me about this. Should I bring Aleesa?"

"Yes. I would love for her to come. There will be lots for the kids to do. I have to be there early, but you can bring her a bit later. It starts at twelve and ends at three."

"Okay."

He reached forward. For a second, I thought he was about to grab my waist, but instead, he aimed for the container and picked it up.

"I can never resist your food." He didn't smile, but he was still staring into my eyes.

"I'm glad you like it so much." I waited for him to back away, to settle this tension by just leaving the house and going to his recreation center.

The aluminum crinkled in his large hands, and a pained expression struck him. "Will things be odd between us?" he asked.

I looked at him from beneath my lashes. "Only if you make them weird."

"I do not want them to be weird."

"Do you plan on firing me?"

"What?" He frowned. "No. Why would I do that?"

"I don't know." I gave a half shrug. "It seems likely to happen after what we did last night. Especially if you regret it."

He studied my whole face, from my forehead to my chin. "Do you regret it?"

"I don't know." I paused, and I swear his face was coming closer to mine. "Do you?"

"I don't know either."

"I won't make things weird," I assured him. "If you want, we can pretend it never happened. We can pretend it was just something we both needed at the time, like a drink when you're thirsty, or food when you're hungry."

"But . . . that is not how I want to see it."

I blinked at him, unsure what to say to that.

"It is just . . . Aleesa," he murmured.

"I know. And for her sake, we shouldn't take this too seriously. It'd only hurt her in the end anyway, especially if we fall out or end up not wanting to be around each other."

"You think that would happen?" His eyes saddened. Seeing him this way broke my heart. It was like the mere idea of me *not* wanting to be around him physically pained him.

My heart pumped a bit faster. I wasn't sure how to digest that reaction. He couldn't have cared about me that much . . . could he?

"I don't think it would happen. You're a good person, and I like being around you. *Now*, at least." I laughed.

His mouth twitched. "I feel the same."

We looked at each other a bit longer, then I sighed and took a minor step back. "You should go if you want to beat traffic."

"Right," he said, but he didn't move. Didn't back away. He still eyed me, wetting his bottom lip with his tongue.

Placing the breakfast sandwich down, he cupped the back of my head, and our lips collided when he reeled me forward.

*Yes. Fuck yes.*

I moaned, lacing my arms around the back of his neck as he tangled his fingers in my locs. He wasted no time picking me up so he could plant my butt on the counter.

"Is it bad that I want more of this?" he rasped before consuming my lips again. He used his hands to hoist me forward, then stepped between my legs, kissing me fervently, desperately.

I grappled at his shirt with one hand, using my other to thread my fingers through the hair at the nape of his neck. He cupped my ass, pressing in deeper and thrusting his tongue into my mouth to taste me. "I want to fuck you right here, right now."

"So do it." He had no idea how much I wanted that to happen.

He snatched his mouth away to reach for his belt buckle. I helped him unlatch it before undoing the button of his jeans. Once he assisted me with my shorts and panties, dragging them down to my ankles and removing them, he was between my thighs again.

I watched him grip the base of his dick with one hand while using his other hand to bring my ass toward the edge of the counter.

He started to push his way in, both of us beyond ready for more.

But then we heard a playful shriek and tiny footsteps pounding upstairs.

"Daddy!" Aleesa yelled.

"Shit." Javier pulled away, helping me off the counter before quickly tucking himself away. While he buttoned his jeans and adjusted his belt buckle, I collected my panties and shorts and rushed to the pantry to hide.

Damn it. She wasn't supposed to be awake yet.

"Hola, princesa." I heard him grunt, like he often did when he reached down to pick her up.

"Daddy, why so dressed up?" Aleesa asked.

While he answered her, I slipped into my panties while facing cans of vegetables. I held back a snort. This was comical. Hiding in the pantry from a toddler, all so she wouldn't see her father's penis or her half-naked nanny. I wanted to roll over and laugh at how ridiculous this was. But necessary. Definitely necessary. Javier most likely didn't want to confuse Aleesa, and neither did I.

After my shorts were adjusted, I grabbed a box of Aleesa's favorite fruity organic cereal and stepped out of the pantry.

"Tava!" Aleesa squealed, scrambling to get out of Javier's arms. He placed her on her feet, and she ran to me, throwing her arms around my legs.

"Good morning, my darling," I sang. "You want some cereal?"

"Yes, please!" She pulled away, clasping her hands together while batting her long lashes.

I laughed as I reached into one of the cabinets for a bowl.

Javier collected his breakfast sandwich again before dropping a kiss on her forehead. "I will be back." Pulling away from her, he eyed me again. "Another time?"

I nodded, smiling. "Another time."

I watched him go until he was out of sight. Briefly . . . or so I thought. Aleesa made it seem like I'd looked after him for five minutes or more.

"Tava, I'm *hungry*," she whined, tugging on the hem of my hoodie. "And I wanna watch Mickey Mouse." She paused. "Please," she added for good measure.

"Okay, okay. Working on it." I cleared my throat, trying to rinse away the chaotically excited feeling bubbling inside me.

Goodness. What was this man doing to me?

# TWENTY

## JAVIER

"And I could get kicked in the balls right now, and I bet you wouldn't even notice." Deke snapped his fingers in my face.

I looked away from the group of children in the middle of the gym to him.

"What?" I asked.

"What the hell is going on with you, man?" Deke laughed as he looked me up and down. "You're over there daydreaming like we don't have shit to do."

"Uh, right." I scratched the back of my head.

"Come on, man. We have basketballs to sign."

I followed Deke to the center of the gym, where several volunteers were trying to keep the children calm. All of them had red-and-white-striped basketballs in hand—ones we'd ordered for this day. We were celebrating hitting $1 million in donations at Element, and the gym was packed with not only volunteers and children but also parents, photographers, and vendor stands.

As we approached, the children squealed and became rowdy. Deke grinned as he stepped right in front of them, wrangling a bunch of them into his arms to give them a massive hug.

They giggled, and as soon as he released them, they shoved their basketballs into his face, begging for signatures.

I waved at a few of the kids who approached me, gave them hugs and high fives, and began signing balls too.

"So what were you thinking about over there?" Deke asked, eyeing me before handing a signed ball to the kid in front of him.

"Nothing," I lied, finishing off a signature myself.

"I'm sorry to interrupt," a woman to my left said. She held her phone in the air and waved it. "My daughter's such a big fan of yours. Can I get a picture of you two?"

"Of course." I smiled and lowered to a squat next to the girl. Once the photo was taken, the girl's mother thanked me, took her hand, and shuffled away.

"It was definitely something," Deke carried on, and I really wished he would let it go.

I was not about to tell him that I was thinking about Octavia.

About the night before and how irresponsible we'd been, yet how fucking *amazing* it had been. I was not about to tell him that I woke up with a hard dick and wanted to stroke myself to the thought of her until I came again. I did not do that, of course. I held back—and was glad I did, because it prepared me for what we were about to do in the kitchen . . .

Up until Aleesa woke up and reality sank in.

Octavia and I were in a very tricky situation. The sex we'd had was explosive, and I absolutely wanted more . . . but wanting more was a risk, and I was not sure if it needed to be taken.

Instead of answering Deke, I ignored him and worked through the line of eager children, signing balls and taking pictures until the area was clear. We were finally given a break when the kids ran to the vendors, getting face paint, popcorn, and cotton candy and shooting hoops at the contest area.

"Let me guess." Deke popped up at my side again.

I avoided an eye roll and a sigh. He was *not* going to let this go.

"You didn't look mad when you were zoned out, so I assume you were thinking about something good?"

"It was nothing, Deke. Seriously."

"Come on, Valdez. You can't lie to me."

"I am not lying about anything. It was nothing. Just . . . things about Aleesa." Partly true. I was worried about sleeping with my daughter's nanny. Technically, that situation revolved around her.

A woman approached us, offering two bottles of water. We accepted, and Deke cracked his open and took a few chugs.

I started to open mine, too, until someone across the court caught my eye.

Walking through the doors with my daughter's hand in hers was Octavia. And, fuck . . . What was she thinking? How was any man not going to look at her?

She wore a floral purple sundress that hugged her at the middle and stopped mid-thigh, with open-toed sandals. Her locs were styled in an updo, and of course she had those jewels in them.

She looked like an angel standing there, gazing around the gym, pointing at things as Aleesa bounced on her toes. And call me crazy, but I found it cute that she and Aleesa were matching in color. They did that often. It was almost always Aleesa's idea. She wanted to wear the same colors as her Tava.

When Octavia carried her eyes to the middle and spotted me, she threw her hand up to wave. I waved back, and Aleesa wasted no time bolting across the gymnasium to reach me.

"Daddy!"

I bent down and held my arms out, then scooped her up and raised her in the air. I nibbled at her belly, and she giggled.

"Sorry we're a little late." Octavia met up with us as I placed Aleesa on her feet. "Leesa refused to leave until she found a purple bow to match her jumpsuit."

I chuckled. "That sounds like her."

Octavia turned her eyes to her future brother-in-law. "Hey, Deke. No Vina today?"

"No, but thanks for reminding me of how much I miss her." He laughed as they hugged.

"Deke, is candy here?" Aleesa asked, peering up at him.

Deke gave me a mischievous side-eye before lowering to a squat. "I heard there's cotton candy *and* candy apples. But shh . . . I didn't tell you that."

I narrowed my eyes at him as he stood again. Aleesa's eyes were big as a smile spread across her face.

"Maybe some popcorn," I said, eyeing Octavia.

She nodded as she took Aleesa's hand. "Popcorn it is."

Before she could walk away, I said, "And just a little bit of cotton candy. You know how she is with sweets."

Octavia grinned at that, her pearly teeth catching the light. I almost faltered, seeing that smile in combination with her soft brown eyes. God, why did she have to be so beautiful? Why was I so into her now? Was it because we'd had sex? Had these feelings always been here? I had not felt my heart pump like this in many years.

As she walked away, I couldn't help watching her go. Her ass swayed perfectly in that dress. I caught a few men staring and tried my best not to glare them down.

Deke cleared his throat beside me, and I snapped out of my trance, slipping my hands into my front pockets.

"So Davina was telling the truth," he said.

I reluctantly swung my attention to him. "About what?"

"About you ruining Octavia's date because you might be into her." He put on a big grin as he bumped me with his shoulder. It looked like he wanted to point and shout *I told you so!*

I refused to give him the satisfaction. Though he was right. He was so fucking right. I was very much into this woman.

With a smirk, I said, "I do not know what you are talking about," before walking away to find the Gatorade stand.

# TWENTY-ONE

## JAVIER

The event was a success, and I was thankful for that. Large crowds were not my thing, but they came with my career, and I often had to make sacrifices to keep it running smoothly.

It was one thing to play in a stadium, but it was another to attend events such as the one at Element, with so many people around. It didn't feel like I had a shred of privacy with all those admiring eyes around, so when it was time to go, I was relieved.

Aleesa and Octavia had left long before I had. I could not stop looking for either of them. Of course, I would always be on the lookout for my daughter. But I kept searching for Octavia too. I did not know what it was about her that had me so drawn. Perhaps what we had done had changed things.

Perhaps it had changed *me*.

What I knew for a fact was that I had not gotten enough of her. I wanted more, and that felt wrong to want. But it was true. Wanting more with her was all I could think about, even during my drive home. And this wasn't just about the sex. This was beyond lust. With her I felt a true connection. I felt a vulnerability that I had not felt in a very long time.

Along the way, my phone rang. Octavia's name appeared on my car's dashboard.

"Hi," I answered. "I am just on my way. It took a little longer to—"

"Javier, I need you to get home as quickly as you can, please." Octavia's voice was filled with panic.

I straightened in my seat. "What do you mean? What is wrong?"

"There's . . . well, there's someone here who shouldn't be here. I'm driving away, but . . . please hurry. I called the police, but I don't know when they'll show up. Oh, God." Her breathing became erratic, blowing through my car's speakers.

"Okay, I am coming. Hey, relax. Okay? I am on my way." I wanted to ask her who this person was that had gotten her so worked up, but asking questions probably would have caused her more anxiety, so I kept them to myself.

"Okay," she breathed, calming herself just a bit.

"Is Aleesa okay?"

"Yes, she's fine."

"Okay. Find a safe space to wait for me. I will text you when I have arrived."

"Okay."

I added pressure to the gas pedal. It would take me at least another twenty minutes before making it to my house. I drove fast, glad that I did not get pulled over for it.

When I made it to my street, I noticed a silver Mercedes parked at the curb near my property's gate. A man sat on the hood of the car, dressed in ripped jeans, a button-down tan shirt, and a pair of loafers. His inked arms were folded, and when his head turned and he locked onto my vehicle, I could tell he was nothing but trouble.

Octavia said he wasn't supposed to be around. She must have known him personally to say that. Was he one of those men she'd met on that dating app?

I parked directly across from him, sent Octavia a text, and then climbed out of my car.

The man stood up, dropping his arms and raising his chin to size me up.

"Can I help you?" I asked. It came out as more of a demand.

"Just looking for Octavia Klein. She works for you, right?"

I frowned, not liking her name on his tongue. "Why? Who are you?"

"I told her I would stop by so we could catch up."

I narrowed my eyes. "That is clearly a lie. She called me less than thirty minutes ago and said you were not supposed to be here."

"Did she?" The man stroked his beard, smirking. "So that was her. I knew I wasn't trippin'."

I clenched a fist.

Car tires rolling on sleek pavement sounded behind me, and I looked over my shoulder. Octavia had pulled up again. She parked right behind my car, a good distance away from us.

"Ah. There she is."

"Stay where you are." I grimaced at him before walking toward Octavia's car. She rolled down the window, but not without tossing a wary glance his way.

"What the hell does he want?" Her voice was trembling. I did not like seeing her like this.

"Who is that man?" I asked.

"My ex."

"Do you still talk to him?"

"No!" she exclaimed, gripping the steering wheel so tight her knuckles prodded through her skin. "I didn't lead him here, I swear. I haven't talked to him in years. You have to believe me, Javier. I would never—"

"I believe you, amor. I believe you." And now I was pissed off. I did not know a thing about her ex, but he clearly had no respect for her. And one thing I absolutely hated was a man who did not respect a woman's boundaries.

I looked at Aleesa, in her car seat in the back seat. She had an orange lollipop in her hand but was curiously looking between me and Octavia.

"Hi, Daddy," she said. "Tava got me lollipop."

"Hola, princesa," I murmured. After having so much cotton candy at the event, the last thing she needed was another lollipop. However, it was good that she had it, because I needed her distracted for what I was about to do next.

My eyes shifted to Octavia's again. They were welling with tears.

"O!" the man said, now a few steps closer, with his hands in the air. "Come on, it's me!" I did not like that he was smiling, as if he was *enjoying* how distressed she was.

"Oh, God. Please." Her bottom lip quivered, and she closed her eyes, trying to steady her breathing. "One . . . two . . . three . . ."

I touched her arm mid-count, and her eyes opened wide, connecting with mine.

"Has he hurt you before?" I asked.

She nodded, then lowered her head with shame, as if it were *her* fault that he had hurt her.

Bottling my anger, I pressed my forefinger under her chin and tipped it back up. "I will take care of him."

She tried to smile—truly, she did—but the expression wavered, then collapsed.

"Roll the window up," I said, stepping back and looking at the shithead standing next to my gates. "I do not want Aleesa to hear this."

I heard the window roll up as I stormed toward her ex.

"She does not want you here," I snapped, getting in his face. "Leave now, or I will make you leave."

"I'm not going anywhere until I talk to her," he shot back.

"Get off my property."

He looked around, as if searching for something. "Last I checked, I'm on the street. This road is considered a public area."

He was annoying me now. I did not like to be annoyed, especially by grown men who knew *exactly* what they were doing. Closing the gap, I grabbed handfuls of his shirt in both of my hands and rushed forward until his back slammed against the side of his car.

The man smirked as a deep growl rumbled in my throat. "I said, if you do not leave, I will fucking make you."

"Go ahead, man." He chuckled. "So I can sue the fuck out of you."

"You will not be able to sue me if I break your fucking neck."

"Threats from an NBA player. Bet I could get millions for this."

"Do you think threatening me with that legal shit will stop me? I don't give a damn about any of that." I tightened my grip. "You came onto my property trying to hurt someone who works for me."

"I wouldn't hurt her," he grumbled.

"But you have before." I jacked him forward by the shirt, then slammed his back against the car again. This time, that smug smile of his disappeared. "Tell me why I shouldn't break your fucking nose right now."

As I stared him down, I heard a siren wail. A police cruiser drove past Octavia's car and mine, and parked on the opposite side of the street. I glared at the shitty ex in front of me one more time before releasing his shirt.

I was relieved they had shown up. The last thing I needed was an assault charge for blackening this man's eye. And, trust me, I was very close to doing that. Attacking him any more would have been all over the press, and I did *not* want that kind of negative attention.

"We received a call about a disturbance," one of the officers said, looking between us warily. He was male, White with a clean-shaven face. The other was a Latina officer. She walked around the passenger side, looking between me and Octavia's ex with an inclined brow.

"This man showed up at my property unannounced, and I do not know how long he has been parked here," I told them. "All I know is that he is a threat to me, my child, and *especially* to the woman in the car back there. She said that he has hurt her before."

"He's tripping. I was just about to leave." Octavia's ex started walking toward his car, but the male officer raised a hand.

"Sir, we need you to stay here until we get a grasp of the situation."

He sighed.

"Do you know who this man is?" the female officer asked me. Her pocket had the name Amara.

"He's her ex. The woman in the car."

That seemed to annoy Officer Amara. She frowned at Octavia's ex before saying "I will speak with her and see what's going on and confirm if what you've told me is true."

"Sure," I said.

Officer Amara walked to Octavia's car. Octavia saw her coming and rolled her window down before she drew near. After the officer said something, Octavia nodded and climbed out of the car.

"Do I have to go over there?" I heard her ask as she cut her eyes our way.

"No, sweetie. We can talk right here."

Octavia nodded, rubbing her hands up and down both of her arms. I could not hear much of what she was saying to Officer Amara, but she looked frazzled. Almost broken. Never had I seen her like this.

I looked at her ex, who had his arms folded again. His eyes were harder as he zeroed in on Octavia, looking her up and down. I wanted to gouge his fucking eyes out. I stepped to the left, blocking his view.

After Amara said a few words to Octavia and gestured back to the car, she marched toward us. Octavia slunk her way into the driver's seat again.

"Luther, right?" Amara asked, eyes pointed at Octavia's ex.

Luther nodded. "Yeah."

"The young woman back there said you emailed her a few weeks ago saying you moved to Atlanta."

"Yeah, I did. So?"

"Did she ever respond to you?"

"No."

"And why do you think that is?"

"I don't know." He shrugged. "Probably because she was busy. That's why I wanted to come here and surprise her."

"She said she never told you where she worked or that she was in Atlanta at all. She never gave you her email address and hasn't spoken to you for years. So explain to me how you received her address?" Amara's tone had a little fire in it.

Luther's nostrils flared just a little. "I saw her on TV. I knew she was into being a nanny or whatever, and I saw she was working for this man's kid." He pointed at me.

"So she never spoke to you personally or invited you here?" the male officer asked. His pocket had the name Graham. "Seems to me you don't know how to read the room."

Luther said nothing in response.

"Sir, I'm going to ask you to leave. *Right now*," Amara said, taking a step closer to him. "That young woman just explained to me who you are and what you did to her, and in my opinion, you are a threat and a danger to this family. If you don't leave, I will arrest you for trespassing. Get in your car and go. *Now.*"

"Man, whatever," Luther muttered, heading to his car.

We watched him climb into his Mercedes, start the ignition, and drive away. He stopped his car next to Octavia's and rolled his window down. I started to walk her way—my daughter was in that car—but he yelled "I still love you, O!" Then he peeled off.

Officer Amara scoffed when his vehicle was out of sight. "I can't stand pieces of shit like that."

"Neither can I," I grumbled.

"If he comes back, let us know," Officer Graham said.

"Yes. And in the meantime, I suggest you and the young woman back there file a restraining order on him."

"Okay. I will let her know."

Officer Amara nodded and walked away.

Officer Graham smiled as he took quick steps backward. "Big fan, by the way."

I smiled back. "Thanks."

I reached Octavia's car just as the police cruiser drifted down the street.

"You okay?" I asked after she rolled the window down.

She avoided my eyes. "I think so. Maybe? I don't know."

"I get it. I think you need a moment. Take Leesa to the house. I will meet you there."

She started her car's ignition and maneuvered around my vehicle to reach the gates. I did not miss the way she trembled as she went.

# TWENTY-TWO

## JAVIER

After parking and checking the mail, I entered my house and dragged in a deep breath. The scent of Italian herbs swelled in the air.

I dropped my keys into the glass bowl in the foyer before venturing through. Around the corner, in the living room, Aleesa sat in the middle of the rug, with a hooded dinosaur blanket covering her head, watching TV.

Mickey Mouse asked the viewer if they could spot a duck, and Aleesa pointed and screamed, "Right there!"

In the kitchen, Octavia shuffled through the fridge. I approached the island counter, where the stovetop was. A pot was on top, with steam starting to waft out of it.

Octavia stepped back with a jar of pasta sauce and a carton of heavy cream, kicking the fridge door shut.

I studied her a moment, noticing her hands were still shaking as she tried opening the ravioli. I walked around the counter, touching her hand to stop her. She froze.

"Octavia, look at me."

She shook her head, biting hard into her bottom lip.

"Please."

"I should finish cooking."

"The food can wait."

"Leesa is hungry."

"Okay, I will feed her. But you are in no condition to cook."

She started to pull away from me, but I caught her with a gentle hand around her upper arm.

I tilted her chin with my fingers, and her eyes were filled to the brim with tears. Her mouth quivered, and before I knew it, she buried her face into my chest and released a raw, choked sob.

My eyes stung as I closed my arms around her, feeling her body tremble and the pain travel through her body.

"I'm sorry," she cried.

"It's okay," I whispered, stroking her back.

"I just . . ." Her words failed her, translating to another sob.

I felt something rub across my leg and looked down. Aleesa stood next to us, staring up, her face drooping with sadness.

"What's wrong, Tava?"

Octavia gently freed herself, swiping at her eyes. Even with her tears, she smiled at Aleesa. "Don't worry, angel. I'm okay. I just . . . needed to process my feelings for a second."

I picked Aleesa up and rested her on my hip. Feeling sad herself, Aleesa rested her head on my shoulder. I kissed her cheek, then said, "Maybe a hug will help Tava feel better."

Eager, Aleesa sat up with a big smile and leaned toward Octavia. Octavia bubbled out a bittersweet laugh as she grabbed hold of Aleesa. My daughter closed her arms around Octavia's neck and murmured, "It's okay, Tava."

Octavia closed her eyes, most likely fighting another surge of tears. "Thank you, my sweet girl. Everything is definitely okay when I'm with you."

"I will order pizza," I said, already pulling my phone out of my back pocket.

"No, Javier. You don't have to do that. Seriously, I'm fine. I have one job, and it's to take care of Leesa and feed her good food."

"Octavia." My voice was low but stern.

"I already bought all the ingredients," she went on.

"Octavia," I tried again, still stern.

"Yes?" she whispered, keeping her glossy eyes on me.

"I am ordering pizza for us, okay?"

"Okay," she murmured after a sniffle.

"I am here," I said. "This is not all on your shoulders. Let me take care of you for a change."

She smashed her lips together, and her eyes became watery again.

Smiling, I rubbed a fallen tear off her cheek with my thumb. "Is that okay, amor?" I asked.

A small smile swept across her lips. "Yes. It's okay."

~

After the pizza arrived and we all ate, I told Octavia to relax while I washed Aleesa up and prepared her for bed. I had to fight her on this, of course. She did not like feeling useless.

But she deserved to take a moment for herself—to think about her problems and process the situation that had just happened. She would not have been able to fully do that while handling Aleesa.

Once Aleesa was dressed in her pink nightgown, she rushed to me with a butterfly hair clip in her hand.

"Daddy, look." She raised the clip in the air. "I want to wear this 'morrow."

"Okay." I scooped her up. "You can wear it tomorrow. Are you ready for bed?"

"Yes. Can you lay wif me?" Her voice was so innocent. How could any sane person reject her?

"Sí, mi amor. Come."

I turned off the light. The bed was twin size, so it was always a struggle for me to get my whole body on, but I managed anyway. I wrapped an arm around my baby girl, letting out a long, deep sigh.

I hoped Octavia would stick around for a while, but I would not have blamed her if she went to the guesthouse. I wanted to know more about that ignorant ex of hers and see what more I could do to help.

"Daddy?" Aleesa raised the butterfly clip in the air, observing it in the night-light.

"Sí, princesa?"

"I like Tava."

The center of my chest warmed. "Yeah?"

"Yeah. She my friend."

I lifted my head to study her profile. Her eyelids were drooping, but she held on to the butterfly clip, twirling it in the air so the yellow wings could sparkle in the light.

"Is she Mommy?"

That caused my heartbeat to stutter. "No, amor. I told you who Mommy is. She is right over there." I pointed at the photo tacked to the wall across the room. It was an image of Eloise while she was pregnant. I had taken it a week prior to her giving birth to Aleesa. Eloise had seemed perfectly fine then.

"Oh yeah." Aleesa giggled. And the next thing she said shocked me a bit. "I wan' Tava to be Mommy too."

I swallowed thickly, trying to fight the emotion burning in my throat. I did not know what to even say to that, so I remained quiet.

Eventually Aleesa yawned, lowering her arms and turning over to snuggle in mine. I held her even tighter, staring at the image of Eloise while tears threatened to fall.

# TWENTY-THREE

## OCTAVIA

I'd never been more thankful for having access to a hot tub than at this moment.

The water bubbled around me, creating a soothing roar that eased my racing thoughts and anxieties. I was still frazzled about Luther.

I couldn't believe he'd found me. When I'd driven toward Javier's house and seen him through the window, I'd thought I was going crazy. My whole body went into flight mode, and every alarm rang loudly in my brain.

I drove past the house, just to make sure I wasn't seeing things, but when I circled around, I saw it was definitely him. He didn't get a good look at me, so I don't think he realized who I was. I also didn't have the same car I'd had when we were together. How dare that asshole just show up like that? How did he even find me?

Seeing him triggered me in so many ways. I felt cut open and raw, as if Luther had taken a knife, sliced into my core, and allowed all my organs to spill. For a split second, I'd felt a panic attack coming on, but one glance in the visor mirror at Aleesa and I'd pulled it together as best I could and then called Javier.

Sighing, I picked up my sparkling water and took a sip. At least my hands had stopped shaking. I would've loved a nice, cold glass of wine, but I had plans for a four-hour drive the next day with a toddler. Plus, one glass of wine would've led to two, three, and so on—all so I could erase my darker thoughts.

I took a sweep of my surroundings, trying to center myself and be present in this moment. *Focus on the things that catch your eye.* That's what my therapist often said.

If there was one thing I could say about Javier and his type A tendencies, it was that he had impeccable taste. His modern Spanish-style home was beautiful, but the pool and spa area were next level.

The hot tub was separated from the pool, of course, but not too far away was a seating area with plush black outdoor furniture and a propane firepit with glass panels and decorative silvery rocks.

A massive flat-screen was built into the wall across from the seating, and off to the left was a kitchen equipped with a gas stove, a grill, and an oven. My favorite, though, was the waterfall wall built into one end of the pool. His space was perfectly luxurious, and I soaked up every second of it to clear my mind.

I tipped my head back to look at the stars in the velvet, dark-blue sky. A thump sounded in the distance, and my breath hitched when a door clicked shut. A tall, solidly built silhouette appeared.

Javier walked toward the hot tub, wearing basketball shorts and a solid-white T-shirt. His hair looked like it had just dried and was a dark, beautiful mess atop his head.

When he stopped, he slipped his hands into his front pockets and gave me a thorough look.

"How are you?" he asked.

I twisted around in the water so I could anchor my forearms on the edge and allow my legs to float. "I'm okay. Thanks for asking."

He was quiet for a moment, eyes drifting from my face to the curve of my ass poking out of the water. I'd gone to the guesthouse to change into a black bikini before hitting the hot tub. He clearly liked what he was seeing.

"May I join you?" he asked.

"Of course."

He grabbed the hem of his shirt and pulled it up and over his head. He stepped out of his shorts next and approached the edge of the hot tub with nothing but his boxers on.

"Make room."

Dropping my arms, I smiled as he dipped one foot in after the other. When his lower half was engulfed in water, he stepped to the opposite side of the hot tub.

"I'm glad you came out. I wanted to ask if it will be okay to bring Aleesa with me to Charlotte?"

"To Charlotte?" He settled in a bit deeper. "What for?"

"Davina is cake tasting, and she wants me to join her. If that's taking Aleesa too far, I understand. I don't want to cross the line or make you uncomfortable. I can just tell Vina I can't make it, and she'll understand."

"No, no." He held my gaze before I could pull away. "It is fine. You can take her with you. I have a meeting with Tommy tomorrow anyway."

I raised a curious brow. "Tommy?"

"My manager. He wants to discuss the Bubbles and Swaddles launch and figure out dates for New York."

"Oh. Gotcha."

Bubbles and Swaddles was the company Javier had partnered with to promote skin care products for young children and babies. Aleesa was one of the faces for their brand, and she loved using their items during bath times.

I'd met the owner of the company once, when I went to Miami with Davina last year. Her name was Kyla Cox, and she was a smart woman who reminded me a lot of my sister.

Business-savvy. Confident. Chic. Humble.

I narrowed my eyes at Javier. He was being *too* accommodating about this. "Are you *sure* it's okay?"

"Yes. It will be good for you to see your sister after the mess today, I am sure. And Aleesa would probably enjoy the change of scenery. It will be good for her to spread her wings a bit."

I almost choked on a laugh. "Am I speaking with the same Javier Valdez that hired me?"

"Do not push it."

I snorted a laugh as he battled a smile.

"I just . . . realize how much freer she is when she is with you," he said. "You were right. She *is* adventurous, and one day she will have to explore this world without me. Better that I let her do some exploring now before she starts sneaking out of her bedroom window."

"You know, I don't put that one past her. She'll be sneaking out of her window by the age of seven to catch fireflies or something."

"Oh, man. Do not say that. It makes me sad to know she will not always be this innocent." He put on a smile, revealing a beautiful set of pearly-white teeth, but there was also a whisper of sorrow. "So . . . you really love cooking?"

"I do." I shrugged one shoulder. "I was going to make ravioli tonight."

"I bet that would have been delicious."

"Yeah, but I'll just make it another time."

"Who taught you how to cook?"

"My mom did." I twirled a loc around my finger. "She's always been good at it. She gives something a try for the first time and perfects it. She taught me how to bake my first cake and has saved a lot of her recipes for me."

"Your first cake? What flavor was it?"

"It was a pound cake."

"Ah." He nodded. "And when will you make one for me?"

"Whenever you want it," I said, biting a smile.

He smirked. "Surprise me."

I grinned, and I really wished I would stop acting like a schoolgirl with a crush. "Okay, GG. I've got you."

"So it is you telling Aleesa to call me that," he said with a snap of his fingers.

I giggled. "Guilty."

"What does it even mean?" he asked with a partial smile.

*"Grumpy Giant."*

"Grumpy Giant? *Seriously?*" His eyebrows dipped as he shook his head. "You are telling my daughter that I am a grumpy giant?"

"Of course not." I laughed. "She doesn't know the *true* meaning of it. She just likes saying the letter *G* twice. And for some reason when I say it, it makes her giggle. You have to admit you can be grumpy, though."

"I am not."

"You are. But it's okay. You're *our* grumpy giant."

A boyish smile swept across his face as he lowered his gaze. That had seemed to warm him up inside. My goodness. How had I not realized before how adorable he could be?

I ran my fingers through the water, loving the feel of it flowing between the gaps. The act relaxed me as I drew in a breath and then exhaled.

"So . . . listen. About earlier . . ." I blew a heavy breath, ready to just bite the bullet already. Because I knew that was the main reason he had come out here. He wanted to talk about Luther. "This isn't something I like to talk about, because I want to put it behind me, but I'll tell you because I don't want you thinking you're the problem."

"Okay," he said as more of a question than a statement. He straightened his back, with his eyes trained on me. I couldn't keep looking at him, so I inspected my cuticles.

"I was in a relationship with Luther for three years, and it wasn't a healthy one. I lived with him for one year, and that one year was all it took to realize he wasn't the person for me."

Javier tipped his chin, absorbing the information.

"He had anger issues, and I told him to get help, but he never did." I shrugged, as if it didn't matter anymore. But it did. It always would.

"When you told me he had hurt you, I wanted to bury him." Javier's eyes hardened while his jaw ticced.

"Yeah. I mean, he never, like, slapped or punched me," I told him, hoping that would calm him down. "But he did grab and shove me a few times. The first time, I confused it for an accident. We had both been drinking, so, you know, you kind of excuse it. But the second time he did it, we were both sober. He grabbed my arms, and I told him to let me go. He shoved me so hard that my arm got cut on the metal plate on the doorjamb." I lifted my arm and twisted it, pointing to a slightly raised scar just above my elbow. "It was after that when I realized I had to go. If I would have stayed, he would have become much worse."

Crickets chirped in the distance as I looked away, shame eating me up. Shame because I'd never thought I would become the kind of woman who had endured abuse. I just . . . well, I'd never seen that in the cards for me, and I wasn't sure how I hadn't seen the signs in Luther. When people say love can blind you, they aren't lying.

I could feel Javier's burning gaze on me.

"Crazy thing is, he'd asked me to marry him *right before* pushing me." I huffed a laugh, still remembering that idiot on one knee, acting like I was his world, his precious lady. "When he asked, I told him I needed to think about it, and that clearly didn't sit well with him. He didn't like that I didn't immediately say yes to him. That same day, I packed my shit, took the ring, and sold it at a pawnshop." I reached outside the hot tub and picked up the can of sparkling water again.

"I am glad you escaped that," Javier said. "You were smart to leave. You do not deserve that."

We both went quiet for a handful of seconds. I took a deep gulp of fizzy water.

"Have you noticed the way I sometimes gasp or get startled when you randomly show up?" I asked.

He nodded. "I have noticed and have always wanted to ask why that was."

"Even though this was years ago, I remember Luther popping up, stomping around, slamming cabinets, and shouting—not that *you* do any of that," I added rapidly. "But whenever he'd come around, I always had my guard up. I always felt on edge, you know? Like I would get in trouble just for breathing.

"Sometimes he'd just pop up in the living room after taking a nap or playing his video games. He'd just show up without saying a word. I would be reading or focused on something, with my back to him, so I wouldn't notice him at first, but when I did and gasped loudly or had a jump scare, he'd crack a smile. Almost like he *wanted* to see me scared. Like he was glad to have that kind of power over me. It's different when it's done as a prank, right? To kind of scare someone just to be funny. I did it with Davina all the time. But there was something about Luther's smile that was sinister. It just wasn't right." I squeezed my eyes shut and shook my head. "He was toxic . . . and I thought I had escaped that, but then he showed up here."

"Wow. I am sorry, Octavia." Javier's whole face softened. "Officer Amara said you should file a restraining order on him if you are worried he will hurt you again. I agree with her. I will file one as well. I do not want him anywhere near my family or my property. I will also speak with my manager and see if there is a way he can blacklist him from the stadium. You will just have to provide me his full name."

"Luther Hall," I said. He could take his name and report it to the FBI, for all I cared. "And I'll file one for sure."

"Okay. Good." He gave me a soft smile. "From now on, I promise not to come around unannounced," he assured me. "Especially if you are busy with something. I will let you know I am there."

A smile tugged at the corners of my lips. "You don't have to do all that."

"Yes, I do." He moved closer to me, a concerned wrinkle forming between his eyebrows. "I want you to feel safe here, Octavia. I want you to feel like you *belong*. I will do everything I can to make sure of that."

My eyes burned with tears, but I bit them back. I'd cried enough today. No more tears.

Instead, I moved closer to him, until my breasts were almost touching his midsection. He looked down at me, pink lips parting as he lifted a hand to cup my cheek.

"You deserve to be protected," he murmured.

"I usually find a way to protect myself. I've learned not to wait around expecting to be saved."

"I am glad that you do . . ." He lowered his head, and his mouth inched closer to mine. "But it is okay to allow others to try. To help."

"Others like who?" I asked, breathless. I eyed his mouth as he examined mine. Our faces came closer, drifted apart, then moved closer again. His warm breath ran across my damp chest.

"Someone who cares about you," he rasped. "Someone like *me*."

With those words, I felt like a goner. But when he curled his hand around the back of my neck and brought his lips to mine, it obliterated me to sweet, delicious pieces.

He consumed me, stepping forward until my back pressed to the nearest edge. A moan rose up my throat, and I lifted my arms to drape them over his broad shoulders. He took that as his chance to pick me up in his arms, but our lips never parted.

He clutched my ass in his hands, and a hungry groan vibrated through him. Our tongues collided, our moans entwining. Then he snatched his mouth away.

"Should I stop?" he panted.

"No." I needed this distraction more than anything. I kissed him first this time, slipping my tongue into his mouth, briefly tasting him before retracting. "I want you to take care of me right now," I said on his mouth.

"Okay." His breathing grew ragged as he released me so he could remove his boxers. He slapped them onto the edge of the hot tub while I rushed to take my bottoms off.

When I reached behind my neck to untie the strap of my top and remove it, freeing my breasts, his eyes seemed to spark. He scanned my curves with fascination before giving his head a shake.

"It does not make sense," he mumbled.

I paused. "What doesn't?"

"How fucking *sexy* you are."

I couldn't help my smile.

Once again, he collected me in his arms just to lift me up. I closed my legs around him, and he reached down to grip himself, angling the tip at my center.

When he thrust into me, I released a sharp gasp.

"*Qué rica.* You are so good." His groan was primal and deep, as if he'd been waiting *years* just to feel me again. It'd only been one day since, but for some reason it felt like forever.

Our lips meshed, and he pumped into me, groaning ferociously while I whimpered and moaned into his mouth.

"Fuck. Your pussy is so wet," he panted, stroking faster. He clutched a fistful of my locs to tip my head back, pressing hot, wet kisses on my throat.

"That feels amazing," I breathed as the water sloshed.

"¿Sí?" His breath ran over the crook of my neck. "How much did you think about doing this again, hmm?"

"A lot." And I did. I was tempted to get an orgasm in this morning with Rosie while fantasizing about him but thought better of it.

"I thought about you all night, Octavia." He brought his mouth to the shell of my ear. "I thought about being inside of you again. Seeing your face when you come." He leaned back so our eyes could connect. "You are so fucking beautiful."

"Ugh." I gripped his face in my hands. "Why do you always know the right things to say?"

I kissed him deep, and he gradually slid me up and down the length of him. No longer was he restraining himself. His groans were ravenous while my moans flew into the air, creating their own rhythm.

He stumbled a bit, and the backs of his legs bumped against one of the built-in hot tub seats. When he dropped, I went down with him, our bodies still joined.

"Ride me." His voice was a deep, commanding growl. I began to work my hips, lifting up and down, then rotating in circles as he focused on me.

He felt so big, so insanely good. Every time I rocked backward, I could feel him hitting my G-spot, triggering the pressure. Every time I rocked forward, my clit grazed against his pelvis, sending sparks of pleasure straight to my core. If we kept going at this rate, I'd surely detonate.

I bit my bottom lip, and he gripped my face between his fingers. "Do not hold back," he rumbled. "I am yours tonight, so use me if you need to. Come all over me. I do not care. I just want to see you satisfy yourself."

"You can't talk like that," I breathed, his words fueling me, causing me to ride him faster.

"No? Do you not like it?"

"I *love* it," I moaned.

He held my ass and tipped his head back, allowing me to take complete charge.

"Carajo. Your pussy feels so good wrapped around me."

"Javier . . ."

"¿Sí, amor?"

"I'm about to . . ."

"About to what, mi amor?"

"I'm . . . oh my God . . ." I tightened my arms around his neck and dropped my face into the crook of his neck, but he snapped me right back into place.

"I told you I want to see you," he said.

A cry escaped me as I threw my head back, pulsating and clenching around him. He groaned as I continued chasing my high, still needing more, wanting all of him.

"Shit," he cursed, tensing beneath me. "I'm about to come, Octavia. You are riding me too good."

"So don't hold back," I whispered on his lips.

He was so close. I could tell by the cords bulging on his neck and the fire in his eyes. The way his dick pulsated inside me, as if it suddenly had a life of its own. It didn't help that I was grinding on top of him, dragging him closer to climax. He palmed my ass tighter in his large hands as my lips fell down on his. Before I knew it, he was swearing into my mouth, and his body tensed.

He pushed me upward just enough that he could pull out, then squeezed his eyes shut as he shuddered with his release, cursing in Spanish and groaning in between.

"Oh, fuck." He held on to me, twitching while I settled on his right thigh and delicately kissed his cheek. After several seconds, he asked, "We are getting out of hand, no?"

I busted out laughing as he looked up at me with a lazy grin. "Maybe just a teensy bit. Also don't worry. I'm protected."

He gave a swift nod. "Do you think we should stop doing this?"

"I don't think we have to stop."

"Okay. Because I am enjoying this."

"Well, as long as nothing gets too serious, we should be okay, right?"

His brows puckered. "What do you mean?"

"I mean . . ." I climbed off his lap and searched for my top, floating on the other side of the hot tub. "I guess what I'm trying to say is if we can keep our feelings out of it, we should be okay. I don't want you to think I'm leading you on, for you to expect something deeper from me that I may not be able to give you . . ."

He was quiet for a bit. "Because you no longer trust being with anyone? Because of *him*?"

"You could say that."

He let those words marinate. "Well, I guess we are on the same page, then." He collected his shorts and provided me a half smile. "After Eloise, I do not wish to be deep with anyone else either."

"So . . . I guess we can agree on that, right? Just letting this be for fun?" I tied my top into a small bow behind my neck, but I didn't miss the way Javier locked onto my face, as if searching for a tell—a sign that I might have been joking.

But I wasn't.

Don't get me wrong, this time with Javier was exciting. Honestly, my whole life at that moment felt sort of like a fever dream. Waking up in a beautiful guesthouse. A dream job, taking care of a lovely kid. Using the pool and hot tub and attending free professional basketball games courtside. Traveling to different states and staying in luxury hotels here and there. It was nice . . . but he had to admit that no matter what either of us wanted, this wouldn't last.

One day Aleesa would grow up.

He'd most likely find someone who wanted something true and deep with him—someone who was 100 percent willing to commit. I wished I had it in me to promise myself to someone again, but I didn't see that happening anytime soon, and I didn't want any pressure about it.

Plus, I could never live up to Javier's wife. Based on all the photos of them I saw around the house, it was clear he loved her. He had a whole *child* with her. I could never top that.

"Right," he finally said after some time. "We will just have fun, then. No worries." The smile he put on barely reached his eyes. He proceeded to climb out of the hot tub to pick up his shirt. "I am going to take another shower. Have a good night, Octavia."

He turned away before I could respond and walked to the door so fast that I didn't even get a chance to say good night back.

Watching him go with that slight slump in his shoulders and his head bowed did weird things to my chest. Made it feel heavy and empty all at once . . .

And it hit me after a few minutes that I might have officially hurt Javier's feelings for the first time.

# TWENTY-FOUR

## OCTAVIA

"I think cream cheese is the best option for icing so far. And do you think we should go with red velvet or white cake?" Davina swiveled her eyes to mine as she licked her tasting fork.

"Cream cheese and red velvet," I told her. "Definitely."

She nodded in agreement, pushing her fork into the red velvet for another bite.

I looked to my left at Aleesa, who was sitting in a chair, with cake crumbs all over her mouth. Icing was glued to her fingers, and she began licking each one, with delighted eyes.

"Do you want a wipe, Leesa?" I asked, reaching for her mermaid backpack.

"No, no wipe. No, thank you." Aleesa sucked each finger into her mouth while kicking her feet.

"Are you sure I can't drive to Atlanta, find Luther, and beat his sorry A-S-S?" Davina eyed me, with flared nostrils, working herself up all over again.

I'd told her late last night about Luther showing up at Javier's house, and I purposely did that because I didn't want her dropping everything to come to me. She would have bailed on this entire cake tasting (that she had been wait-listed on for months) just to spend the whole morning in Atlanta with me. I'd refused to let her do that.

"You can try, but he's not worth it." I blew a sigh. "I'm going to file a restraining order when I get back."

"Good." She licked icing off her fork's prongs. "Can't believe the police had to get involved. Like, seriously? What was he thinking? What kind of man does that?"

"He's *not* a man, Vina. He's a child in a man's body, who throws tantrums when he doesn't get his way."

"Facts." She sighed. "Well, do you wanna tell me what else is wrong?"

"What do you mean?" I sat up taller in my chair. What was she hinting at? Did Javier talk to Deke and now she knew something? "I'm fine."

"No, Tavia, you're not. That dumbass showed up and shook you all up."

"Yeah, and I'm over it. F-U-C-K him." I glanced at Aleesa.

"So what else is bothering you?"

"Why would you think something else is bothering me?"

"Is it work?" she asked, ignoring my question.

"No, Vina."

She was quiet a moment, studying me, looking for any tells. "Well, it has to be *something*. We're at a popular bakery, and you're not commenting on any of the designs? Aahing over the consistency of the icing? Ogling the cupcakes? That's so unlike you."

"I just had a long night, that's all. I'm tired."

"What were you doing?"

"Nothing," I returned quickly. "I just couldn't sleep. What's with all the questions?"

She gave me a suspicious look. She was still searching me for lies. She then pointed at Aleesa with her fork. "Javier was okay with you bringing his precious?"

"Yeah, he was cool about it. He had a meeting with his manager today." I picked up my fork and pierced the prongs through the moist chocolate cake.

Okay, sure. Vina was right. Something else *was* bothering me, but it wasn't fuckboy Luther. I kept thinking about the night before, being in the hot tub with Javier. How he walked away. The disappointed look in his eyes. I wasn't sure if we would be on good terms or not, but after seeing him this morning, it felt like we weren't.

He'd given Aleesa a kiss, glanced at me with a forced smile, and then left the house. No *Goodbye*, *See you later*, or anything.

"Octavia, please look at me." *Damn it.* Davina was once again using her big sister voice. It was clear she had an idea of what might've been wrong with me. And the crazy part about my sister was when she had a hunch, she was *never* wrong.

I reluctantly shifted my gaze to meet hers.

After studying me carefully for a beat, she looked across the room at the baker and wedding planner, who were deep in conversation, before leaning in closer to me.

"You did something with him, didn't you?"

"With who?" I asked, playing dumb.

She scoffed. "You know who." She bobbed her head at Aleesa. "Tell me what's going on. I don't like seeing you like this."

I dropped my fork and slouched back in my chair. "Okay, fine. But I'm going to need you to not overreact."

She threw her hands in the air. "I never overreact."

"Yes, we did something."

She gasped, eyes stretching wide. "Tavia!"

"Oh my gosh, I just told you not to overreact," I countered.

"I'm sorry, I just—I had a feeling!" she whisper hissed. "Deke called me after the charity event yesterday and was saying he noticed something different about Javier. He said Javier kept looking for you during the event, and when you told me he interrupted your date that other night . . . well, now it's all starting to make sense."

"Wait. *Really?*" I asked. "He kept looking for me?"

"According to Deke, he definitely was. I told him that Javier was probably looking for you because you had Aleesa," Vina went on, "but Deke *swore* something else was going on. He said something had changed between you and him. Said y'all were flirting, girl. Now I get it." She couldn't contain her grin.

"Okay, fine, it's true. But y'all shouldn't make a big deal about it. It's just for fun right now. Nothing serious." At least, I hoped we would still have fun. I wasn't quite sure after last night.

"Okay, I get it." She bobbed her head. "And that makes perfect sense for both of you, considering your pasts."

"Exactly." Why couldn't Javier see it that way?

After thinking about it last night, I realized he'd expected a different answer from me. He'd told me he didn't want us to stop having our fun . . . but what did he think would happen the more we had sex?

Someone would become attached, and I was going to make damn sure it wasn't me. And the last thing I wanted was to hurt his feelings if he asked for more. Why ruin a good thing?

Besides, what good would a relationship between a broken woman and a widower be?

"So this is part of the reason why you're moody today?" my sister asked, folding her arms.

"I'm not moody."

"You are."

"Okay, I might be. Sue me."

"I *will* sue you if you don't tell me what's up."

Something rattled on the other end of the table, and out of instinct, I reached over to grab Aleesa's plate before it could topple and hit the floor.

"Sowwy, Tava," Aleesa said in an apologetic little voice.

"It's okay, love." I watched her climb out of her chair just to stand at my side.

"Can I have iPad?"

I sighed. "If you get the iPad, you can only watch it for *ten* minutes, okay? You watched too much of it in the car, and your dad will never shut up about it if he finds out."

"Okay." She smiled at me, almost like she knew I'd forget and she'd fly right past her ten-minute limit. That happened more often than I cared to admit.

I dug into the backpack for her iPad and set it up on the table with the kickstand.

"Kids now are like little geniuses." Davina watched Aleesa as she moved her finger around the screen. "Imagine if we would've had iPads at her age. What do you think we would be like now?"

"That's a good question." I laughed. "We'd have probably taken over the world."

Davina snorted.

I drew in a deep breath through my nostrils before releasing it through parted lips.

"Okay." I leaned closer to my sister. "The truth is that last night, we did *explicit* things in the hot tub. But right after, he said he wanted those things to keep happening. I told him it could as long as we didn't get too deep or serious, you know? When I said that, it seemed to bother him, though."

"Hmm." Davina took a moment to mull that over. "Why do you think it bothered him?"

"I don't know, but you'd think the last thing he wants is something even remotely close to a serious relationship. Especially with his *nanny*."

"Maybe he's just wanting a connection. Doesn't mean it has to be serious. And he probably doesn't see you as just *the nanny* anymore, Octavia. He might see you as family now."

"Family members don't fool around."

She gave me the stink eye. "You know what I mean."

I rolled my eyes.

"Look." She rested an elbow on the table and looked into my eyes. "You've bonded with both of them. You've been around them for over half a year. You're beautiful, smart, and kind. I'm truly surprised it took this long for something to happen between y'all, honestly. Me and Deke were betting on the timing. Looks like he won. *Again.*"

"Well . . . it wasn't supposed to happen," I informed her. "And he initiated it."

"Really? You sure it wasn't you?"

"No, it wasn't me! He kissed me first."

She laughed. "I'm just saying."

"Don't do that." I pointed a finger at her, narrowing my eyes. "Don't act like I'm some hoe ready to jump into any man's bed."

"I never said that, but you do have the tendency to take what you want."

That was true. I liked what I liked. But still.

I folded my arms. "*Anyway*, I think I should just tell him we need to stop now before we take it too far."

"What do you mean by *too far*?"

"I mean . . . I don't want either of us trying to fall for each other or whatever." I waved my hand, as if this topic wasn't actually weighing heavily on me.

It was. A whole lot.

Maybe because no matter how much I tried to deny it, deep, deep, deep, deep down, I did want to fall for someone again.

I was just scared.

"Tavia, I've told you a million times that every man is not like shitty Luther. That fucker never deserved you," Davina said in a lower voice. "It's okay to want more with someone else."

I shook my head.

"He was one horrible, rotten egg," she went on. "So what if things get a little serious with Javier? Would that be such a bad thing?"

"That's an interesting question, coming from a woman who recently had a hard time letting another man in."

"Not the point," my sister shot back, fighting a smile. "I'm just saying, if he wants you and you want him . . . why not?"

"Because at the end of the day, I'm the woman he hired to take care of his child. He can get tired of me, meet someone else, and then fire me. It'd be like I never even existed to him."

"Those are your insecurities and fears talking. Besides, with an attitude like his, I doubt he'll be meeting anyone else anytime soon."

I couldn't help my smirk. "What about his wife?" I asked. "I can't compete with the mother of his child. He could compare me to her. Expect me to be like her . . ."

"Stop that. No one's asking you to compete with her or to be anything like her." She scratched above her brow with the tip of her French-tipped nail. "I mean, are there times when I compare Deke to Lew? Yes. But my therapist told me that was natural and that I shouldn't feel guilty about it. And Javier could think of comparisons in his head, but as long as he doesn't try and change you or bring things she did into your conversations to intentionally make you feel ashamed, it shouldn't matter."

Hmm. I guessed she had a point.

"Deke always used to say he never thought he'd live long enough to see the day Javier moved on," said Davina. "That says something. To me, it says Javier trusts you and that he must *really* like you. He may not know what he wants from this whole thing with you right now, but from what I'm hearing, he *does* like you. Hell, he crashed your date! Literally cut off the chance for another man to have you. If that doesn't scream it, I don't know what will, girl."

I blinked at her a few times before lowering my eyes to the thin cake slices on my plate. "So . . . what do you think I should do?"

"I think you should just let things happen. Let life do its thing." She popped another piece of cake into her mouth. "And I tell you this from experience, sis: trying to run from something that brings you joy, even if you feel like you don't deserve it, won't save you. It'll ruin you and make your life miserable."

And yet . . . I was still terrified of that, because joy wasn't an emotion that walked alone. Sorrow lingered right behind it, ready to storm in and sweep you away when the slightest crack formed.

# TWENTY-FIVE

## JAVIER

"Headphones? Check. Water cup? Yes. Barbie with pink hair? Check. Oh, shoot!" Octavia cursed under her breath as she shuffled through Aleesa's overnight bag. "No, come on."

"What is it?" I asked as her frown became more evident and her hand went deeper into the bag.

"I forgot her bedtime books."

"It should be fine. She will be okay for two nights without her books, Octavia," I said.

"She begged for those books, Javier. Once she realizes I don't have them, she'll flip." She pulled away from the bag and folded her arms. "You *know* she will too."

I looked from Octavia to Aleesa, who was currently occupied with a flavored-water juice box and Cheez-Its in a snack pouch. Her iPad was already set up on the back of one of the private plane seats, and her seat belt was clicked into place. She was all ready for takeoff and perfectly content now.

But Octavia was right. Once bedtime rolled around, she'd have an episode when she realized her favorite books weren't there.

Aleesa was not a fan of sleeping in new places. She loved our home and especially her bedroom. Most times when we traveled, she had a hard time adjusting to new settings, so those little comforts like bedtime books and Barbies mattered.

"You are right." I pinched the bridge of my nose. "We will make time to stop by a bookstore before her bedtime." I craned my neck to look out the door that revealed the tarmac. "Where the hell is my sister?"

"I am so glad there is wine," my mother said, waltzing from the back of the plane with a bottle of pinot grigio.

I shook my head. "Má, it is twelve in the afternoon."

"This is needed! Hijo, you know I get way too anxious on these things you call planes. You are lucky I am even here for this." She placed the bottle down on a nearby table.

"I never asked you to come. You invited yourself," I reminded her.

She scowled. "Do not get smart with me."

Octavia huffed a laugh as she tucked Aleesa's bag under her seat.

"That is funny?" I asked, folding my arms.

"A six-five giant getting told off by his petite five-foot mother? Comical." Octavia chuckled. "It's good to know you still fear her."

She was right. I *did* fear my mother at times. Any sign of disrespect toward her and I knew to expect a shoe to smack my head.

"I am just saying, you should not be back there, Mamá." I put my attention on my mother again. "Let the flight attendant do her job. I am sure she does not mind helping."

"The flight attendant is taking too long." My mother ducked off again, only to return with a mechanical bottle opener. She got to work opening the bottle right away as Margery, our flight attendant, appeared.

Margery's eyes widened, then swung my way, apologetic and a bit panicky.

"I am *so* sorry, Mr. Valdez. I was storing your bags and didn't realize—"

"Do not worry about it, Margery. It is not your fault my mother is impatient."

Margery smiled, though her cheeks were bright red. "Is there anything else I can get you all?"

"Xanax?" I joked, eyeing my mother.

This time, my mother did remove her flip-flop to chuck it at me. I dodged it just in time, and it smacked into one of the walls.

Octavia broke out in laughter. My mother, of course, was scowling at me again. Aleesa giggled.

"Do you see what I put up with, amor?" I smiled and winked at my daughter.

"I pray mi niña doesn't grow up being so rude like her father."

Something caught my ear, and I looked out of the door of the plane again. Coming up the stairs and into the jet was Catalina. She wore a pair of sunglasses, a crop top, and jeans. Her hair was all over the place, as if she had just been running or something.

"Finally," I said as she stumbled onto the jet. "What took you so long? We were supposed to take off twenty minutes ago."

"I know, I know." Catalina waved a dismissive hand as she plopped down in one of the seats. "The Uber driver's car got a flat tire. I had to run the rest of the way."

"Aw, man. I'm glad you made it," Octavia said.

"Yes, and you are here now. That is all that matters." My mother handed Catalina a glass of wine, and my sister gladly accepted it. My mother then glanced at Octavia, giving her a weird up-and-down look.

"I would ask you, Octavia, but I do not think it is wise for you to drink on the job."

Octavia pursed her lips, looking from my mother to me.

"She can have a drink if she would like, Má," I said. What the hell was that about?

"It's okay." Octavia forced a smile. "She's definitely right. I don't want a drink right now anyway. It's fine." She glanced at my mother a few times, slightly confused. Then she took the seat next to Aleesa.

I frowned at my mother, and she finally looked at me.

"What?" She threw her hands into the air, trying to be innocent.

"Pórtate bien, Mamá." I gave her a stern eye, insisting that she behave.

Yes, I feared my mother in certain ways, but I also knew that she did not care much for my nannies. She always assumed they wanted more from me or were flirting with me. She could be overwhelmingly protective.

"I did nothing wrong," she muttered in Spanish. She rolled her eyes, taking a long sip of wine.

Octavia was looking between us, brows puckered, trying to figure out what we were talking about.

"Are we ready to go now?" I asked, looking between all of them.

"Ready," Catalina said.

"Yep," Octavia answered.

My mother strapped in, performed the sign of the cross, and then took another big gulp of wine. "I am ready," she said.

I swear, that woman drove me crazy. Hell, all the women on the plane drove me crazy.

I took the seat across from Aleesa (diagonally across from Octavia), swapping out her iPad for a coloring book and crayons. Because I could not help myself, I stole a glance at Octavia, who was asking Aleesa what the color names were for each crayon she pointed at.

Things had shifted since the night of the hot tub. That had happened a full week ago. I noticed that when she took care of Aleesa, she would not be downstairs with her as much. She would be in Aleesa's bedroom, the playroom, or the theater room. She also spent more time around the pool, took more walks, and hung out with Aleesa in the guesthouse.

It was clear she was trying to avoid me. I could only blame myself for that, really. It was not like I'd expected things to evolve into more with Octavia. I wanted what she wanted—something simple and easy that did not sink too deep.

No, I was not looking to be in a relationship or to be committed, but hearing her immediately reject anything even remotely serious between us, before even giving it a real chance, made me wonder if what we were doing was worth it. And maybe that was because a tiny part of me, buried deep down, was open to the idea of us growing closer.

But if we did not grow closer, would she even remember me if I never saw her again? And would I be okay with watching her walk away? What if she went back on her word and ended up with that terrible man, Luther, again? And even if that happened, why did I care so much what she did with her life?

I was definitely thinking too much about it. Truthfully, I was just a lonely man who did not know how to handle this delicate situation with her. If I came on too strongly, she would pull away. If I didn't come forward at all, she would assume I did not want her around.

This was a hard game to play, so for now, I just followed her lead.

And I guess right now, that was to practice avoiding each other as much as possible and keeping things professional.

# TWENTY-SIX

## OCTAVIA

New York City is a bustling beauty that deserves exploring.

Too bad we'd spent most of the day stuck in traffic, trying to make it to our hotel. We'd stumbled into three wrecks before finally making it. By the time we did, it was nearing five in the evening and everyone was starving.

We made our way up to our reserved penthouse suites first to drop the bags off. The two rooms Javier had booked were right next to each other, and each suite had two bedrooms.

"Are you sure you do not want this room to yourself?" Javier asked as I dropped my bag on the floor of one of the rooms.

"Javier, come on. Look at this bed." I gestured to the enormous king-size mattress. "Aleesa won't take up even half of that."

"She can always sleep with me if you want your own space," he offered.

"It's all right, I promise."

"Okay, okay." He looked at me, eyes going up and down. Not only were they curious, but I noticed a hint of desire too.

I tried not to react to his heated stare. Things had been a bit tense on the plane. First, with Paola giving me the stink eye and being way colder to me than she had been at Aleesa's birthday party, then with

Javier sitting across from me during the flight. I'd felt him looking at me a few times and tried my best to ignore it.

I wasn't sure what to say to him, so instead of speaking, I dug into my suitcase to pull out my toiletry bag. "I'm gonna freshen up before we eat."

"Sure." He nodded and started to turn, shoulders slumping again.

No. This couldn't be it. We couldn't keep going like this. It was going to kill me.

"Javier?" I called.

He paused, glancing at me.

"You promised things wouldn't be weird between us."

He started to frown, but instead his face softened. With a gut-deep sigh, he walked deeper into the room.

"It is not weird," he murmured. "I just . . . well, I am not sure what you want from me, Octavia. I do not know how far to take things with you."

I pursed my lips. Those seemed like such loaded statements.

"Do *you* even know what you want?" His eyes were gentle but mildly confused. "I just do not want to overstep. That is all. You said you did not want us to get too serious, so I am giving you some space. Plus, you are the one who has been avoiding me and creating this weirdness."

"I haven't been avoiding you," I countered quickly.

He gave me a sarcastic look that said, *Really?*

Okay. Maybe I had been avoiding him a little. After that conversation with Davina, it had really struck me that there was something more I was feeling for Javier. It wasn't just lust. We'd only had sex twice—and yes, those two times were *incredible*—but even before that, I'd felt something.

This *something* had been deeper and much more intricate, and I think sleeping with him had solidified that somehow. Add onto that the fact that he was so quick to defend and protect me from Luther, and yes . . . I was feeling things for this man that I didn't want to explore again.

A part of what made me hesitant was that I wasn't sure I could trust another man after Luther had shown his true colors. How could I like—or even *love*—another person when I was such a terrible judge of character?

I had been so blinded by love and all its audacity with Luther. How could I let someone else in when the idea of falling for them was so terrifying? What if Javier lost interest in me? Or he noticed more of my flaws and pointed them out like Luther had? What if he decided I wasn't worth wanting *more* with?

My feelings were caught up in this difficult web, and I didn't know how to free them. That was a little nerve-racking to realize—knowing my feelings could be dictated by someone else's again. Knowing my emotions were no longer just . . . *mine.*

I cared about Javier. I cared *too much*, when all this could come crashing down around me at any given moment. So, to me, keeping a distance felt like the smart thing to do. Distance was best for clarity's sake . . .

However, my sister was right. Trying to avoid what I really felt was making me miserable. I missed him and found it so damned hard to accept that.

"Okay, fine." I wrapped my arms around myself. "I'm sorry if it feels like I've been avoiding you."

"You have," he replied. Then he smiled and lifted a hand to stroke my chin. "But it is okay. Let's just start over."

"Davina says I should just let this thing between us take its course . . ."

His hand stopped mid–chin stroke. "You told Davina about us? That we have slept together?"

"Yes," I responded warily. "She's my sister. I trust her with my life. Is that a bad thing?"

"Well, no . . . but now I know for a fact that Deke knows and he's going to rub it in my face the next time I see him. Ay Dios."

I huffed a laugh. "Oh, you can count on that."

He smiled, running the pad of his thumb across my bottom lip. "How about this . . ." He curled that same hand around the back of my neck. "We start fresh. We go about this with little-to-no expectations. In fact, we do not ever have to talk about what we expect again. As you said, we can just let this take its course. See where it goes. Okay?"

I nodded, relieved to hear that. "Okay."

"And tonight, we will eat dinner, I will take you and Aleesa to the nearest bookstore, and we will hang out in the hotel the rest of the night. When she falls asleep, you and I can watch a movie, or play a card game, or whatever you want to do to make yourself comfortable."

"Okay, now I know you're just trying to get laid again," I teased. "What woman *wouldn't* love the sound of that?"

His lips curved into a smile. He studied me intently, as if he were searching for all the answers to his problems and hoping to find them within me.

"I do not want you to be afraid of being honest with me, Octavia." His voice was deep and soft. "I do not know all of what that hijo-de-puta ex of yours did to you, but I am not him. Okay? I will *never* hurt you."

Every single part of me warmed up to his words. I wanted so badly to cry. He had no idea how much that meant to me to hear.

"It's hard for me to be honest with people these days," I admitted. "And I don't know if I can actually trust *this*." I used my hand to gesture between us.

"Why do you say that?"

"Because all of this can come to an end, Javier. Do you really think we're going to be able to do this forever? Sleep around? Pretend what we're doing is no big deal? Eventually, Aleesa will go to school and she won't need me as much anymore."

"But *I* will." His voice was sure, confident—as if he didn't need to think about it. As if it had always been right there, on the tip of his tongue. My heart thumped quickly again.

Listen, I'd developed a lack of trust in people—especially men—but Javier was slowly restoring my faith. I wanted to fall to my knees for this man.

"I do not want you to go anywhere anytime soon," he told me. "I want you *here*. I want to be around you for as long as I can, and if that sounds selfish, I do not care. So do not worry about the future. Focus on what is happening for us right now. Yeah?"

I swallowed all my emotions down, refusing to ruin this tender moment with my tears.

His words were so powerful, though.

So sweet.

So beautiful.

I wished they were real and tangible so I could catch them, hug them, and then tuck them into my pocket to hold on to forever.

"So we'll really just have fun with it?" I raised a curious brow. "No expectations?"

"Yes. Just don't get weird on me again."

I laughed. "I promise I won't."

"Good." He laid a kiss on my lips, and I sighed behind it.

Damn, I missed his lips. It'd been a solid week since I'd last felt them. Perfectly supple and full. He was a damn good kisser too. I laced my arms around the back of his neck, deepening the kiss.

"Oh, and also," I said when our lips separated. "I think your mom might hate me."

"She does not hate you. She is just protective."

"But you noticed that on the plane, right? She didn't act that way toward me at Aleesa's party."

"No, she did not. She tends to get hostile when she thinks my nannies are seeking more. Many in the past have tried it—wanting to get closer to me, clearly all for one thing."

"You don't think that about me, do you?"

"Absolutely not. You have been the most genuine of all of them."

"Did you do anything with any of them?" I couldn't help but ask. It was going to kill me not to know.

"Hell, no."

"Swear."

"I swear. You are the only one I have ever felt anything for. But even if our circumstances were different, I am certain we would have connected in some other way."

"Aw. That's a sweet way of looking at it."

"Daddy!" Aleesa squealed from the living room. "iPad is dead!"

He let out a weary chuckle. "Let me get to her." He placed another kiss on my lips, one that was so deep and passionate my toes curled in my sneakers. "You go ahead and freshen up. I will get her ready."

"Okay." I drew my bottom lip in, sinking my teeth into it.

I watched him make his way toward the door but was surprised when he stopped, twisted around again, and came back to me. He gathered my face in his large hands and brought his mouth down to kiss me one more time.

I melted in that moment like butter in a skillet. I gave in and kissed him back, laughing behind it.

"You're much more romantic than I expected, Valdez," I murmured when he let me go.

His thumb skimmed my bottom lip, and he wore a smirk that was too sexy for his own good. "There are a lot of things about me that are unexpected, amor. You just have to stick around long enough to see what they are."

# TWENTY-SEVEN

## OCTAVIA

Dinner was impeccable, of course. I'd expected nothing less from one of the pickiest men I'd ever dealt with.

The picky man that I couldn't stop looking at or thinking about.

Paola still gave me the cold shoulder or ignored me altogether. I didn't know what the hell her problem was or why she was making sudden assumptions about me. Catalina, on the other hand, had no problem chatting me up and even shared some of her chocolate cake with me.

After eating, Catalina and Paola decided to take a walk to burn a few calories and to sightsee. Javier, Aleesa, and I were picked up in a black car that took us to a massive bookstore on Broadway.

Javier led Aleesa to the children's section right away. I was about to follow them when a book on one of the stands caught my eye. This had been bound to happen. Of course I was going to get distracted. I was a bookworm in a store full of *books*.

I wasn't sure how long I stood at that section, browsing every romance-novel cover and debating on which I wanted to take with me. There were so many options—too many, really. The books I decided to grab were gorgeous and had amazing premises and plots. At one point, I wondered if it would've been too much to buy *six* of them.

"Just one," I told myself as I picked up one of the novels and scanned the back cover again. Besides, I didn't have enough space in my suitcase for six.

"It's me," Javier called, causing me to spin around. He wove his way through the aisle with Aleesa on his shoulders. There were no books in either of their hands. "Just letting you know I'm approaching."

I held the book to my chest with a grin. "Thank you for that."

He gave me a nod and a half smile.

"Did you find anything for Leesa?"

"No." A deep sigh left him as he removed her from his shoulders and placed her feet on the ground. "All she cares about are the toys."

"Of course she does." I laughed. "Let me give her a try."

I collected her hand, and we made our way through the aisles until we came across the children's section. There were so many books lined up on the shelves. I could see how this could be overwhelming for a four-year-old.

"Here, Leesa. How about this?" I plucked a book titled *Night Owl Kisses*.

Aleesa gave it a scan, then nodded. "Yes. I like ow's."

"Okay, great. What else do you like?"

"Bears," she answered. "And candy."

I busted out laughing. "All right, let's see if we can find a book about one of those."

"Me again. I've got a book right here." Javier's voice carried our way. He stood on the other end of the shelf we were near, holding up a book with an illustrated Black girl on the cover, wearing pigtails and licking a lollipop. The title was *Sweet Suzie*.

"Oohh! Candy!" Aleesa bolted for her dad and threw her hands up. "Lemme see. Lemme see." She paused when Javier cocked a brow, waiting for the magic word. "Please," she added with a playful giggle.

He handed the book to her, and she was instantly mesmerized as she flipped through the pages.

"Nice one," I noted, approaching him.

"See. I am not completely useless."

"I never believed you were." I sent him a wink.

Javier studied Aleesa a moment before bringing his gaze up to mine again. "You know we are not only here for Aleesa, right?"

"No?"

"No. I saw you looking at the books and did not want to interrupt you. You can pick out whatever you want too. I will get it for you."

"Oh—no, Javier. I won't let you do that. You pay me enough. I can buy my own books, really."

"I saw you trying to choose between three or four of them." One of his eyebrows inclined.

"Well, yeah. It's hard to choose sometimes."

"Well, that is what I am saying. You do not have to choose. If you want them all, I will get them for you."

"Seriously?" I deadpanned. "So if I go back over there and pluck out ten books, you'll buy them *all*?"

He chuckled. "Ten seems a bit extreme, but yes. It would be no problem."

"Ten is *not* extreme for a book lover. That's us just getting started."

He continued laughing. "I am being serious. Get as many as you want." He caught Aleesa's hand before she could make a dash for the toy section.

"You know books aren't cheap, right?" I challenged. Because why was he doing this? A guy had never been willing to buy me as many books as I wanted.

"Octavia." His voice was firm, and his eyes held steady on mine. "Cost is nothing to me, and I do not want you to worry about it either. Consider this my way of saying thanks for taking such good care of my daughter."

"But that's my job. And you pay me very well for it."

"Octavia," he scolded again. "Are you really going to stand here and argue with me about not buying you something you love?"

"I don't mean to argue, I just . . ." The center of my chest warmed as I struggled to find the right words. "Why are you being so nice to me?" I suspiciously narrowed my eyes at him.

"Would you rather I be grumpy? Because I can be. I am *very* good at it. You said so yourself."

I laughed. "Absolutely not."

"Okay then."

Holding on to Aleesa's hand, he stepped closer and raised his free hand to stroke my upper arm. It was a soothing touch. Couple that with the way he looked into my eyes, and every part of me felt gooey and warm.

"I want you to have a good time, and I want you to be happy. That is all. Now go." He cocked his head, gesturing for me to get to it. "Find me when you are ready, amor."

That was another thing. Calling me *love* in Spanish. One hundred percent endearing. I'd thought he was only using it for sex, to enhance the moment, you know? But he was still calling me it . . . and I secretly loved it. Lord. He had to stop this. It was too much for me to handle right now.

I bobbed my head and walked away, because if I didn't, I was going to jump on that man and climb him like a tree.

# TWENTY-EIGHT

## JAVIER

Octavia selected five books because, in her words, she did not "wanna be greedy." Right after we checked out, she jumped to throw her arms around my neck and then kissed my cheek.

"Thank you," she whispered in my ear.

She did not know how much that small act meant to me. To feel appreciated for something. To feel wanted by a woman and cared for.

I tried my best not to think too much of it—she was simply thanking me—but it was hard not to think about it when she looked at me with those big, sparkling brown eyes.

Or when she bit her bottom lip.

Or when she stared at my mouth, like she wanted more than just a peck on the cheek.

After leaving the bookstore, Octavia somehow convinced me to stop at an ice cream parlor. This was a bad idea. Everyone knew not to feed a four-year-old ice cream with sprinkles at eight o'clock at night.

"I'll tucker her out so she burns it off, I promise." Octavia sat down at a table near the window, and I joined her.

"This is very hypocritical, you know?" I leaned back, watching as she handed Aleesa a cup with a vanilla scoop and sprinkles. "We literally just bought a book for her about eating less sugar. Plus, she had a lot of Catalina's chocolate cake during dinner."

I never thought that I would be the parent who was a stickler about sugar, yet here I was. But honestly it was because Aleesa literally seemed to turn into some hyperactive gremlin when she consumed too much candy or sweets. I am not even kidding. She would scream with excitement, get the zoomies, giggle hysterically, beg me to watch some random dance move that made absolutely no sense. It was cute at first but became exhausting very quickly.

"I'll wear her out *and* double brush her teeth. Will that help?" Octavia brought her spoon to her mouth and licked the fudge away. I didn't dare look away as she did it.

"Are you trying to distract me from this topic by seducing me?"

"What?" she shrilled. I smirked. "You're crazy. I'm simply enjoying my ice cream." She gave the spoon another lick, this time curling her tongue around the top. My dick spasmed as I saw her pink tongue glide over the curve of the plastic.

"You are something else, Octavia Klein."

"In a good or bad way?"

"I am not sure yet."

"I hope it's good." She winked. "Leesa, how's your ice cream, angel?"

"Mmm . . . it's yummy," my daughter answered. Then she cheesed hard to show us all the rainbow sprinkles stuck to her teeth.

"Yeah," I scoffed. "Good luck brushing all of that out."

Octavia giggled.

~

We'd finally made it back to the hotel, and sure enough, Octavia had tuckered Aleesa out. Before our ride showed up, she'd taken Aleesa outside the ice cream parlor, thrown her over her shoulder, and zoomed back and forth along the sidewalk. Aleesa squealed and giggled until she was breathless.

People probably thought Octavia was a little crazy for it, running around with a four-year-old, making airplane noises and all. It wouldn't have been a method I'd use to calm Aleesa, but I appreciated it.

It was interesting to watch Octavia with Aleesa. How she did things so differently from me yet produced the same result. With her around, I realized maybe I didn't have to be so controlling and overprotective. Maybe I could learn to let some of that go . . . if I could also learn to trust that there was still good in this world. Good people like her.

Aleesa was already rubbing her eyes during the car ride, but as soon as we reached the elevator of the hotel, she threw her hands up at me and begged to be picked up. Once her cheek rested on my shoulder, I knew she was a goner.

Octavia had gotten her washed up as quickly as she could, helped her into her pajamas, then laid her in the bed. Aleesa did not even need a bedtime story. She had been so deliriously sleepy that she had not fought it.

"She's down for the night." Octavia walked around the corner and entered the living room. "She snores like a grown man."

"And you are sure that you want to share a bed with her?" I laughed.

"Ah, it'll be all right."

"You are very good with her, you know?"

"It's nothing." She waved a hand, as if it were no big deal.

"No, I am serious." I sat on one of the barstools near the kitchen counter. "All of her previous nannies would look so drained after dealing with her. They could not really keep up with her energy. But you do, and you handle it well. If anything, it is Aleesa who cannot keep up with *you*."

She laughed at that last statement. "I guess it's just in my nature. I told you I love kids. I try to see the world through their lens. Everything is so big and new and exciting to them. It's a beautiful thing, seeing so much hope and curiosity in their eyes."

"Yes, well, I feel like I should be paying you more for all that you do. Those meals you make are always more than I expected."

"Javier, please." She walked my way, stopping at the barstool right next to mine. "I don't need more money. What you give me is fine. Plus, you provide for the meals, so technically I'm not coming out of pocket for any of it."

"But the meals are always so nourishing and detailed. Even down to your garnishes. That must be time consuming."

She laughed. "Look at it this way: I love cooking, and you have a nice kitchen that I *love* making a mess in. It's my pleasure." She grinned as I nodded with a crooked smile. "So what should we do now?" She swept her gaze around the penthouse.

"What do you want to do?"

She gave the question some thought. "Honestly . . . I think I just want to decompress and read one of the books I bought. It's been a long day."

"I don't see the harm in that."

"Okay. Let me get comfortable first."

She sauntered away, only to return about fifteen or so minutes later in a fresh set of pink pajamas with cupcakes on them. Her face was shinier, which meant she had probably washed it. Her locs were also now in a ponytail.

"Cute pajamas," I said as she made her way to the paper bag full of books on the table. As she shuffled through it, I stared at her ass.

*Did she take her panties off? Fuck me.*

"What will you do?" she asked, carrying one of the books to the sofa. She curled up on one end while I cleared my throat and pretended I wasn't just thinking about her with no panties on.

"I am going to have a drink." I had requested that the hotel send up limes and tequila while we were out. I made my way to the minibar, grabbed a silver tequila, and carried it to the kitchen. I poured two glasses, mixed tequila with a splash of lime juice, and carried both toward her.

"For me?" She smiled, accepting the glass I offered. "Tequila is my favorite."

"I know."

She quirked a brow. "How do you know?"

"You were drinking it the night you had that date."

"Oh—right. The date you so rudely interrupted. You know I will never let you live that down, right?"

Smiling, I walked away, but only to get a book out of the paper bag—one that I'd bought for myself. It was a self-help book on learning how to *not give a fuck*. According to Octavia, I needed to learn how to "chill out and let things be" sometimes. She swore reading this book would help me.

Returning to the sofa, I picked up her stretched-out legs and lifted them.

"Hey—" She started to protest, until I placed her legs on top of my lap and held on to one of her ankles. Her mouth clamped shut, and her eyes softened.

"Okay if I read too?" I asked.

She batted her lashes a few times, then fought a smile as she brought the rim of her glass tumbler to her lips. "Smooth move, Valdez."

After a big sip, she placed the glass down on the coffee table, then settled into the sofa. It was cute watching her crack the book open with such a satisfied smile.

It was like reading brought her nothing but pure joy. I was not a big reader, but I did read a lot of parenting books, biographies, and sports articles. It was nice trying something new . . . *with* someone new.

A strange thought struck me. I realized I had never done this sort of thing with Eloise. We had never sat in peace and quiet, with nothing but the sound of turning pages and soft breaths.

Eloise was always active, always wanting to dance and sing and drink. She was full of energy and life, and I loved that about her because I was quiet and antisocial—she'd balanced us.

But this was nice too. I found myself mindlessly caressing the top of Octavia's foot with the pad of my thumb. I studied her toenails, which were painted white. She had really cute toes.

Something Octavia had said earlier circled back in my mind. She'd mentioned how she saw the world through Aleesa's eyes. Just like children, she enjoyed the simple things in life and cherished them. She was not a woman who asked for much. She simply used what she had and flipped it into something grand.

Hell, she had made something as simple as lounging on a sofa and reading a book feel wholesome and monumental. For what felt like the first time, I could see life through her lens. I could see that peace was what she truly craved in life and holding on to that was important to her.

When I realized I was stroking her skin, I turned my gaze to hers. She was already looking at me.

"What?" I asked.

"This feels very . . . *intimate*," she murmured.

"Is that a bad thing?"

"I don't know," she replied in a soft voice. "Maybe not if I actually like it." She studied my face for quite some time, then pulled her legs away so she could twist her body the other way and rest her head in my lap. I wrapped an arm over her as she exhaled and opened her book again to read.

"Javier?" she called after a few quiet minutes.

"¿Sí, amor?"

"Thank you for making me feel safe." Her voice was thick and didn't sound like it normally did.

*Wait.*

I looked down at her. "Octavia, are you okay?"

She remained quiet.

"Octavia, look at me."

She shook her head.

"Please."

Sniffling, she sat up and slid her gaze my way. Tears lined the rims of her eyes, and when she blinked, they all came streaming down.

"I'm sorry," she cried, turning away. "It's so stupid for me to cry right now. I hate when I get all emotional like this."

"Hey, no. It is fine. Look at me." I collected her face in my hands before she could try and make her way to the far end of the sofa. "I do not think it is stupid. You are human. You can cry whenever you want to."

"I shouldn't even be crying." She sniffled. "Like, seriously? Crying because a guy chooses to *read* with me?"

"Is that a bad thing?" I asked, a little hesitant and confused. "Is there something else you want me to do? Do you want to be left alone while you read or—"

"No—I *like* that you're in here." She grabbed one of my hands, pulling it from her face to squeeze it. "I just . . . I guess I feel silly, because most guys would try and initiate sex or something. But you don't . . . and you haven't. At least not yet. You're just so patient and calm and accommodating. I'm not even your girl or whatever, and you spoil me. You don't realize it, but you do. No guy has ever taken me to a bookstore and let me get whatever I wanted. No guy has ever been this patient with me. It's all so simple, the things you do, yet they mean *everything* to me."

"Oh. I see." I remained quiet as she wiped her tears away with her free hand. "But these things, Octavia . . . they are the bare minimum. You do realize that, right?"

She seemed a little confused.

"A real man is *supposed* to be patient with you," I explained. "They should be calm with you, so that you feel calm too. A man should always want to accommodate you, and if he can manage it, he should spoil you every single day. He should want you to feel safe at all times."

"But most I've dealt with only do nice things when they want something out of it." She paused and pursed her lips. "Maybe that's just my trauma speaking. But regardless, I don't get that vibe from you. I feel like you actually . . . *want* to be around me. And I have to admit, this is a very new experience for me, so I guess . . . well, I guess I just don't know how to handle it."

"Well, you are right. I *do* want you. But, hey, what did we say? No expectations. Okay?" I wiped her falling tears away. "Do not worry about handling it. Let's focus on being here, in this moment. Let's just *chill out and let it be*."

She hiccuped a laugh. "It's so annoying when you use my words against me."

I laughed, too, then brought my lips to hers, giving her a slow, deep kiss. She sighed behind it, then climbed onto my lap, settling her body against mine. I lowered my hands, skimming them down her back and along the curve of her ass.

"You deserve good things," I whispered on her lips.

"Tell me again," she pleaded before diving in for another kiss.

"You deserve good things, amor. You deserve everything."

She moaned. "It'll take some time for me to embrace that."

I cupped the back of her head, tangling my fingers in the locs at the nape of her neck and consuming her. Giving her everything.

I was not sure how we managed to get our clothes off, but it happened, and neither of us dared to slow down. When she was only in her bra and I was in my boxers, she knelt on the floor to get between my thighs. Her fingers wrapped around the waistband of my boxers, and she tugged downward.

"Octavia," I breathed in warning. "Are you sure?" I did not want her to think she had to please me just because I had said all that. I was not looking for a reward of any kind.

"Yes. *You* deserve this." She looked up at me beneath her lashes, still trying to pull my boxers down. I tilted my hips, and she didn't stop until my boxers had been tossed aside. Then she wrapped one soft hand around the base of my dick while the other cupped my balls.

I cursed under my breath as she lifted herself higher on her knees. When she took me into her hot mouth, the back of my head tipped backward and a deep groan escaped me.

She slurped and sucked, pumping my dick and massaging my balls. I picked my head up to watch her. Her eyes were already on me. It was like she was making love to me with those eyes, all while having me deep down her throat.

I clutched a handful of her locs, drowning in pleasure as she dropped her head and took me deeper, gagging just a little, before coming back up for air.

"Fuck, you are too good," I groaned.

She moaned, sending a strong vibration along the length of my dick. Her hand pumped faster, her tongue swiveling around the thick tip, and all it took was one more swallow from her to make me quake and for a deep groan to break free.

I gripped the back of her head as I came, lurching forward and cursing. I could feel all of it spilling down her throat, hot and swift. Her mouth was fucking magical, wrapped all the way around me, taking me whole. As if she could be more perfect, she swallowed every drop while peering at me, as if seeking approval.

"Yes," I breathed, twitching as she lapped her tongue around me again to clean up the mess. "You are amazing. So, so amazing."

When she released me with a pop of her lips, I hauled her back up to my lap, and she laughed as I kissed the crook of her neck. Greedy myself, I placed her on her back on the sofa, spread her legs apart, and ate her pussy.

And damn, was she delicious.

# TWENTY-NINE

## OCTAVIA

There was knocking in the distance.

I groaned as I rolled over on the bed, only to bump into a large, warm body. I blinked through bleary vision, and when it cleared up, I saw Javier lying next to me, eyes shut and mouth slightly ajar.

I took a look around, realizing I was in his room of the penthouse suite—and in his bed.

The knocking started up again, louder this time.

"Shit." I rolled over, scrambling for my phone on the nightstand. It was seven thirty in the morning. Who the hell was knocking this early on a Saturday?

I climbed out of bed—completely naked, might I add—but not before hissing Javier's name.

He groaned, and instead of waking up, he turned onto his side and burrowed himself deeper beneath the comforter.

"I swear you sleep like a bear," I muttered. I hurried through the hallway and searched for the pajamas I'd worn last night. I found the cupcake-print shorts first. My shirt was behind the sofa.

The knocking resumed, this time with a voice on the other end. "Hijo, it's me! Open the door," Paola called.

*Oh, double shit.* His mother was on the other side of the damn door, and here I was standing naked in the living room. I hastily slipped into my shorts.

"Tava?" I whipped my head up to see Aleesa now standing in the living room. "Ewww!" she squealed. "You naked!"

It didn't help that she had a fit of giggles afterward. Good thing she was young. She'd never remember seeing her nanny naked . . . I hoped.

I slipped into my shirt as Aleesa wandered toward one of the floor-to-ceiling windows to stare at the skyline. Then I hurried to the bathroom to grab a robe and thrust an arm into each sleeve.

"Coming, Paola!" I had no time to tie my robe as I rushed to the door and unlocked it.

When I opened it, Paola narrowed her eyes. Then she scanned me, taking in the robe hanging off my shoulder as well as a bit of rumpled pajamas beneath it. I bet my locs were a hot mess because I fell asleep without my bonnet.

Javier and I had several more tequila shots and read for a bit more, then we took a break to talk about random things, like his last season of basketball and how he wanted to build a garden so Aleesa could learn how to grow her own food.

After that, all I remember was his large body on me again and his tongue sweeping through my mouth. How had we even made it to the bedroom?

With Paola was Catalina, who stood a step or so behind her mother, with her phone in hand and a pair of cat-eye Versace sunglasses on. She looked at me over the sunglasses, then suppressed a laugh as she slipped her phone into her back pocket.

Paola frowned at me, clearing her throat. "Buenos días, Octavia." She greeted me with a cold, hard, cheerless voice. "Where is my son?"

"He's still sleeping," I answered, pulling up the robe to cover my shoulder, then self-consciously folding my arms over my chest.

"Well, he should wake up soon. We are just stopping by to let you all know we ordered room service for everyone to enjoy a nice breakfast." Her eyes flicked up and down again. "Javier said he wanted to view the billboard at nine, right?"

"Yes, I think so." I tried racking my brain for the answer. My mind was still stuck on last night . . . on her son's *you-know-what* inside *my* you-know-what.

"Well, we'd better get a jump on it to beat traffic." It was Catalina's turn to speak. Paola was still frowning at me.

Aleesa padded across the room and pushed by me to get to her grandmother.

"Ay, mi niña!" Paola scooped Aleesa up and hugged her tight, making sure their cheeks smushed together. Fortunately, that frown of Paola's had disappeared. "You hungry? Hmm?"

"Sí," Aleesa said with a giggle.

"Sí, I bet you are. Come with abuela. I'll get you fed." Paola swung her eyes to me, looking me up and down once again. This time, I swear she was looking at me with pure disdain. "Wake my son for me, yes?"

I nodded. "Will do."

Catalina and I watched them go until they reached the door of the next penthouse suite. As soon as Paola opened that door and went inside, Catalina put her focus on me again.

"Long night?" She wore an amused smile.

I tried reading her eyes, but with those sunglasses on, she was unreadable. Hey, at least she wasn't glaring at me to death like her mom.

"Sort of," I answered.

"I bet." She snickered before turning on her heels. "Come over for breakfast when you're ready. And tell my bonehead brother to get up."

Yeah. They definitely suspected something about us.

~

After a shower, I gathered my hair into an updo, then got dressed in a gray jumper and Nike Dunks. When I left the bedroom I was *supposed* to share with Aleesa and carried myself into the living room, Javier was there.

He stood in the kitchen with a mug of coffee in hand . . . and no shirt. Just boxers. God, this man was impeccable. Those six abs, that tan skin, the natural V-cut just below his abdomen. Those long, thick black lashes as he looked under them to find me. He had bed hair . . . and I had never felt so attracted to a sleepy human.

"You are staring," he said before taking a sip of coffee.

I shifted on my feet. "Kinda hard not to when you look like *that*."

He fought a smile. "Like what?"

"Like an Argentinean snack. I mean, really. God wasn't messing around when he made you. Just gave you all the green flags."

He laughed, setting his mug down on the countertop. "You flatter me, Octavia. You really do." He walked across the room to approach me. "Where's Leesa?"

"With your mom. They stopped by a little bit ago. She said she ordered breakfast from room service for everyone."

"Oh, she ordered it, huh? Is she also paying for it?"

I laughed as he placed a hand on my waist. "Doubt it."

"I doubt it too. That woman loves spending my money."

"Hey, listen . . . I think your mom and sister might know about us." I tucked a loc behind my ear. "Like, they probably suspected something before, but now I think they know."

"Why do you say that?" he asked.

"Well, your mom gave me a look when she stopped by. Kind of like she was annoyed with me. I was still in my pajamas, and I think she's putting two and two together. And Catalina was laughing like there was some kind of inside joke happening."

"Okay." He seemed confused by my confession. "Did they say anything about it?"

"No, but what if they start hating me or something? They seem really protective of you and Aleesa."

"They can be," he said, "especially my mother. But I am a grown man who can make his own choices. Trust me, they know not to overstep."

"So, you're basically saying they *will* end up hating me." I rolled my eyes. Men truly did not understand how women operated. "Got it."

"No. I am saying do not worry too much about it. When I am ready to tell them about you, they will respect it. In the meantime, let them think whatever the hell they want."

"That's a whole lot easier said than done, Valdez."

"Fine. I will talk to them. Okay?"

I smiled. "Okay. Thank you." I checked my watch for the time. "Well, I'm going to head over to that lioness's den. You should get ready. Catalina said we should leave soon if we want to beat traffic to get to the billboard."

"Right." His attention traveled past me, focused on the skyline. "The billboard."

"That isn't a very excited response."

"No, no. I am excited. I just am not looking forward to the crowds. But I want pictures so that Aleesa can be reminded of these moments."

"It'll be fine." I pressed up on my toes to kiss his cheek. "Now wash your ass and come eat. Don't leave me in there to drown."

"What if what I want to eat is right in front of me?" He placed both hands on my waist, then twisted us around. When he lifted me up and placed my butt on the countertop, I yelped.

"Javier, did you not have enough last night?" I laughed.

"Have enough? Of you?" He kissed the bend of my neck, then the area just below my collarbone. "That could never be possible."

"No?"

"No. I will *always* want more. I am insatiable when it comes to you."

It was dumb of me to think, but I wondered if he'd said the same thing or something similar to his wife. Surely, he'd felt the same way about her.

*Nope. Remember what Davina said. Don't compare yourself.*

Shoving the thought aside as best I could, I cradled his face in my hands and placed a soft kiss on his lips.

"We'll have plenty of time later."

He wasn't done, though. Before I could wriggle away from him, he caught my mouth again, kissing me so deeply that I wanted to say *Fuck it*, rip my clothes off, and let him have every inch of me.

Who cared if his family was waiting? Who cared if his mom got mad? They could wait ten minutes longer.

Javier Valdez was the kind of man that could make any woman melt if he truly wanted her. His dominance, his accent, his body . . . it was all an addictive cocktail. One that I was becoming more and more thirsty for by the day.

By some miracle, we decided to behave.

He helped me off the counter. "Go," he said, lowering a caress to my butt before spanking it. "Before you end up needing another shower."

I bit back a smile as he gave my butt another squeeze.

Seriously. Don't ask me how I managed to leave that penthouse intact.

# THIRTY

## OCTAVIA

Bubbles and Swaddles had nailed it.

It was clear the owner, Kyla, was doing great things with her company, because we were now all staring up at one of the New York billboards with her brand's name on it.

Thousands of people would walk past this. Thousands would see the photo of the famous Javier Valdez holding Aleesa, who wore a hooded towel and was cheesing from ear to ear.

In the image, Javier smiled at his daughter, holding her close, as illustrated bubbles floated around them. His signature was stamped in the bottom right corner.

Far below the billboard and at just the right angle, I took a few pictures of Javier with Aleesa on his shoulders. Both of them wore big, eager smiles. They were so cute together, really. And he made such a great father.

I captured more photos of him with his mom and sister included, then a few candid shots of Aleesa, who did several princess poses with duck lips. I swear I loved that little girl.

When we all had had enough, we found an Argentinean bakery within walking distance, to catch a coffee and a quick sit-down.

"Ever had a cañoncito?" Javier asked, offering me a flaky cream-filled pastry.

"No, but it looks good," I said, taking it graciously. "What's in it?"

"It is filled with dulce de leche. It is very good, especially when it is warm."

Excited, I bit into it, and the flavors instantly burst on my tongue. "Oh wow."

"Right?" Javier grinned.

"Oh yeah. This is amazing." It was perfectly flaky, with a hint of butter that melted on my tongue. And the filling was creamy and sweet but not overly so.

He handed Aleesa a palmerita and was about to sit when his phone rang. Withdrawing the phone from his pocket, he checked the screen, then blew a slightly agitated breath. "I have to take this. Keep an eye on her?"

"Of course."

He cut his eyes to our left, looking at Paola and Catalina, who were leaving the counter with their orders.

"Be right back," he said, then walked out of the bakery.

I watched as he marched back and forth in front of the window with the phone glued to his ear.

"So, how long?" Catalina's voice caught me off guard as she twisted one of the chairs at my table around and sat on it backward. She rested one arm on top of the chair while biting into a frosted chocolate doughnut.

"How long what?" I asked.

"How long have you and my brother been sleeping together?"

My heart dropped. I swear it felt like it was sitting in the pit of my stomach now. "Um . . . I—I don't know what you mean, Catalina."

She smiled behind another bite. "You know *exactly* what I mean."

I pressed my lips, looking from her to Paola, who was coming our way. She zeroed in on me, and my heart shot back up into my rib cage and pounded dangerously hard.

"I had a feeling." Catalina shrugged. "And for the record, *I'm* not angry about it."

"You're not?" A whisper of relief filled my veins.

"Hell, no. If anything, this is good for my brother. Maybe not the fact that you're Aleesa's *nanny*, because that's stereotypical as hell, but still . . . I think this is good. Even better because I actually *like* you."

Paola took the seat across from Aleesa, diagonal from me. "What are we talking about?" she asked, dumping a packet of sugar into her coffee.

"How happy Javier has been lately," Catalina answered.

"Hmm." Paola made a face as she began stirring her coffee with a wooden stick. "I am not sure if it is true happiness he shares with her."

"Má," Catalina said with a sigh. "We talked about this."

"No, it's okay, Catalina," I interjected, holding a hand up. "I understand why she may not be happy about me and Javier's situation."

"Yes, because that is exactly what this is. A *situation*." Paola's voice was hard, the wrinkles around her mouth more visible. "Yesterday, on the plane ride, I thought I was being crazy. He kept looking at you, and you kept looking at him. Then I see you this morning almost half naked under a robe, and . . . well, it was all very unprofessional. It became *very* clear that, yes, my son may be sleeping with this woman."

I wasn't sure what to say to that. I mean, I could've cursed her out just for being rude about it, but I had respect for my elders. And she had every right to be upset that her widower son was sleeping with his nanny. Catalina was right. It was beyond stereotypical, but that's just how it was.

Paola took advantage of my silence. "Are you using my son?"

My eyebrows stitched together so tight they may as well have conjoined. "What? Ms. Valdez, I would never use him or anyone."

"Every woman says that." She sniffed. "Look, I do not have a problem with you, Octavia. You are a great girl, and you take really good care of my granddaughter." Her voice lowered as she pinned her cold brown gaze on me and leaned forward. "But if I find out that you are using my son or manipulating him in *any* way, I will come after you myself."

"Ms. Valdez, I promise you I would never—"

"¡Mamá, basta!" Catalina hissed at her mother, with a hard glare. "Seriously. *That is enough.*"

Once again, Paola sniffed. Then she took a sip of her coffee.

I lowered my gaze to my lap. Half of me wanted to snap on her. The other half—the stronger part of me—chose to respect her. She was just being protective, and that was fine. She was a mom. He was her only son. I could understand. That didn't give her the right to be a bitch to me, though.

"Do not take what she is saying the wrong way, Octavia." Catalina reached across the table to touch my hand. "I personally think you should be proud," she said with a small laugh. "Do you know how hard it is for a woman to make my brother happy?"

"What do you mean?" I found myself asking. "Wasn't he happy with his wife?"

Catalina rolled her eyes while Paola scoffed.

"It is hard to be happy with someone who is not even happy with themselves," Paola muttered, taking another swig of her brew.

Wait, wait, wait . . . *what*? "What are you talking about?" I looked between both women.

"What she means is, their marriage wasn't as perfect as you might be thinking," said Catalina.

"Exactly." Paola placed her coffee down to fold her arms. "Eloise was a nice person, but she was not good for my Javier."

"And deep down, I think he knew it," Catalina added.

The bell above the front door chimed, and Javier entered the bakery again and meandered his way to our table. Catalina sat up taller, and Paola unfolded her arms.

His eyes locked on Aleesa first, and when he saw she was secure, he found me. There was light in his eyes and a faint smile gracing his lips.

"Gah, the way he looks at you." Catalina shook her head as she rose out of his chair.

Paola stood as well, but before she passed me to reach one of the utensil stations, she leaned down and brought her mouth close to my ear.

"You better not break my son's heart. Understand? He does not deserve that again."

*Again?*

I blinked up at her, wanting to ask what she meant by that, but I didn't have the chance. Javier was back, taking the seat Catalina had just risen from and picking up his cañoncito.

"Great. It is cold now," he grumbled.

"I need to peep!" Aleesa shouted.

*Peep* was what she said when she actually meant *pee*.

"Come on, love." I grabbed her hand and escorted her to the bathroom, then let her do her business while I stood outside the stall. She hummed some random tune: such a young spirit, with no worries in the world. Meanwhile my mind was running wild with thoughts.

What did Paola mean when she said he didn't deserve to be hurt *again*? What had his wife done that had hurt him? Or did she mean that because Eloise died, he was hurting?

I wasn't sure, but something told me it had a deeper meaning than just his wife's death. Something told me there had been a strain between him and Eloise that only Catalina and his mother knew about.

"Tava?" It was now I realized Aleesa had opened the stall. She stared up at me with big, curious green eyes. "What's wrong, Tava?"

"Oh, it's nothing, angel. Nothing. Come on. Let's wash those hands." I guided her to the sink, helped her wash up, then left the restroom.

Before I sat at the table with Javier again, I glanced at Paola. She sipped from a coffee cup, this time not appearing as stern as she regarded me. If anything, she seemed a bit remorseful and had more of an *I did what I had to do to protect my family* sense about her.

However, her eyes screamed one very specific thing.

*Please do not break my son.*

# THIRTY-ONE

## JAVIER

The trip to New York was much needed. I realized that after we had returned home and my family dumped their bags by the door. They all plopped down on the sofas with big sighs and yawns.

Aleesa, although exhausted, had been content with the trip and had hardly cried. She had needed one bedtime story Saturday night to settle down, and after that, it was lights out.

Octavia had seemed to grow closer with Catalina in a matter of hours. They caught a few drinks at the hotel bar Saturday night, after Aleesa fell asleep. They invited me, too, and my mother insisted that I should go and find a woman to flirt with (I rolled my eyes at that) while she kept an eye on Aleesa. Something had told me Octavia needed a moment to herself, so I had stayed in the hotel room.

I was not sure what it was, but Octavia had looked at me differently after visiting the billboard. I noticed admiration and understanding, but there were also questions in her eyes. Those brown irises burned with curiosity.

There was even a moment on the plane ride home when she started to ask me something but clamped her mouth shut and changed her mind. It had made me wonder if my sister had said something to her about my past.

I would not have put it past my sister. She had a bad habit of trying to make people understand me, like she had to take responsibility for my lack of sensitivity in certain situations.

"I can order dinner for everyone," Octavia said, with her phone already out. "Do sub sandwiches sound okay?"

"That is perfect," I said.

"You've got it."

Aleesa climbed onto my lap and hugged me around the neck. "I sweepy, Daddy."

"I know you are, princesa. After dinner, we will get you to bed."

Catalina went to the wine fridge for two bottles of red, then poured glasses for herself and my mother. She offered one to Octavia, too, but she turned it down, insisting that she wanted to make sure Aleesa was tucked away first before shifting into adult time.

The bell to the gates rang about an hour later.

"That's probably our food. I'll get it." Octavia rose from the sofa and made her way to the front door.

"So, big bro . . ." Catalina said with a sigh as she sat beside me. I noticed her voice was quieter than usual. "The babysitter, huh?"

I frowned at her. "What?"

She cocked her head to the left. "Octavia. She makes you happy?"

"Why are you asking that? She is here for Aleesa, and yes, she makes *her* happy."

My sister scoffed. "Please, Javier. Don't play dumb with me. I talked to her last night. I know what's going on. She's smitten, by the way."

I glanced at my mother, who was sitting on the floor with Aleesa, helping her build a tower with jumbo blocks.

"Do not make a big deal of this, Catalina," I returned in a low voice. "You or Mamá. Please."

"I'm not. But for what it's worth, I like that you're smiling again. I can't even remember the last time I got to see all of your teeth."

I chuckled. "Shut up, Cat."

"I'm just saying." She took a long sip of wine. "With her around, though, do you think about Eloise and—"

"Javier?"

I turned to the sound of Octavia's voice. She stood near the start of the foyer, with confusion twisting her features.

"What's wrong?" I asked, standing up.

"There's a man at the door. He said he needs to speak to you . . . and that it's urgent."

"Did he say what his name was?"

"No," she said as I approached, "but he said you'll know it when you see him."

*"What?"* I walked around her and made my way through the foyer. At the end of the hall, the front door was cracked open just a sliver, allowing a slice of light to spill onto the waxed floor. I could see some of the person's shadow through the crack. Gripping the knob, I pulled the door open wider.

When I saw the familiar man in the suit and tie, with tan skin and nearly black hair, my entire mood deflated.

"Javier." He removed his aviator sunglasses and tipped his chin, revealing dark-brown eyes. "I think it's about time we have a chat."

It was him. Rafael Acosta.

The man whose mere existence had caused me to lose sleep for almost a year.

The man I'd wanted to kill with my bare hands.

The man Eloise had cheated on me with only a few months before she died.

# THIRTY-TWO

## JAVIER

"What the fuck are you doing here?" I growled, stepping onto the porch.

Rafael backed away, throwing one hand up to try to calm me. "Just relax, all right. I just need to talk to you."

"Showing up at my doorstep like this is *not* the way to reach me."

"Well, you didn't have to open the gates." He shrugged and smirked.

"You have five seconds to tell me why you are here, or I am going to punch that stupid smirk off of your fucking face." I took another step closer, clenching my fists. He took one backward, the back of his foot nearing the edge of the stoop.

The door creaked behind me, and Octavia and Catalina rushed out, eyes wide and worried.

"Listen, I just dropped by to tell you that I know about Aleesa. Okay?"

"What are you talking about?" I snapped.

"I think that she might be my daughter. Not yours."

My heart sank like a rock to my stomach. Catalina gasped behind me. I clenched my fists tighter, feeling my nails pierce my palms as my throat became raw and thick.

No. That could not be true.

"What the hell are you talking about?" Catalina demanded, walking around me to get in Rafael's face.

He took a step down. Three more and he'd be off the stoop.

"What? Did he not tell you about me and Eloise?" Rafael flashed an arrogant smile at Catalina before putting his focus on me again. "I guess it makes sense. Don't want to taint her reputation."

I shoved past my sister and gripped the lapels of his suit, then stormed down the steps until I was on flat ground. I threw him down and dropped to my knees, ready to beat the shit out of him . . . until I heard the one voice that always centered me.

"Daddy!"

I froze, fist midair, then twisted my upper body to see my mother standing on the porch, with Aleesa in her arms. Aleesa's eyes were wide and panicked as she studied me. My mother stared at Rafael, her face warped with confusion.

I hurried to a stand, breathing raggedly.

"Jesus, now I see why Eloise wasn't happy with you." Rafael got up and dusted himself off. "All that anger can't be healthy."

"Fuck you," I spat. My whole body was vibrating with rage.

"Look, I hate to bring it to you this way, but I felt it would be best to hear it from me personally and not some random person showing up at your doorstep. I already went to court to file a petition, and soon you'll be served. I've also requested a paternity test so that it can prove I am her father. If I am, I would like to discuss custody."

"Why the hell are you doing this?" I said, trying hard not to let defeat drown my words. "Why *now*?"

"Trust me, I hold nothing against you. But *if* I am her father, I deserve to be in her life just as much as you do."

"You are *not* her fucking father," I snapped, pointing a finger at his face. "Eloise would have told me if she suspected that you were! You were not there during her pregnancy. You were not there when Aleesa was born. You were not there when Eloise died after giving birth to *my* daughter. I was! I've been here every single day. She is *mine*, and I'll be damned if you take her from me."

"I had no idea she was pregnant until I heard she'd died during labor. That's when I thought about the timing of it all and added it up. I had a feeling the child she had could be mine, but I wasn't too sure, and my conscience has been weighing on me a lot more lately. What kind of man would I be if I just keep living my life as if I don't have a child? Come on, Javier. Look at her."

He gestured to Aleesa with a mock smile.

I didn't look. I glared at him instead, refusing to back down.

"As soon as I saw her on the sidelines at your games, I could see it. I mean, of course, it could go either way, but the older she gets, the more I see myself in her. That most certainly isn't your nose, and that dimple in her chin . . . *seriously*." He pointed at the dent in his chin, one eerily similar to the very small dimple in Aleesa's.

"Trust me, I know you've been through a lot, and a part of me wanted to leave this alone, but . . . it doesn't sit right with me that I may have a child in this world and I don't even get to know her. I thought long and hard about it, and I knew you'd fight me on this, so that's why I filed the petition first."

"You do not deserve anything," I growled, closing in on him again. "You were a mistake that Eloise made. You do not deserve to be anywhere near *my* daughter."

"Well, I have no doubt that she is my seed, Javier," he said, partially laughing. "The timing of when Eloise conceived is just . . . it's too close. With all the traveling you were doing that she *constantly* complained about, there is just no way Aleesa can be yours."

Before I could react, Catalina stormed around me to slam her hands into Rafael's chest. "Get the fuck out of here!" she barked, shoving him further away. "Now!"

He stumbled backward but caught himself. Then he chortled. "Fine. Whatever. I thought we could be cordial about this and do what was best for Aleesa, but you all clearly don't want to play nice, so I'll leave." Rafael sighed and raked his fingers through his too-perfect hair. "We'll see what the paternity results are and then what the judge has to say, whenever we have the hearing." He stepped backward, eyes going past me. "Aleesa, I'll see you soon, okay, sweetie?"

I wanted to jack him up by the collar. I wanted to choke him to death—I swear I did. How dare he come onto my property, dropping a bomb like this? Telling me that she may not be mine? How dare that motherfucker come to *my* house, trying to take *my* daughter away from me?

This was unbelievable. How could Eloise do this to me? How could she not tell me that Aleesa may not have been mine?

A judge would never allow this. Not when I was there for Aleesa when she took her first breath. It was *my* name on her birth certificate. She was *my* baby girl . . . there was no way he would be able to get her. No damn way.

We watched him stroll away and climb into a black Tesla. He tooted his horn as he drove around the fountain. I didn't look away until his taillights were completely out of sight.

"Hijo." My mother rushed down the stoop to reach me. "What is going on? Who was that man?"

"You heard who he was, Má." My hands shook violently. I wanted to punch something. Break something. This couldn't be happening.

"How can that be?" Mamá's voice trembled. "Tell me this is not true, hijo. Por favor."

I could not bear to look at her. Instead, I stormed into the house and did not stop until I reached the living room. I paced back and forth, in circles, my mind racing and my heart pounding way too hard and fast.

"H-how, Javier?" Catalina's voice was soft. I stopped pacing to look at her and the two other women standing a few feet away. I looked at Aleesa too. She continued watching me anxiously. "I . . . I knew Eloise wasn't happy for a long time and that she might've slept with—"

"I didn't think it needed to be said, Cat!" I yelled. "Yes, Eloise slept with him. Yes, she was unhappy. But Aleesa is *mine*, do you hear me? All this time, I have raised her, and she—no, he *has* to be lying and is doing this to mess with my head! She is my daughter, and he is not getting her!" I stomped toward my mother to collect Aleesa. "Give her to me."

Aleesa gave my mother a wary look but leaned toward me so I could grab her.

"I think we should keep her with us until you calm down a bit, Javier," Octavia murmured as I marched around her.

"Do not tell me what to do with my daughter," I grumbled, storming toward the stairs. "You are not her mother. You do not have the right."

"Javier!" Cat's voice sparked with rage now. "I know you're upset, but you don't have to be an asshole."

"No, it's fine, Cat." Octavia held up a hand as I hiked up the stairs. "He's right. This is none of my business. I'll give y'all some space."

"Octavia, please," Cat called after her.

I continued to my bedroom and locked the door behind me. Then I cursed under my breath because I did not mean that. I truly, sincerely had not meant to say that to Octavia. She was the best thing to have happened to me in *years* other than Aleesa, and she was just trying to help . . .

"Fuck," I cursed again, sitting on the edge of my bed.

Aleesa began to cry as she held on to me. "Daddy, I scared."

"No, no, amor. I am so sorry," I whispered. "Do not be scared. You are okay."

Her bottom lip poked out as tears streamed down her cheeks. And when she closed her arms around my neck and held me even closer, I broke down in a sob. I buried my face in the small space between her head and shoulder, hugging her tighter.

If Rafael got custody of Aleesa, I was going to lose her.

The one person in my life that I loved unconditionally—that I would do *anything* for—I was going to lose. Was it not enough losing my wife? It was as if God was punishing me for something I had done. But I was a good person. No, I was not perfect, but I was a decent human with morals and heart.

I sobbed a little louder because this was not fair.

Life was never fucking fair with me.

# THIRTY-THREE

## OCTAVIA

Once again, I was fucking crying.

I knew Javier didn't mean what he said. He was angry, hurt, and shocked. We're all responsible for our actions and the things we say, but he was blindsided and I don't blame him for getting so upset, especially about one of the most important people to him.

But that didn't make his words hurt any less.

I lay on the bed in the guesthouse, curled up, with a blanket covering me. I had my phone with me and saw there was a missed call from Davina. I told myself I'd call her later, when my mood lifted.

Squeezing my eyes shut, I inhaled deeply before exhaling. It was this exact exercise, learned in therapy, that I heavily relied on when things felt intense in my life.

After Luther, this exercise became necessary but wasn't enough, so I returned to therapy.

All the yelling he did. The mean comments he made about my desires, like deriding how I wanted to get my degree in childhood development, or mocking my first gig as a nanny for a six-month-old. His attempts to startle me, just to get a rise out of me.

My therapist had told me I was smart for leaving him, but she had also told me in order to move past it, I had to take moments to breathe.

Now I tried blocking the thoughts about Luther out, so I thought about Javier and Aleesa.

But the idea of them circled around to someone else.

My father. Aaron Klein. I hated that I had lost him so young.

Remembering my daddy brought forth a different kind of pain. I still remembered a lot about him, like the way he'd play hide-and-seek with me and Davina, even when he was tired after working long shifts. The way he praised every piece of artwork I brought home from school.

I remembered his hugs and forehead kisses.

He was the first man in my life that I could trust and feel safe with . . . and then came Javier. Our weekend in New York proved that I could trust him a bit more and that I could be vulnerable with him. That was scary because I kept thinking *What if he drops the ball? What if he does something that turns me away or makes me nervous to be around him?*

And then he went and said: *"You are not her mother. You do not have the right."*

I knew I wasn't Aleesa's mom, and I'd never tried to be. It was never my intention to replace her mother, to discredit her, or anything.

What hurt was that Javier took his anger out on *me*. His words were like weapons that penetrated my heart. I wondered if that was how he felt. Like I was trying to replace Eloise?

A knock sounded on the door, and my breath hitched as I sat up. I wiped my tears away with the back of my hand, waiting to see if the knock would happen again as my heart banged in my chest.

"Octavia," a deep voice called.

I frowned.

"Go away, Javier," I said loudly enough for him to hear.

"I will not go away. I want to talk to you."

"I'm not in the mood to talk."

There was a stretch of silence so long that I thought he was going to walk away. But then he said, "I am *so sorry*, mi amor. I did not mean a word I said to you. I swear."

I felt a flutter in my stomach and also the urge to flick the stupid butterflies away for falling so easily for his apology.

But this was Javier, and Javier was not the type to bullshit anyone. What you saw was what you got with him, no sugarcoating.

"I was just upset," he went on. "It was wrong to take that out on you. Please, Octavia. Open the door."

"Why should I?"

"Because I want to look into your eyes and apologize the right way. I do not want to be behind a door and blocked from you. I . . . I just need to see you."

A sigh escaped me. This time I didn't have the urge to knock the butterflies away. Instead, I took the stairs down from the loft and walked barefoot through the guesthouse.

I paused and drew in a deep breath before unlocking the door.

Javier lifted his head up as soon as I cracked the door open. Whatever was left of my guard instantly lowered when I caught sight of him.

God. It pained me to see him like this, with his eyes so red and his lashes damp. He almost started to tear up again, but I opened the door wider to throw my arms around his neck.

With a shaky breath, he held on to me as I hugged him tight.

"I am sorry," he whispered in my ear. "I did not mean it. I swear, I did not mean it."

"I know," I whispered back.

He pulled away, but only so he could clasp my face in his hands. "Do you forgive me?"

I blinked to fan my tears away. "Yes, I forgive you."

"Okay," he responded, sounding relieved.

I stepped back, and he followed my lead, entering the guesthouse. He had to duck his head to do so, but he managed. I held his hand and walked to the sofa so we could sit.

We sat in silence for a while. My thoughts were so loud and sharp, and I was positive his were too.

"Listen," I said, squeezing his hands. "I know I didn't birth Aleesa, and I know I can *never* be Eloise. I don't wish to be her or to try and replace her, to make you regret or resent her—none of that. But you should know that I would do *anything* for Aleesa. Okay? I would *die* for her. Do you hear me?"

He nodded. "Yes, I hear you."

"I can't be her mom," I continued, "but I *can* be someone who is there for her through thick and thin. I can be someone who is there for her no matter the situation, just like a loving parent or caregiver would be. Why? Because I *love* that little girl. I love her so much, and *nothing* that you say or do to me will *ever* change how I feel about her."

His throat bobbed as tears accumulated in his eyes. "I understand, and again, I am so sorry." He stroked my cheek with his thumb, a small smile tugging at the corner of his lips. "You mean so much to me and Aleesa. *So much.* And yes, I know you did not birth her, but you treat her as if she is your own, and I am very thankful for that." His lips twisted, but he didn't dare let me go. "I know you probably have the urge to leave now, but there was no way I could let you walk away from me without at least apologizing to you face to face. If you want to go, I will not stop you, because I understand."

I could hardly see him through my blurring vision. I blinked, causing the tears to roll down my cheeks and drip onto my lap.

"I'm not leaving," I assured him. His eyes filled with a splash of relief. "But I am scared that you'll realize I'm not good enough for you. And I'm also scared because every time I think I'm safe with someone, life proves me wrong and I realize I'm better off alone."

"You do not have to be afraid," he murmured. "I am right here, Octavia. I am not going anywhere. Please trust me on that." He paused, studying my eyes as I did his, both of us coming to a silent understanding. His gaze dipped as he contemplated his next string of words. "Truthfully, I do not feel good enough for you. You heard Rafael. Eloise was not happy with me. I had one job and that was to make her happy, but I failed."

"Why was she not happy?"

He released my face, dropping his head and giving his lap a slight scowl. "She never wanted me to join the NBA. We met in our home country—Argentina—before the United States noticed me when I was twenty-four. When I got drafted, she did not want to come here. But by then, we were engaged, and she knew we needed to stick together as a couple. With all the traveling I did, though, she was lonely. She would come with me sometimes, but she became tired of bouncing around so much and wanted more stability. That was understandable. I believe that is what many women want.

"She told me all the time that she wished we could go back to Argentina to be with her grandmother. Her grandmother was all she had, but she passed away two years after Eloise did. But when Eloise was alive, I suggested she look for something to do that could fill her time. So . . . she got a job as a designer's assistant. And that is how she met Rafael—her new boss."

"How did you find out about him?" I asked.

"Eloise told me everything about them a few weeks after we found out she was pregnant. Rafael is wrong about the timing. Eloise and I may have been on shaky ground, but we were still sleeping together. And back then, before she found out, I had no idea she had even cheated." He paused for a second, brows stitching together. "I remember she made this really big breakfast one day, then she sat down at the table with me and said, 'Javier, I have something to tell you.' I knew by the look in her eyes it was not something good. But she told me everything. She told me how a relationship started with Rafael. How she did not mean for it to happen. She kept saying that she felt so alone when I was away and that he made her laugh and kept her spirits up. Just so many things that I did not even realize."

"Wow."

"Yes, and I was angry for a while," he said. "But she was pregnant, and it felt best to work on our marriage and figure out how to become a better man for her. She said she had ended things with him way before finding out, so I just assumed that Aleesa was mine. I . . . I mean, I had no doubts, and she never said there may have been a possibility of him being the father. Things seemed okay after we got past that rough patch and focused on becoming a family. We made plans and tried not to think about those negative things."

He went quiet for a bit.

"I feel like a man would know if a baby were not theirs. I mean, there would have to be some kind of doubt, right? I never had that feeling with Aleesa. In fact, when I held her in my arms for the first time, I truly felt like she belonged with me. Her eyes were so big, and she was so alert. And it was like we had connected in a soulful way. She did not cry. She just stared at me, as if I were the only person in the world she wanted to look at. I was so proud that I helped create someone so beautiful."

He paused, drawing in a shaky breath. "But with all of that overflowing joy came immense pain. Eloise hemorrhaged and died the same day."

"Oh my God." I cupped my mouth. "Did she birth her at a hospital? Couldn't they stop the bleeding?"

"No. They tried but could not stop it. There was just too much. She became nonresponsive, and they told me to leave the room with Aleesa. The next thing I know, a doctor is telling me she could not be saved. But what really gets me is that only a few minutes before it happened, Eloise looked at me and smiled with tears in her eyes. She told me she loved me and that I was going to be a great father. It was almost like she knew something bad was going to happen to her."

"Oh, Javier." I leaned in and hugged him tight. "I'm so, so sorry. That's so traumatic. I can't believe that happened."

"Sometimes I cannot believe it either."

I held on to him for a solid minute, my mind racing about that tragedy. No parent deserved that after giving birth. Though beautiful, our bodies had a bad habit of betraying us when we least expected. This was absolutely horrible to hear.

I leaned back and held his hands again, blinking my tears away. "What Eloise said is true. You are a great father, and no matter what happens, we're going to fight *really* hard for Aleesa. Okay? No matter what that paternity test says, we're fighting."

His eyes crinkled around the edges as he peered into mine. "You would fight for me?"

"Of course I would. And if I need to, I will vouch for you in court. We're not letting that arrogant dick take her away. Fuck that."

Javier laughed. "Well, that is good. I appreciate you saying that, babe."

Once again, my stomach was full of butterflies. "Did you just call me *babe*?"

"I did. Why? Do you not like that name?"

"No, no. I do like it," I said. "I just didn't think that word was a part of your vocabulary."

"Would you rather I call you *baby*?" he asked, leaning in to kiss my cheek. "Or *honey*? Oh, wait, no—*sweetie pie*, or however Americans say it?"

I snorted. "Please stop. If you call me *sweetie*, I'll get the ick."

"The ick? From me?"

"Yes, 'cause then you'll sound like a sixty-year-old man trying to holler at me."

He chuckled as he reeled me toward him. I eased onto his lap, draping my arms over his shoulders while he sat back.

"I'm here for you. You know that, right?" I asked in a soft voice.

"I do. Thank you."

"Good." I kissed his warm, soft lips.

"And I promise you are safe with me," he murmured, grazing his mouth across my chin. His lips pressed to the crook of my neck, then he created a trail of hot, delicate kisses to my collarbone. When he skimmed his hand up my back, I tipped my head back, absorbing all his affections.

"So does this mean I'm not fired?"

He came to a halt, and I dropped my head so our eyes could connect again.

"Stop doing that."

"Doing what?" I teased.

"Pretending that you are just the nanny. You and I both know you are becoming much more to me than that."

"Oh yeah? What am I then?"

He studied me briefly, eyes softening.

Then he said, "You are becoming *my everything*."

# THIRTY-FOUR

## JAVIER

Six days had gone by since the paternity test was taken. I had been nervous during every single hour of those days. I hoped, truly, deep down, that I was the father and would not have to deal with Rafael or the court.

But ever since that idiot had shown up on my doorstep, I had found myself staring at my daughter, looking for features that matched my own. She looked a lot like Eloise, and I always figured Eloise had a stronger genetic pull than I did. I thought Aleesa's nose resembled mine, but perhaps that was just in my head. Just a way for me to find some kind of similarity.

If a man is proud to become a dad, he does not spend time looking for what parts of him might be missing in his child. He accepts it all. Embraces it all. Because in his mind, it does not matter what his kid looks like—he still loves them.

"I think I'll take Aleesa to the park." Octavia's voice sounded behind me as I stood on the deck, staring at the trees in the distance.

I peered over my shoulder. She was concerned, her face pinched just a bit and her eyes swimming with sympathy. That whole week had been off for us.

"That would probably be good," I said. "I am sure she is tired of being around the house."

"She might be. Do you want to join us?" she offered. "Maybe a change of scenery will help clear your head a bit. You've been cooped up all week."

I turned around, forcing a smile. "I am okay, Octavia. You guys go."

She sighed before nodding. "Okay. Well . . . let me know if you need anything."

I watched her go back into the house. When the door clicked shut, I walked to one of the cushioned outdoor chairs and sat down.

I was not sure how long I sat there before I heard the door creak on the hinges again. This time I saw my mother walking out, carrying a tray with both hands.

"You need to eat, hijo." She brought the tray my way and set it down on the side table near me.

"No tengo hambre," I muttered.

"I do not care if you are not hungry. *Eat*," she demanded, taking the chair on the other side of the table. "You have hardly eaten all week. I am worried about you. It does not help that Octavia makes all those eccentric meals. You have Spanish blood in you. You should tell her you do not eat those things."

I shifted my gaze up to meet hers. "Go easy on Octavia, Mamá."

"I am going easy on her," she countered swiftly.

"No. You have been giving her trouble all week. You may think I do not notice the way you act toward her, but I am not blind. All she is trying to do is help."

"Well, she is a little *too* helpful, in my opinion. People like her are clearly after something."

"She is not after anything," I snapped, feeling my eyebrows pull together. "She almost did not keep the job as Aleesa's nanny because of me. If she had not connected so much with Leesa, I am positive she would not have stayed. A woman like that does not need anything from me."

My mother said nothing in response, but she held my stare.

"Besides, her sister is well off," I went on. "And her sister is about to marry Deke, who is my best friend. If she needed to gain money or wanted to capitalize off of anyone, she would do it with them. But she does not do that, and she does not think that way. Why? Because she is not the type to take advantage of people. So stop being rude to her and start accepting her, Má. She is not going anywhere. Not if I can help it."

My mother sat back in her chair, folding her arms across her chest and sniffing. She turned her head, looking at any and everything but me.

"You really like her, then?" she asked after stewing for a minute.

"Yes," I answered. "I *really* like her. And I want her to be happy while she is here. She is a really nice, thoughtful, supportive person. You would know that if you actually gave her a chance, Mamá. Cat likes her, and you know she will find a reason to hate anyone. I am sure you can learn to like Octavia too."

My mother pursed her lips, but I did not miss the way the rest of her face softened.

"Well . . ." Finally, she focused on me again. "That is all you had to say. I will try to be nicer to her from now on."

"Not try. *Will.* Okay?"

She tutted. "Fine. I *will.*"

I smiled. "Gracias."

Pushing out of the chair, she said, "Eat." She returned to the house while I glanced at the food on the tray. Eggs over easy, Argentinean sausage, and tortillas with a side of salsa verde.

This was one of my favorite meals . . . but I could not find it in me to bother eating. Instead, I picked up the coffee and drank it, allowing the warmth to soothe a tiny bit of me.

~

When I was finally ready to go in the house, I brought the tray with me and placed it on the kitchen counter. As I did, I heard the front door close.

Catalina stepped around the corner seconds later, her face sweaty and a little pink. Her hair was in a dark ponytail, a white headband on her head. She wore leggings and a sports bra.

"Went for a run?" I asked.

"Yes." She lifted a hand, holding up a single piece of mail. "I think this is it, Javi."

My pulse clogged my ears as she approached me. My mother popped off the sofa and scurried in our direction. Cat started to hand me the envelope, but I held up a hand, walking around the counter and sitting on one of the stools.

"I . . . I cannot open that," I mumbled.

"Do you want me to?" Cat asked.

I nodded my head, glaring at the floor.

My sister drew in a deep breath and started to open it. Only the sound of crinkling paper filled the dreadful silence. After it was open, she cleared her throat. I looked up as she removed a single sheet of paper from the envelope, unfolded it, and began to read.

She looked at me with watery eyes and did not have to utter a single word for me to know the truth.

"Oh, Javi," she whimpered.

"¿Qué?" My mother snatched the paper out of Cat's hands and scanned it rapidly. Then she yelled, "No! Oh no!"

Her cry was loud, striking at every nerve in my body. I climbed off the stool and caught my mother as she started to buckle. I was not sure why this feeling of numbness had rinsed over me. I tried to blink, to let the feelings take root, but my body refused.

"Hijo, no," she whined. "No. Not this."

"It is okay." I held my mother when she threw her arms around me. Then I looked at Cat, who had tears skidding down both her cheeks. I opened one of my arms so she could step in, but she waved a hand before bolting out of the kitchen.

Cat was never really big on showing her emotions, so I held my mother instead. Because not only did she need me, but I also needed her. I guided her to the sofa so she could sit again, then I returned to the kitchen, spotting that single sheet of paper on the floor.

It was shocking how one little piece of paper could change your whole life. This one little thing was going to leave a stain in my memories.

I stared at the paper for a while, debating with myself if I actually wanted to see the results. What did it matter if Rafael was the biological father? I was the one who was there for Aleesa. She only knew me as her dad. That would change nothing in that regard. All it would do was hurt to see it.

And yet . . . it still mattered somehow. It mattered to know the truth—to face it head-on.

Bending over, I snatched up the paper and blinked quickly to clear the blurriness in my eyes.

There were two sections on the paper. One with my name and Aleesa's below it, and another with Rafael's name and Aleesa's below it.

Probability of paternity for Rafael Acosta: 99.99%
Probability of paternity for Javier Valdez: 0.00%

The truth was right there . . . and I swear I had not felt this much pain since Eloise died. It felt just like that again, like my heart had been ripped right out of my chest and then shoved down my throat.

My wife had been taken away from me . . . and now the same could happen with my daughter.

It was a good thing Aleesa and Octavia were not home. If they'd been here, they would have witnessed my true anger—the raw, primal, blazing part of me that I did not like to reveal.

With the numbness fading and my anger seizing me, I picked up one of the barstools and slammed it on the ground, breaking it to pieces.

# THIRTY-FIVE

## OCTAVIA

"All right, you got it?" I watched as Aleesa picked up her miniature pink purse.

"Yep. I got it." She grinned at me, holding the purse close to her chest. It was her latest obsession, bought by her auntie. It was also covered in dirt now. I'd tried cleaning it with a wipe, but dirt still clung to the threaded edges and even near the straps.

I held Aleesa's hand and headed for the front door of Javier's house. I pushed my key into the lock and gave it a twist, let her in first, then shut and locked the door behind us.

It was now that I realized how quiet the house was. It was a little too quiet, honestly. No TV running. No music playing. No commotion in the kitchen from Paola, who loved cooking just as much as I did. It was dead silent.

Aleesa ran through the foyer, Crocs slapping on the floor, and disappeared around the corner, yelling, "Abuela!"

Well, that was good. Paola was still hanging around.

I placed my satchel and keys down on the foyer table, then walked along the marble floors. Just around the corner and seated in the living room were Catalina and Paola. The TV was off, and their smiles were strained as they watched Aleesa take out a collection of rocks from her purse.

I swept my gaze around, from the kitchen to the dining area. Then I took a few steps back, peeking around one of the corners to where the deck was. Javier was nowhere to be found.

Catalina noticed me first and turned her head. She tried her best to smile, but it didn't reach her eyes.

"Everything okay?" I asked, stepping closer.

"Not quite" was all she said.

"Where's Javier?"

"Sitting by the pool."

Paola glanced at me with damp red eyes. "Maybe if you join him with Aleesa, Octavia, he will feel a little better."

A heaviness wrapped around me. There was no spite in Paola's voice. No mild hostility. This couldn't be good. "The results came in, didn't they?"

Both women nodded in unison.

*Fuck.*

"I'll check on him. Leesa, wanna help me find your daddy?"

"Yes!" She trotted toward me with the purse, taking hold of my hand. "I show Daddy my rocks."

I walked through the hallway that led to the door for the pool area. When we stepped outside, I noticed Javier sitting on the edge of the pool, with his feet in the water and his head down.

"Daddy!" Aleesa hurried to him, causing him to pick his head up and find her. When he saw her, the biggest smile swept across his face.

"Hey, princesa." He wrapped an arm around her, holding her close.

"I got rocks," she said, opening the purse and letting him see her collection.

I met up with them. "Are you okay?" I asked him.

"Not really," he answered, not bothering to look up.

"I'm so sorry, Javier."

He said nothing in response, but he did release Aleesa and pull his legs out of the water so he could stand.

"I will take care of Aleesa for the rest of the day, yeah?" he said, finally. "I might take her out for some lunch or something, and I can also handle her tonight." He gazed at his daughter with the saddest eyes. "I just want to spend as much time with her as I can. Hopefully it will distract me."

"Okay." I rubbed his arm, and he finally met my eyes. "I understand. I'll be around. Just let me know if you need me."

He gave me a weak smile, then quickly picked Aleesa up and carried her into the house.

Javier did take her to lunch and returned about two hours later. He seemed so numb. Any conversation his mom or sister tried to have always resulted in him answering with one word. He zoned out for the majority of the day unless Aleesa did something to draw his attention to the present.

He didn't bother eating dinner. I had to bring him water bottles just to make sure he was staying hydrated. It was almost as if he felt *nothing*. He was quickly becoming this shell of a person that I hardly recognized. It was heartbreaking to witness. No one would have blamed him for pouring out all he felt. If anything, we'd have joined him.

When it was Aleesa's bedtime, Javier did as he said he would and handled it. I gave him some space when he took her upstairs, but after a good twenty minutes, when I realized he was still up there, I got off the couch and searched for him.

I checked his bedroom first, thinking maybe he'd gone to lie down after putting Aleesa to sleep. His bedroom was vacant. I went to Aleesa's room next. The door was partially cracked, but I saw him in there.

Normally, Javier would lie with Aleesa in her bed if he hung around, but this time he was squatting in front of her bed, with one hand on her arm as she slept. He stared at his daughter for a while, then he lifted something that was in his hands to look at it. It was too dark to figure out what it was he was holding. All I knew was that as soon as he laid eyes on it, he cupped his mouth and suppressed a loud sob.

His body shuddered with the quiet cry. I could tell he didn't want to wake Aleesa up, but he also didn't want to leave her side. He was breaking. Breaking into a million pieces.

Everything in me felt like it'd unraveled, seeing him this way. My heart ached for him—this man who had lived such a hard life. I was certain he didn't deserve any of this, and yet he was faced with test after test. Loss after loss.

When he fell on his knees, with his head bowed, still sobbing, I pushed the door open and met him at his side, dropping on my knees as well and wrapping both arms around him.

I pulled him toward me, wanting to comfort him, to show him that I was there—that he had support and would make it through this hard time. He didn't resist me. His face fell into my chest, and I held him close as his tears dampened my shirt.

This was such a quiet, painful cry. I could feel all his hurt coursing through his body, all the agony, all the pent-up frustrations swirling through him and escaping through his tears.

My eyes welled with tears too. I blinked them away, doing my best to stay strong for him. I glanced at Aleesa, who was still sound asleep, and then lowered my gaze.

The object Javier was holding was a picture frame. And inside the frame was an image of him giving the camera a tired yet proud smile while holding in his arms a swaddled baby in a pink cap.

The photo was taken right here in this very room.

This time around, I couldn't hold back.

I let my tears fall and hugged him tighter.

# THIRTY-SIX

## JAVIER

"I can't believe I am here." I groaned, dragging a palm over my face as I sat in the waiting area of the law firm office.

Cat sighed beside me, folding her arms.

It had hurt to see Rafael's name spelled out as Aleesa's biological father on that paper. To have that truth shoved in my face like that was painful, especially when all these years, I'd thought I had done *one* thing right. That one thing being Aleesa. The light of my life. A gift for every single one of my days. I thought I had truly helped create her, down to the DNA.

This truth changed nothing for me, though.

I was still her father, and I was not giving her up.

"This is so fucked up," Cat muttered. "I can't believe Eloise wouldn't at least *mention* that he might be the dad."

"Because she knew it would devastate me." Eloise was a lot of things, but she was not cruel. She made mistakes—we all did—but she did love me and only ever wanted the best for me . . . whether she was in the picture or not.

I looked into my sister's eyes as she stared into mine. "I don't give a damn what the results are. She is still my daughter, and she is still your niece. That will never change."

"I know, I know. I'm just . . . I'm fucking worried. What if he manages to get visitation rights or something? What if you have no choice but to share her with that dipshit?"

"I am hoping it does not come to that."

"Mr. Valdez?" The secretary stepped around a corner. "Mrs. Whitfield is ready to see you now."

I stood, rubbing the palms of my hands over my jeans to get rid of the dampness. I looked at my sister again, and she looked right back at me, nodding to encourage me, but it was impossible not to see the apprehension in her eyes.

We walked through the hallway until we reached a spacious office with a view of the Atlanta skyline. A massive desk was on one side of the room, with a cushioned leather chair behind it.

Standing next to the desk was the family attorney I'd reached out to—Christine Whitfield, a tall, thin woman with blond hair pulled into a sleek bun and porcelain-white skin. Her lipstick was apple red, and she had electric-blue eyes that were a bit intimidating.

She was the best in Atlanta when it came to custody battles. She was also expensive as hell, but I wasn't putting a price on this matter. I'd give up every fucking penny if it meant Aleesa stayed with me.

"Mr. Valdez." Christine met up to me, stretching an arm and offering me a hand. "So lovely to meet you. Thank you for coming in."

"Thank you for agreeing to squeeze me in to your schedule. And please, call me Javier."

She smiled. "Javier it is." Her eyes turned to Catalina. "And this is . . . ?"

"Catalina, Javier's sister." My sister took Christine's hand and shook it.

"Lovely to meet you, Catalina. Please have a seat, both of you."

We sat in the chairs on the opposite side of Christine's desk while Christine plopped down in the large leather seat and cleared her throat. "Can I get either of you anything to drink? Coffee? Tea?"

"No, I'm okay."

"Same," Cat replied.

"Very well. So, let's just jump straight into this. You mentioned a bit of your situation to me over the phone, but I want to understand the whole story. Your name is on Aleesa's birth certificate, correct?"

"Yes, it is."

"And I can safely assume you were there during her birth?"

"I was. I drove Eloise to the hospital and everything."

"Okay, that's good. That shows consistency."

Cat cut in. "I'm sorry, but I have to ask. How can this guy just come in and try to take her away? She's four years old now, and not once had he shown up before."

"Well, Rafael claims that Javier's wife may have purposely withheld that he could be the father, which means he never had a fair shot at raising Aleesa. Given the timing of it all, it makes sense that he would search for the truth—especially if he cared about Eloise. And now that the paternity results have proved he is Aleesa's biological father, it gives him legitimation, which means he can request visitation and even custody rights."

"That's bullshit," Cat muttered.

Christine was quiet a beat. "It is very much bullshit, but that's the United States for you. The good thing is that we have been assigned a decent judge—one that looks at the best interest of the child and not so much biology. You have taken good care of Aleesa since she was born. You have the proof and four years of being a father under your belt. Aleesa, I'm sure, has been happy with you, and all she knows right now is that *you* are her dad. Introducing Rafael could potentially confuse her and lead to behavioral issues down the line, and that is the last thing the court wants for a child.

"Judge Dalton has a weak spot for children. She will only want the best for Aleesa, and anyone looking at this from the outside will know that Rafael getting any kind of long-term custody is harmful to Aleesa because he is a stranger to her. Custody, in my opinion, is out of the question. But visitation is a different beast, because if Rafael proves he is worthy enough for Aleesa to get to know on a personal level, the judge may insist that Rafael get the opportunity to visit her on a consistent basis."

"I don't want him to have *anything* with her," I grumbled. "I could not look at that man every single time he came and be okay. He slept with my wife. He ruined my life once, and now he is trying to do it again."

"I understand your frustrations, but sometimes that is the way things go, and I want you to be prepared for that, Javier. Okay?"

I clenched my jaw, hating that cold, hard truth.

"Until the hearing, I want us to focus on building the best case possible. So far, I believe we have a solid argument. You've been a primary caregiver for Aleesa, and the court takes into consideration the emotional bonds, stability, and whether the environment the child is being raised in is a comfortable one. You've provided all of that for her plus more. We need to show that removing her from your care would be disruptive and harmful."

"So what do I need to do to fully prepare?" I asked.

"Right now, all you can do is practice being calm and patient. Judges appreciate and respect parents who put their children's needs above their own. That means no lashing out, no public bashing, and *definitely* stay away from the media. Something tells me news about this will come out. Rafael may tell others, and that word will spread."

"Damn it," I hissed. "I do not need Aleesa mixed up with the media."

"That will be frustrating, but the best you can do is keep yourself and Aleesa out of the public eye. Honestly, the fact that he came to your home and confronted you with such a sensitive matter proves that he is not fit to be in Aleesa's life. It was unexpected and reckless, and very clear that he was trying to provoke and anger you. Nothing about that screams 'stability' to me."

"Right," I said, combing my fingers through my hair. "Well, if you think we have a solid case, fine. I'll try to keep calm and focus on Leesa. When will we know the date of the hearing?"

"We should know within a couple of weeks. I will keep you updated as much as possible."

"Great."

"Wonderful." Christine stood, and Catalina and I followed suit. When she escorted us out of the office, she smiled and said, "I'll be in touch."

Cat and I walked out of the building and headed to my car. Once I was behind the wheel and she was buckling herself in, I gripped the steering wheel with both hands and pressed my forehead to the top of it.

"Hey." Cat rubbed a hand across my back. "You got this, hermano. You've survived so much. I have no doubt you'll survive this too."

"Sí," I murmured, picking my head up. "It is just this *life*, Cat. It is so hard and so unfair. I know that many people have it much worse, but I do not understand why things can never be simple. First our piece-of-shit dad leaves us on our own, then I finally get some footing, find Eloise, but she ends up unhappy with me and then *dying* before we could fully fix it. And now there is Aleesa. What if she grows up, resents that I am not her real father, and would rather be with him?"

"That will never happen." Cat's voice was firm. I looked at my sister, and tears lined the rims of her brown eyes. "She will see you have always been good for her. She will love you. And that love a girl has for her father never goes away. I mean, look at me." She huffed a laugh. "I hate our dad for leaving, and yet a part of me still wishes he would come around and make up for lost time. No matter what, Aleesa will always love you. I have no doubt in my mind about that."

"I hope so."

"I *know* so. Now let's go home. Má is making empanadas today, and I'm starving."

# THIRTY-SEVEN

## OCTAVIA

Rossi's was a sports bar in Atlanta with way too many screens and a long line of liquor on the wall behind the counter.

Davina and Deke were already in Atlanta together, and after speaking to her, I insisted that we all needed to hang out. I figured Javier needed the break, and I hadn't seen my sister in weeks.

It'd been two weeks since Javier's meeting with his lawyer. He said he was okay, but I could tell this situation was weighing heavily on him and disrupting his days.

Paola had returned to Argentina but had made plans to come back whenever the hearing happened. Catalina was still in town and was currently watching Aleesa so I could take a "break." I told her I didn't need a break and that taking care of Aleesa was no issue at all, but she insisted and said she wanted to spend some quality time with her niece.

"I think that's some bullshit." EJ McCoy slammed his glass of beer down on the table as he locked his eyes on Javier.

I'd only met EJ once, and that was after one of the Ravens games. He was the starting point guard for the team and the kind of guy who didn't take life seriously. He was definitely a playboy, and it was men like him that I avoided like the plague.

He seemed nice enough, though. If Javier and Deke hung around him often, he had to be a good person beneath all that cockiness. Even more so since Deke had invited him to join us tonight.

"You've been her dad since the beginning, man," EJ went on. "I swear the system is fucked up. No one should just come onto the scene trying to claim kids unless the current parent is trash or something."

"Seriously," Davina chimed in. "I don't understand how he can waltz in and demand this. Does he not realize how hard this will be for you and Aleesa?"

"Oh, he realizes," Deke muttered, head shaking. "He just doesn't care. Dude sounds like a true piece of shit."

"My lawyer believes he will not get custody, so that is good." Javier sighed. "But she does think visitation may be a possibility."

"Stupid," Deke grumbled. This news seemed to really be bothering my future brother-in-law. Part of the reason could have been that he, Javier, and Aleesa were very close.

But another could be that the subject of dads was triggering for Deke. Davina had told me a few things about Deke's childhood in confidence, and after hearing about it, I couldn't blame him for being upset. Hell, I was upset for him. He didn't deserve what he'd gone through.

"I don't like this for you at all, man," Deke said as Davina held his arm, rubbing soothing circles on it with her thumb. "I'm sorry you're going through this."

"It's all right. Somehow, I am staying motivated and keeping my head clear." Javier took a swig of beer. "It is best for Aleesa that I do."

"So when's the hearing?" Davina asked.

"Well, my lawyer requested an expedited hearing because we want this settled before the season starts, if possible. I should hear from her in a few days."

"I really think you have a strong case." I took Javier's hand and squeezed it. He met my eyes, and a soft smile swept across his lips. "You'll get through it. I'm sure of that."

"With you by my side, I definitely will." Javier smiled, squeezing my hand back.

I felt all mushy and warm from that smile and couldn't suppress my own. Our eyes lingered on each other's, and it wasn't until billiard balls clashed in the distance and a group of people cheered in a far corner of the bar that we snapped out of it.

I took my hand away, and Javier cleared his throat, then picked up his beer and sipped again. I collected my tequila-and-pineapple drink and took a swig myself. I didn't miss Davina's grin or the way Deke wiggled his eyebrows.

"Told you so," Deke said.

"Do not start, Bishop." Javier fought a smile.

"So you two are a thing now?" EJ pointed between me and Javier.

"Do not worry about it," Javier answered.

"Nah, I'm gonna worry about it." EJ sat up in his chair with a grin. "'Cause I'll be honest, I didn't think you'd *ever* get with a woman again with that stick up your ass."

Deke reached over to slap EJ on the back of the head. "Shut up, EJ."

"Bruh, slapping me on the head is getting old. You know that, right?"

"Obviously not if it shuts you up."

"Exactly. And why are you even here?" Javier questioned. "I am surprised you are not sleeping around with one of your fans."

"I'm becoming a changed man, you feel me?" EJ dusted imaginary lint off his T-shirt. "These women are getting too dramatic. Y'all didn't hear about that one girl who tried to trap Javeon in her apartment with him? The police had to get involved. Nah." EJ's head shook. "It might be time for me to settle down before I end up trapped too."

Davina laughed as she sipped her margarita, then she turned her attention to me when Deke asked EJ, "How the hell did Javeon get caught up in that?"

"You okay, sis?" she asked.

"Yeah, I'm fine," I said. "It's just a lot for everyone. I keep thinking if that guy gets visitation or even custody, I probably won't be able to see Aleesa as much anymore."

I glanced at Javier, who was still going back and forth with EJ and Deke. EJ said something that made Javier and Deke howl with laughter. I smiled.

"But at least he's smiling," I murmured.

"It's a good thing he is. You guys definitely needed this. How are things between you two?"

"We're doing just what you said. Going with the flow, letting it happen naturally."

A warm smile claimed her lips as she cut a glance at Javier again. "He's going through this battle, but I have to tell you, sis, I don't think I've *ever* seen him smile like this before. He seems so content, even with all that's going on. I don't know what you're doing to him, but it's making him very happy. And you . . ." She reached across the table to hold my hand. "Your eyes are so bright, and you looked so confident when you walked into this place. I love seeing you like this. I love that you're embracing life again."

"I love that we *both* are." I held her hand tighter. "You and me, sis."

"Still a little scary, though, right?" she said in a low, playful voice.

"Um, hell yes it's scary." I bubbled up a laugh. "I mean, this guy *apologizes* right away for his mistakes and holds himself accountable. I didn't think men still did that."

My sister laughed. "The good men do."

"So it's getting serious, huh?" Deke asked. He was looking between me and Javier. Javier wrapped an arm around me as he gave me his attention, waiting for my response.

"We're not putting any titles on it," I said, holding his gaze a few seconds before focusing on Deke. "But it seems to be getting there."

"Well, don't get any ideas about proposing to her at my wedding, Valdez," Deke said.

Javier scoffed. "Why would I do something like that?"

"I'm just saying." Deke tossed his hands into the air. "Some people do it and think it's a romantic gesture. That shit is selfish—unless you ask the bride and groom, of course. Can't just take away from their big day like that."

"Can I hook up with somebody at your wedding?" EJ asked, smirking.

"Absolutely not," Davina countered. "Keep it in your pants."

Deke snorted. "Get the fuck outta here."

EJ threw his hands into the air. "I swear I can't win, man. Next time we do this, I'm bringing a girl. I feel like a third wheel right now."

"What girl?" Davina asked. "Is there someone in particular?"

EJ seemed to hesitate. "No. Just whoever."

I looked at Davina at the same time as she looked at me. We both knew he was lying.

A group of women shrilled in the distance, and EJ examined them over his shoulder. Three women eyed him right back, smiling and batting their lashes.

"I think that's my cue, ladies and gents." EJ rose from his chair. "A foursome sounds about right, doesn't it?"

"You are terrible," Javier groused with a slow and exhausted roll of his eyes.

"What happened to not getting yourself trapped?" Deke watched EJ push his chair in. "'Cause that, my guy, looks like a huge trap."

"One more night of living won't kill me." EJ took off just as quickly as he spoke, ducking under the velvet ropes to leave the VIP section.

A waitress appeared and set down a new round of drinks. I had no idea when someone had put another order in but was grateful for it.

"Let's make a toast," I said, raising my glass.

"Okay." Javier picked up his drink with his free hand. "To what?"

"To amazing futures. To happiness . . . and hope."

Javier looked at me for so long I thought I'd said something wrong. Then a smile tugged at one corner of his mouth, and he lifted his glass. "I like that."

"To amazing futures, happiness, and hope." Deke lifted his glass too. Davina followed suit, and we all met in the middle with a clink, then sipped right after.

Being around my sister and Deke made me feel a whole lot better. Seeing them together made me realize just how powerful love and hope could be. Those two things were what fueled them, what had created their bond, and what had placed them exactly where they were now. Committed and 100 percent in love.

As Javier pulled me deeper under his arm and I rested my head on his chest, I thought for once that I could have it too.

Hope. Happiness. And eventually *love*.

Once we made it through this battle, we'd be stronger and better.

Nothing would be able to stop us.

And I was very much looking forward to that.

# THIRTY-EIGHT

## OCTAVIA

"Tava, I want strawbebbies." Aleesa sat in the grocery cart, pointing at the fruit section.

"Strawberries it is." I collected two containers of them.

"And mangoes," Aleesa added, grinning.

I snorted a laugh, turned for the mangoes, and snatched up a few.

As I placed them in a bag, my phone buzzed in the back pocket of my jeans. I pulled it out and saw a notification from *BOBBLE*. Davina swore this app was going to be the death of me, but it wasn't my fault that celebrity gossip was so entertaining. It always shocked me, the things famous people did with their lives.

Normally, I'd have been quick to open the app, but when I saw the headline, my heart dropped to my stomach.

> Not His Daughter? The Scoop on the Custody Battle Between Javier Valdez and Fashion Designer Rafael Acosta

"Fuck. No, no, no."

Aleesa let out a sharp gasp. "Tava say bad word!"

"Oh, sorry, angel. Ignore me." I opened the app, only to see an image of Javier in his basketball uniform. Of course they'd chosen the worst picture possible of him. He looked tired and sweaty in the image, and it was most likely one taken toward the end of one of his games.

I scrolled down a bit more and found an image of Rafael Acosta posing on the red carpet. He looked spiffy, neat, and put together. I didn't like this at all. And something in my gut told me *he* was the reason *BOBBLE* even had the scoop on their custody battle.

How else would anyone know? No one who knew Javier was leaking this anywhere. It had to be Rafael, and he was most likely doing this to mess with Javier's head, to throw him off, and to make him angry.

"Um, let's get the macaroni and chicken and head out of here. I need to call your dad." I tucked my phone away and gripped the handle of the cart, my heart racing.

I had to call him right away. If he found out on his own, there was no telling how he'd react.

# THIRTY-NINE

## JAVIER

Deke, EJ, and I decided to spend the day practicing at Element.

Deke wanted to kill time before a flight to London, and I wanted to blow off some steam and forget about the upcoming hearing that I now knew was happening in less than a month. And EJ . . . well, he was just bored at the moment and had called Deke a few hours earlier to see what he was doing. As always, Deke had invited him.

Sometimes I felt sorry for EJ, I could not lie. He was always desperate for his life to be busy so he would not have to think about his reality. And his reality was that he was lonely. He was adopted, with no siblings; had White parents who did not understand what it was like being a Black man in America (despite his career and how much money he made); and had grown up very confused about his identity.

Although we teased him often (because, just like a little brother, he could be exasperating), we had nothing but love for him. And we never denied him whenever he asked to hang out with us.

Regardless of trying to blow off steam, my mind reverted back to Aleesa. I did not know when the hearing would be, but I knew it was coming, and I needed to be as mentally prepared for it as possible.

Deke and I played defense while EJ played offense. EJ managed to circle both of us and shoot a two-pointer. The shot landed effortlessly, and he ran backward, pinching the shoulders of his shirt and popping them upward.

"Told y'all. You can't stop me! Who's next?"

Deke dribbled the ball but said, "I'm about to wrap it up. I have to meet D before my flight."

"You are pussy whipped, man." EJ chortled. "Both of y'all."

"You sure you're not just jealous?" Deke cocked a brow, smirking.

"Not at all." EJ scooped up his water bottle. "If I want to, I can find a girl to settle down with by next week."

"Yeah, okay." I scoffed. "Hell would freeze before that happened." I lifted my shirt and wiped the sweat off my brow. Deke took one more shot and landed it. I collected the ball and returned it to the cart while he and EJ gathered their things.

"Whoa . . . hold on. This can't be real." EJ stood from his chair just as I dug into my gym bag for my phone. I had two missed calls from Octavia and three text messages.

"Big J, you might want to stay away from the internet today." EJ's voice, for once, was serious. So serious I had to look at him to make sure he was okay.

I frowned. "What are you talking about?"

Deke's brows dipped as he looked from me to EJ. Then he stepped up to EJ's side, and EJ turned the screen of his phone toward him.

Deke read whatever was on it, and his eyes widened. "Shit."

"Yeah," EJ muttered. *"Shit."*

Deke made his way toward me. "EJ's right. Ignore your phone and go straight home, man."

"Why? What are you not telling me?"

"*BOBBLE* dropped an article. And the context of it will piss you off. Trust me. You don't want to read it."

"What does it say?" I asked through gritted teeth, though I had an idea. I just did not want to consider it.

Deke hesitated as EJ approached us.

"Deke?" I demanded.

He sighed. "It's about your custody battle. And it doesn't seem to be siding with you."

"Let me see it."

EJ hesitated but handed me his phone. I saw my picture and read the header, but when I saw Rafael's face, I clenched my left hand so tight my nails bit at my palm.

I handed EJ his phone back, then snatched up my gym bag. "I need to go."

"Yeah, go ahead," Deke said. "Hit me up if you need me, man."

I threw the strap of the bag over my shoulder and hauled ass out of the gym. I did not stop until I reached my car, but when I left the parking garage and noticed the people standing outside of it with cameras, my throat filled with heat.

Hot, irritable heat.

I could hear them shouting my name, asking questions, yelling Aleesa's name. Security was keeping them on the crosswalk so I could safely exit, but that didn't stop them from snapping photos with their annoying cameras or hollering louder.

I did not stop driving until I made it to the freeway. When I did, I gave Octavia a call.

"Finally," she answered with a heavy breath. "Are you okay?"

"I am fine. I may not return to Element for a while, but I am fine. Where are you?"

"I'm at the house. Aleesa just went down for a nap."

"Did anyone bother you today?" I asked, gripping the steering wheel tighter. The sheer thought of someone harassing her and my daughter pissed me off. The paparazzi were hounds. I knew they would do anything for a good picture. I saw it often with Deke, and one thing I knew for certain was that I did not want that kind of attention from the media. That was why I stayed away from it if I could. I did not even bother with social media, because people loved to take any little thing out of context.

"No," Octavia answered, much to my relief. "No one bothered us. I saw the news and came straight home."

"Good," I breathed. "I do not understand how this is happening. This was supposed to be a private matter."

"Oh, I know *exactly* how this happened," Octavia grumbled. "Rafael looks shady. He's probably telling the whole world about it. Doesn't help that he's some well-known Georgia clothing designer. With your name tied to his, he's probably trying to garner publicity."

"Of course he would fucking leak this," I growled. "I will fucking kill him."

"No, Javier, listen to me. That is *exactly* what he wants. You are a great dad, and he has to find a reason for the court to give him more than visitation. He wants you to do something wrong so he can use it in court. You can't let him."

"He has been ruining my life, even before Aleesa was born. He thinks he can just boast about this? Now the whole world will know that my wife slept with him! That she cheated on me with him! He is trying to humiliate me! I do not care what the rest of the world thinks of me, Octavia—I truly don't—but I care about what my daughter thinks! What my family thinks!"

"Your family knows you, and they love you. They will never look at you differently, baby."

The burn in my throat settled to a simmer. Hearing her call me *baby* anchored me because it sounded so sweet coming from her. I believe that was the first time she'd called me that.

"Do me a favor and breathe," Octavia went on. "Take a few deep breaths and focus on Aleesa. Focus on her future and what you want for her. Everything you do is for her, right?"

I exhaled. "Yes."

"So keep your attention on that. Forget Rafael. Forget *BOBBLE*. Focus on what's right in front of you."

I loosened my grip on the steering wheel, shaking my head. "I swear you are like a therapist."

She giggled. "Davina says the same thing."

"Well, she is right." I dragged in a few deep breaths and exhaled again through parted lips. "I am coming home, amor."

"Great. I'll see you soon."

When the call ended, I clenched my jaw. I knew exactly where Rafael worked. I could have easily turned this car around, sped my way to his building, stormed inside, and punched him square in his face.

But Octavia was right.

I needed to focus on what was in front of me. And what lay ahead and waited for me was my daughter and a woman who I was becoming fonder of by the day. There was my home, which I had made comfortable for Aleesa, and the unconditional love that she had for me and that I had for her.

Rafael did not have any of that.

With that in mind, I calmed my nerves, settled my rage, and continued forward, ready to go home and be with my girls.

# FORTY

## OCTAVIA

As soon as Javier arrived, I gave him a hug, then served him a big bowl of chicken stew. We ate together at the dining table while Aleesa napped upstairs.

I'd had lo-fi music playing earlier, and normally I turned it off when he arrived, but I figured he could use the noise to tune out some of his darker thoughts.

"This is very good," he said before shoveling another scoop of stew into his mouth.

I grinned. "Thank you."

A stretch of silence passed between us. Moments later, Javier's spoon clinked against the edge of his bowl, and our eyes connected again.

"I am sorry that you have to go through this too." His lips pressed. "You do not deserve to deal with my issues."

"Don't worry about me. I'm fine."

"I do worry about you, though. You did not sign up for any of this."

"I signed up to take care of Aleesa. And if that means pushing through a stupid custody battle that is a complete waste of all our time, then I'll be here."

He went quiet again. "I will understand if you want to leave."

"Do you want me to leave?"

The skin between his eyebrows wrinkled. "Of course not."

"Then stop saying that. I'm staying, and we're seeing this through."

"Why would you want to do that with me? Why bother dealing with my stress?"

"Because you're a good person, Javier. And I really, really like you. Plus, I love Aleesa, and I'm not letting her deal with this alone either. She understands something is going on, you know?"

His eyes stretched with surprise. "Does she?"

"Yes. She asks questions."

"What kinds of questions?"

"She asks if you are mad. If you are sad. She doesn't understand the full scope of what's going on, but she knows something is troubling you. And that little girl is the biggest empath I have ever been around. She absorbs emotion and feels it all."

"Oh." His chin dropped. "I did not realize. I will talk to her later. Let her know everything is okay."

"That would probably help. I've been telling her the same too. She's still happy." I smiled as he raised his chin again. "And she still loves her daddy."

That brought forth one of his smiles. "I am glad that I can trust you."

"Always."

"That will never change, will it?"

"What? You trusting me?"

He nodded.

"Never."

He sat up higher in his chair, then flicked his fingers, gesturing for me to come to him. I walked around the table edge to reach him, and as soon as I did, he placed his large hands on my waist, guiding me down to his lap. I wrapped my arms around his neck and settled in, breathing in his scent. He'd been sweating, that much was clear, but there was still that hint of deodorant, that warmth of masculinity.

"If my questions bother you, I am sorry," he murmured in my ear. "I have to remember that not everyone in my life is out to hurt me."

I rubbed the heart of his chest. "Eloise really broke your heart, didn't she?"

He lowered his head, but I didn't miss the small nod. "I really did try with her. I tried to make her happy and to give her the best life. Basketball was what I was good at, and it gave us the life we had always dreamed of. But it does not matter how much money you make, or how big your house is, or how shiny your cars are. If someone does not want to be happy, they will not be. Apparently, Eloise felt something with Rafael that she did not feel with me. I guess that is what hurts me the most. Knowing that she had to look outside of the home and life we built to find whatever it was she was seeking."

I stayed quiet, letting those words simmer.

"When I think about it, though," he went on, "Eloise and I were probably not meant to be. We married young and fast and grew apart long before her situation with Rafael. I just refused to admit there were bigger issues, because ignorance is bliss and all. It is just a shame that my ignorance cost us so much." He released a ragged breath and held on to me tighter. "But at least with you, I can feel happy again."

My heart thumped a beat faster. "Are you just saying that because you're in a vulnerable state right now?"

"No, Octavia." He leaned back so he could stare into my eyes. "I mean it. I am happy with you. I am so lucky that I get to come home every day and see your face. I am grateful that you are here and that I can talk to you. When I look back over the last few years, I wonder how I was getting by without you."

My throat felt suddenly raw. "Aww, Javier."

"Maybe you do not realize it, but you have changed mine and Aleesa's life, Octavia. If anything were to ever happen to you, it would break us to pieces. So yes." He tightened his arms around me. "With you, *I am happy*. And I hope nothing ever takes you away from me."

I held back my tears. "No one has ever said something that sweet to me. Did you take a crash course in romantic things to say to women?"

He rumbled a laugh. "I did not, and that course sounds like it would be absolute torture."

I giggled behind a soft, slow kiss.

Groaning, he slid a hand past my waist to cup my ass.

Before our kiss could deepen, we heard our favorite disruptor.

"Tava!"

I laughed on his mouth as Aleesa came skidding on her butt down the stairs.

# FORTY-ONE

## OCTAVIA

The following week, I had a few errands to run and didn't want to take Aleesa out of the house too much. The paparazzi were being ridiculous, and it didn't feel safe bringing her out.

I mean, who stooped so low as to show up at Aleesa's ballet studio just to see if Javier was around? And the only reason I knew this was because the instructor and owner of the studio called to inform Javier. She said she'd kicked the stranger out and called the police on them for trespassing.

Javier figured he would pause Aleesa's classes until things settled. That drop from *BOBBLE* had created a massive mess.

My first stop was at a bakery, where I bought a box of cupcakes with vanilla frosting. The family needed a pick-me-up, and I damn sure could use something sweet to tide me over. Afterward, I stopped by a grocery store for more of those crackers Aleesa loved, then I made my way to the bank.

When I left the bank, I noticed a commotion across the street. My bank was in downtown Atlanta, almost in the heart of the city. Across from it was an ivory tower with police cruisers lined up in front of it. I walked to my car and got behind the wheel, but my eyes swung back to the busy building. That's when I noticed someone coming out of the front doors.

No, there were *two* people. One of them was awfully familiar and being detained by a police officer.

"Oh shit," I breathed. Because this wasn't just any person. It was *Luther*.

I climbed out of the car, watching as the police hauled him toward the back door of one of the cruisers.

"They're fucking lying!" I heard Luther yell as I jogged across the street. "I didn't take shit! They're lying!"

A crowd had formed, and I stayed in the back, peeking through the gaps between several heads. The officer shoved Luther into the car and slammed the door on him.

"He was a new hire, right?" I heard an Asian woman ask to my right. I noticed she was wearing a sky blue shirt with the word *CordTech* stitched to the heart of it.

"Yeah," a guy said over his shoulder. He wore trousers and a button-down short-sleeved shirt. "Frank was the one who hired him. Lucas—no, Luther. I heard that guy was really smart, but also really stupid apparently."

"What did he do?" the woman asked.

"Embezzled money from one of the accounts. He should have known those things are *always* monitored. Doesn't matter how good you are with coding."

Wow. Luther had gotten arrested for embezzlement.

Honestly . . . that didn't surprise me. Luther was greedy—always wanting more money, flashy cars, big chains. The man in the trousers was right. Luther was very book smart, but very fucking dumb in all other aspects of life.

"Excuse me." I stepped closer to the man as the woman walked away. "I couldn't help overhearing. How long do you think someone goes away for something like that?"

"Oh, I don't know." The man shrugged as several people dispersed. "Maybe a good eight to ten years. I heard he was pushing out a few hundred a week, just enough to slip under the radar during biweekly evaluations. That probably accumulated to the thousands."

"Wow. What an idiot," I said.

"I try not to call people names, but . . ." The man held up a hand, smirked, then dismissed himself.

I neared the curb just as the police cruiser Luther was in drove away. As it rolled by, Luther turned his head a bit, looking through the corner of his eyes out the window. He did a double take when he noticed me. His eyes became bigger, and his jaw dropped. Shame settled on his shoulders.

I lifted a hand and waved him off with my middle finger.

*Good fucking riddance.*

When I returned to my car, I sat for a moment. It felt wrong to smile about someone's demise, but I did. I smiled because I had been worried for *weeks* that Luther would show up, despite the restraining order I'd filed on him.

Every time I pulled up to the house, I was afraid that he would be waiting there. Or worse, that he would get through the gates somehow, like Rafael had, and corner me.

But now, I would be the least of his worries. And if he did get eight or ten years under his belt, a lot could change for me.

For the first time in a long time, I felt nothing but pure relief knowing those fears I carried could rest.

At least for now.

# FORTY-TWO

## JAVIER

Three weeks later, and it was time for the hearing.

I stood in my bathroom, fixing my tie and doing my best not to feel irritated. I still could not believe this was even happening but was glad it was sooner rather than later.

I could hear Octavia talking to Aleesa downstairs. It was clear she was giving Octavia a hard time, so I finished up and joined them.

Octavia was sitting on the floor next to Aleesa, who was pouting, with shiny eyes. When she caught sight of me, she ran my way from the living room and closed her arms around one of my legs.

"What is going on?" I asked, picking her up.

"She wants to go with you." Octavia blew a mildly frustrated breath as she stood up.

"I see." I focused on my daughter. "Lo siento, princesa. I have to go, but I will be back very soon."

Aleesa placed her head on my shoulder and began to cry.

Damn. I did not want her to cry. Not on this day. It was already going to be hard enough.

Octavia smoothed her dress down. "I can take her to the park," she offered. "One of the smaller ones with less people. I think she's getting tired of the pool and bubbles."

"Yes. That will be good. I'm sure she will like that."

"Okay." Octavia reached for Aleesa, but my daughter was not having it. She kept her head glued to my chest instead, now whining.

"Go on, amor," I murmured, handing her over to Octavia.

Aleesa cried harder.

"It's okay. You're okay, love. I've got you. We'll get on the swings. How does that sound?"

Aleesa's cry weakened, but her eyes never left me. Guilt ate at my heart. I hated this. I would have done anything to stay and console her. Clearly this custody battle was affecting her too.

"I don't want swing. I want slide," Aleesa demanded.

"All right." Octavia couldn't help laughing at her mini protest. "We'll go down the biggest slide, then, my love."

At that, Aleesa calmed down and closed her arms around Octavia's neck. I couldn't help smiling at the interaction.

Octavia shifted her attention my way while rubbing soothing circles on Aleesa's back. "Good luck today, okay?"

"Thanks." I leaned down to kiss her.

"Ew," Aleesa quipped.

Hilarious considering she wasn't even looking at either of us. My girl was too smart for her own good.

Octavia blushed while fighting a smile.

"See you later, okay?" I told her.

"'Kay."

If I stood around any longer, I would break. I knew I would. Knowing I had to go to this court and prove my case—prove that I was a good father—was destroying me inside. I was losing sleep to the thought of Aleesa spending time with Rafael.

I was not a selfish person, but if he spent time with her, I did not see how that would benefit her at all. Not only that, but he had slept with a married woman. He had tried to take my wife, and he likely would have succeeded if Eloise had not felt so guilty about what she'd done.

I could only imagine what it would have been like if Eloise had chosen him. What would I have been like? Would I have been angry? Depressed? Would I have even continued playing basketball so passionately? I most certainly would not have Aleesa, and after spending the last four years with her, I could not imagine living the rest of my life without her.

When I made it to my car, I drew in a breath, exhaled, and started the ignition. And as I drove to the courthouse, I kept my thoughts calm and my heart set on my daughter.

I would prove to them that she did not need the change.

I would do what I had to so that my life could go back to normal.

# FORTY-THREE

## JAVIER

"Are you ready?" Christine swung her attention to me as we stood outside the courtroom.

"I guess so," I said.

"Good. Remember what I told you. Keep your answers simple and concise. No need to elaborate."

"He hardly ever elaborates," my mother said, standing a few steps away.

"Mamá, please." Catalina sighed.

"What?" She threw a hand into the air. "It is the truth, no?"

Christine smiled. "Rafael's lawyer will try to point out your flaws. Don't get angry. Count to ten if you feel yourself growing angry, then answer as best you can."

"Okay."

"Great." Christine gripped the door handle and pulled it open. "Let's win this thing."

I followed her inside, not surprised that Rafael and his lawyer were already seated. Rafael examined me over his shoulder, and I swear he smirked before putting his focus ahead again.

Mamá and Cat sat a row behind me. Out of nowhere, my heart began hammering as I swept my gaze around the mostly empty courtroom. I had never imagined I would be in one, yet here I was. Stuck in this place, about to be questioned about my fucking parenting.

The bailiff announced the judge, and a woman with tan skin and graying hair made her way to the bench. Judge Dalton was thin lipped, with serious eyes, and according to my lawyer, this judge did *not* mess around and did *not* like her time wasted. If I could, I would have told her this whole case was a waste of time and to let it go. Rafael wasn't worth her energy one bit.

Judge Dalton gave us a breakdown of the rules of her court, and unfortunately, I was called to the stand first.

I sat with unease, remembering Christine telling me not to look in Rafael's direction. It was hard not to, considering how badly I wanted to knock his fucking lights out, but I managed.

"Hi, Javier," Christine started. "Can you tell the court how long you've been Aleesa's father?"

"Since the day she was born," I answered.

"So that makes her how old?" asked Christine.

"Four years old."

"Can you explain what it has been like raising Aleesa?"

"Well, when she was a baby, I would wake up in the middle of the night to feed her, and if I could not or if I was away for a game, I had my mother or sister around. I play games with her. We color and do lots of puzzles. I taught her how to swim. I read her favorite books to her. And when I am unable to be home, I have a live-in nanny that takes very good care of her. It is not an easy job being a parent, but I would not trade it for anything in this world."

"It's incredible you manage to handle so much while being a professional athlete. You're right. That's definitely not easy."

"It is not."

"Mr. Valdez, how would you describe your relationship with Aleesa?" Christine asked.

"We are very close. I know all of the things she likes, and she looks to me when she is scared or in need. She is . . . well, she is my daughter, and she calls me her dad. She does not know any different. Though Rafael is her biological father, she and I have a bond worth more than blood."

"What do you believe would happen if she were taken from you and placed in the care of a man she doesn't even know?"

"It would destroy her. She does not know a single thing about him, but she has known me since the day she came into this world. Ripping her away from everything she knows would break her heart and confuse her, and I do not believe that is in her best interest. She already struggles with sleeping in other places outside of our home when we happen to travel."

"So would you say that placing Aleesa in an *unfamiliar* environment with an *unfamiliar* person would be more harmful than beneficial to her?"

"Yes, it would be harmful. One hundred percent."

"I believe so too. Thank you, Javier. No further questions."

Christine trotted away to our desk, and in my periphery, I saw Rafael's lawyer stand and mosey his way around their desk.

When he stood in front of me, I avoided a grimace. He looked like the type to represent a man like Rafael. Expensive suit, hair oily and gelled back, no beard or mustache, and a sketchy look in his eyes.

"Mr. Valdez, you are aware that you aren't Aleesa's biological father, correct?"

"Obviously," I said.

"Answer with a yes or no, Mr. Valdez," Judge Dalton said.

I sighed. "Yes, I am aware."

"Do you believe blood relation is important in determining the best interests of the child as well?"

"Blood is not everything. Love, care, and being there every step of the way is what matters most in my opinion."

"But how could the biological father have been able to love and care for Aleesa if he wasn't aware of her birth?"

"He was not made aware because my wife clearly did not want him to be the one taking care of Aleesa." This time, I glared at Rafael, who wore a smug smile and had his arms folded.

"Unfortunately, your wife is not here with us to attest to that," the lawyer said. I clenched a fist in my lap. "The biological father never had the chance to be involved with Aleesa. Does he not deserve a chance?"

"Not in my opinion. She is perfectly fine where she is."

"And that, too, is your opinion, Mr. Valdez. Would you say Aleesa is safe in your home?"

"Yes."

"Are you sure? Because according to Mr. Acosta, he was tackled by you and shoved by your sister. That sounds quite violent."

"Objection, your honor," Christine called. "Firstly, there is no proof of this happening. Secondly, Mr. Acosta came onto Javier's personal property to inform him that he was filing for custody of his daughter—a little girl he has been attached to for four consecutive years. I have no doubt he was intentionally provoking Mr. Valdez, his family, and threatening their safety."

"Sustained. Rephrase the question or don't ask it, Mr. Cameron," said Judge Dalton.

"Very well." Cameron smirked. "Is it possible, Mr. Valdez, that the reason you do not want to share custody of Aleesa is because of your dislike for Mr. Acosta?"

"No. I do not want to share custody of my daughter with him because I do not trust him."

"Why not? What has Mr. Acosta done, outside of his affair with your wife, that makes you believe he cannot be trusted?"

I hesitated with my response, shifting my gaze to Christine, who simply shook her head and mouthed the word *breathe*, and then to my mother and sister, who sat side by side with worried eyes.

"To me, it shows that he makes poor decisions. He chose to sleep with a married woman and got her pregnant. A man like that does not deserve to raise a daughter."

"That was over four years ago. Are you saying Mr. Acosta is not capable of learning from his mistakes?"

"No. But my wife made her choice. She wanted me at the hospital during Aleesa's birth. She wanted me to sign the birth certificate as Aleesa's father. She clearly thought the same thing about Rafael's character if she did not feel the urge to at least alert him that he could be the father."

"Or perhaps your wife felt ashamed, Mr. Valdez. Did you think about that?"

"Objection, your honor. We are not here to discuss Mr. Valdez's deceased wife or her affairs. We are here to seek the best solution for Aleesa."

"Sustained. Remove the last question from the records," Judge Dalton commanded. "Mr. Cameron, I expect you to conduct yourself professionally. There will be no further questions about the mother of the child."

"Of course, your honor. No further questions."

"Mr. Valdez, if the court were to grant the biological father visitation or partial custody, how would you handle that?" Judge Dalton asked me as Cameron walked away.

"If you want me to be honest, I would not like it, Your Honor. I believe that keeping her in my care is what is best for her. I do not care if she grows up and learns the truth about who her biological father really is. If she decides that she would like to get to know Rafael, that will be her choice, and I will not stop her. But right now, I do not think it is fair to throw that wrench in her life." I noticed my eyes had drifted as I provided the explanation. I looked at the judge again, raised my chin, and said, "If it comes down to it, though, I will do what the court decides is best for my child."

Judge Dalton nodded sympathetically as she regarded me.

"Thank you for your honesty, Mr. Valdez. You may now leave the stand. We will take a fifteen-minute recess, then proceed with Mr. Acosta on the stand."

I walked up to the desk, where Christine was collecting papers in her folder. "Great job, Javier. You spoke calmly and kept your answers simple. Judge Dalton will take your behavior into consideration, considering how sensitive this situation is for you."

"I hope so. I just feel like I did not say enough."

"You said more than enough. Trust me."

I slid my gaze to Rafael and his lawyer as they left their desk and sauntered toward the double doors.

Rafael nodded at me.

I grimaced.

I wanted to bury him in the fucking ground.

# FORTY-FOUR

## JAVIER

The fifteen minutes seemed to fly by.

Before I knew it, we were back in the courtroom, and Rafael, along with his smug grin, took the stand.

I hated sitting there, listening to him make his pleas. Listening to him as he tried to garner sympathy from the judge, saying how badly he wanted to be a father and how he'd already missed important stages of Aleesa's life.

And the worst part about it was that Judge Dalton seemed to be falling for it. That serious mask she wore slowly morphed to an expression full of understanding.

That was almost enough to send me into a spiral.

When Christine approached Rafael, she did not take it easy on him, but he knew what to expect. He answered all her questions with ease and continued pulling at the judge's heartstrings.

He was trying to prove he was a good person who deserved to know his biological child . . . and, fuck me, it was working for him.

By the end of it, I felt defeated. Weak.

My lawyer gave her closing statements, and so did his.

It wasn't until I was inside my car that I realized my hands were shaking. Perhaps that was why Cat tried to insist that she drive me home before I even made it to the car. I probably should not have turned down her offer.

She and my mother had driven a rental car together to reach the courthouse and were on the way to my home.

I held on to the steering wheel, feeling hotness build behind my eyes.

"No," I muttered.

I would not cry. Not over this.

I started the ignition, and once my hands stopped shaking, I left the parking lot. But I didn't go home. I went to a place I hadn't been to in a very long time.

After parking and climbing out of the car, I made my way through the cemetery and didn't stop until I reached Eloise's grave.

Her headstone read:

**ELOISE LILIANA GOTERA VALDEZ**
**LOVING MOTHER, WIFE, DAUGHTER, AND FRIEND**
**1989–2019**

There were no flowers for her—only dead leaves and weeds. Her grave had been neglected, and guilt punched me straight in the gut.

I lowered to a squat, and because I could no longer hold back my tears, I dropped my face into my hands and released them.

"I do not know what to do, Ellie." I raked my fingers through my hair, studying the name carved into her headstone. "I have done everything right by Aleesa. I take care of her. I protect her. I love her so much, but now he might get her, and that is not fair to me."

I was in too much pain to rant in English anymore. It all came spewing out and translated to: "Why could you not just love me? What was so bad about me that you ran to him? You hurt me so bad, but I forgave you because you gave me our perfect little girl. You made her mine, and I thought I would be able to hold on to that forever . . . but now he will probably take her too. I deserved better. I deserved better! I know I am not perfect, but I did, Ellie. I deserved so much better than what you gave me."

A guttural sob left me as a deep ache settled below my ribs.

Silence wrapped around me. Wind caused the leaves to rustle, and cars drove by in the distance. Birds landed on branches, mindless survivors. It was all so calm, so peaceful . . . and yet my sadness morphed to anger.

This was why I was so mad at the world. People claimed I was grumpy and hard to deal with—that they did not understand me. *This* was why.

How was any of this fair? Even from the start of my life.

It was not fair that my father had left me, my mother, and my sister when I was only eight years old.

It was not fair that my wife had lost so much love for me, despite my efforts.

It was not fair that I'd had to assume all responsibility when she passed away.

It was not fair that I'd had to become a single father, and not by choice.

It was not fair that, after I'd embraced the role and loved Aleesa more than anyone or anything in this world, she could now be claimed by someone else—a man that I *hated* and a man who did *not* deserve being around her precious soul.

Footsteps sounded behind me, and I peered over my shoulder.

Shock hit me when I saw Octavia and Aleesa approaching. I swiped my tears away and stood up as they walked in my direction. Octavia's brown eyes were soft but sad. Aleesa was smiling at first, but when she saw my state, her smile drooped.

She tugged her hand out of Octavia's and trotted to me. I lowered down so I could catch her. I held her in my arms—I held on for dear life.

"Mi niña," I whispered, smoothing her hair back. "I love you so much. *So, so* much."

Aleesa tightened her arms around my neck, holding on for a few seconds before releasing me and leaning back so she could see my face.

She was smiling again. She ran a hand over my cheek, rubbing a tear away. "No be sad, Daddy."

I smiled back, then kissed her cheek.

I faced Octavia next, hating that she was seeing me like this. So weak, pathetic, and broken. She stood a few steps away, wringing her fingers in front of her.

"Sorry if we interrupted," she apologized.

"It is okay. I was about to leave anyway." I cleared my throat. "How did you know I was here?"

"Catalina called, said it might calm you down and cheer you up if you saw Leesa. She sent me this address and said she was sure you'd be here."

I huffed a humorless laugh. "My sister knows me too damn well."

Octavia closed the gap between us, placing a hand on my arm. "Are you okay?"

"Not really," I admitted.

"Anything I can do to help?"

I thought about that for a moment, looking from her eyes to Aleesa's green irises. "I think we need to get away for a few days."

Octavia gave me a funny look. "Like a vacation?"

"Yes. I do not want to think about what the judge's decision will be. And if I am forced to share visitation with Aleesa, I want to spend all the time I can with her while I have her."

A smile swept across Octavia's lips. "Then we'll do that. Where do you want to go?"

"I think we should go to a place Aleesa is slightly obsessed with."

"Uh-oh." Octavia laughed, knuckling Aleesa's cheek to make her giggle. "Let's hope we survive it."

# FORTY-FIVE

## OCTAVIA

Of course, the place Javier was referring to was Disney World.

But you know what, I'd never been before, and I was a *huge* Disney girl. *The Princess and the Frog* would always be my favorite, with *The Lion King* as a close second.

We caught so many rides and ate so much food. Between the ice cream, the candy, and even the churros, Aleesa was in heaven.

We spent two days at the amusement park, having the time of our lives, wearing Mickey and Minnie Mouse ears and eating way too many carbs.

Seeing Javier carry Aleesa on his shoulders, witnessing the fireworks in her eyes as they burst at night, I saw the proof of how much he loved her. He was the perfect father. I hoped the judge would realize that not a single thing was missing from Aleesa's life and that she was fine where she was.

It hurt my heart to think he would miss out on more time with her. It was enough losing time to travel for his games. He complained about that a lot and wished things were different or that Aleesa could simply travel with him, but it wasn't realistic.

Regardless, Javier did seem to forget about the custody battle for a while.

After those days at Disney, he booked a rental and drove us to the Florida Keys, where he'd reserved a high-end hotel. We spent that day teaching Aleesa how to play Putt-Putt, walking the beach, and then eating deliciously greasy pizza for dinner.

Aleesa was beyond exhausted by the time we returned to the hotel. I gave her a bath, put her little bonnet on, and let her rest in a room with bunk beds.

When she was asleep, I blew a sigh of relief and left the room.

I had expected Javier to be in the living room, but he wasn't. Instead, he was standing on the balcony, with his arms folded, peering out at the dark ocean ahead.

I slid the door open and shut it behind me before standing next to him. "She passed right out."

He smiled. "Good. She seemed to have a really great time."

"She definitely did."

Javier draped an arm over my shoulder, bringing me closer to his body. A balmy breeze caressed my skin, and I laid my head on him, so content with this moment.

This feeling.

This *safeness*.

When I was in his arms, I wanted to be nowhere else.

"So, I do not want to scare you, but you realize you are no longer my nanny anymore, right?"

I tipped my chin to look at him. "Oh really? Are you firing me?"

"Yes. You are one hundred percent fired as my nanny," he answered with a playful tone. "I do have another position you can fill, though, if you are interested."

"Oh yeah?" I looped my arms around his waist. "What's that?"

His warm brown eyes connected with mine. "I want you to be the one I wake up to in the mornings. The one I hold when I need comfort, and the one you look to for the same thing. I want *you* to be the one I continue feeling this happy with."

"So, you're offering me a position as your girlfriend?" I asked, mildly teasing.

He smirked. "Well . . . I do not want to put a title on it, since you seem to hate those so much, but . . ."

"Ask me."

He removed his arm from around me so he could hold my hands. "Octavia Klein, will you be my girlfriend?"

"Hmm, I don't know. Your life's a little complicated. I'll have to give that question some thought."

His face twisted with confusion. "Wait . . . are you being serious?"

Oh goodness. I forgot that he took things literally sometimes. Language barriers and all.

"No, I'm not serious. I'm kidding!" I laughed. "*Yes*, Javier Valdez. I'll be your girlfriend."

Chuckling, he leaned down to place a deep kiss on my lips. "Will it scare you to hear that I am in love with you?" His voice was warm and deep.

My heart picked up in speed, and my smile slipped.

"Okay, I see that it does scare you," he added quickly.

"No—I'm . . . I'm *not* scared, that's the thing." I held on to his hands tighter. "I thought if I heard a man say those words to me again, I would be terrified. I figured I would get cold feet and run . . . but I don't want to run away from you." I released his hands to run my fingers along his jawline. "I don't want to run, because I'm pretty sure I'm in love with you too."

"Pretty sure?" he teased.

"Okay. *Really* sure."

He laughed. "I am happy to hear it. But just because I want this does not mean I want to place all of my burdens on your shoulders."

I gave him a look that said, *Really?*

"If you mean taking care of Aleesa, she is not a burden. She is a blessing. As for everything else you have to deal with, those are just distractions. No matter what, I'll be here, because I want you." I kissed him. "I want *this*. I've wanted something like what we have my whole life."

He put on a boyish smile. "That means a lot to me to hear you say that. I promise that I will not disappoint you or ever hurt you like your ex did."

"You could never hurt me like he did. You're ten times the man he was, baby."

His hands dug into my hips as our lips met again. "Call me that again," he rasped.

"What? *Baby?*"

"Sí."

I couldn't contain my grin. "Okay . . . *baby*."

He grinned, nuzzling his nose into the crook of my neck. "Even your voice turns me on."

"So, I'm really fired, huh? No more pay?"

He threw his head back to laugh, and it was so nice seeing him this joyous and at ease.

"Fired as the nanny," he said, entwining his fingers with mine. "Hired as mi novia. In this position, you can have whatever you want."

"Ohh, *novia*. You make it sound so sexy."

He lowered his hands to my waist. "I will show you *sexy*. Come here."

I yelped as he picked me up, then laughed as I circled my legs around his waist.

He carried me back into the hotel suite and went straight for his bedroom, placing me on my back and sinking between my legs.

We got rid of our clothes piece by piece between deep, passionate kisses, and before I knew it, he was angling himself just right so he could sink into me.

A moan left my lips as he cupped the back of my neck, thrusting carefully with deep grunts. His face hovered above mine as he took control, and that night, he truly made me his.

There was no doubt about it anymore. No more questions, comparisons, or wonders.

I was his, and he was mine.

That night something burned between us that was impossible to explain. But if I had to, I would say that my chest was on fire—no, that my whole *body* was on fire for him. We were combusting in the best way, and the only thing that kept the flames contained were three simple words . . .

"I love you," Javier rasped on my lips. "Te amo mucho, Octavia."

Tears slid down the sides of my face. I cupped his cheek while the nails of my other hand dragged down the length of his back.

"I love you too," I whispered.

I realized in that moment that this wasn't like all the other times we'd had sex before. Yes, all the other times had been incredible, but this was special. This was deep and blissful and powerful.

This was . . . *making love.* I had never experienced such a thing before. I never realized how amazing it could feel, combined with joy.

Now I understood why so many people were desperate to make love.

Because this was personal. It was emotional. It was deep.

I never wanted it to end.

*Safe,* I thought. *You're finally safe, girl.*

Javier pulled out when he came, groaning in my ear and making me clench. His come dripped on my pelvis, and after stealing another kiss, he got up to get a towel and wipe it all away.

Next, he climbed back onto the bed and centered his face between my thighs, clutching my hips in both of his large hands.

"Be still, novia," he murmured.

Before I could nod, react, or do anything, his tongue skimmed through the lips of my pussy.

And I kid you not, it was the best head he'd ever given me.

# FORTY-SIX

## JAVIER

The getaway with Octavia and Aleesa was perfect. I had not realized how much I'd needed to escape, but just being away from Atlanta for a few days was a relief.

I felt no pressures while roaming the streets of Disney. And getting one-on-one time with Octavia was a true gift. I loved being with her. With her around, life felt whole and right. Yes, it was still hard, but having a woman like her made processing it so much easier.

Sometimes I expected the ball to drop with her. I feared that one day she'd wake up and realize she did not have to deal with the things I was going through. That she'd pack up her belongings, give me notice, and walk right out the door. Or worse, that she would find another man, just like Eloise did, and want him more than me.

That was my insecurity talking, but it was true. It was a fear I could not ignore.

But, like I'd told her, that was because I lacked trust in many people. That was something I was working on, though. Octavia suggested that I try speaking to a therapist. I was not quite ready to do that yet, but she was right. Plus, it would be worth the shot if it meant I could find peace within myself.

It shocked me that I could feel so content with her and Aleesa around, yet when I was alone and my mind ran in circles, I hated myself for all the mistakes I'd made. I hated myself for not being a better husband. I regretted accepting the offer to join the Ravens and moving to an entirely different country. Perhaps if I had stayed in Argentina, Eloise never would have felt so alone.

But life works the way it's supposed to, and Eloise's path had already been paved. So had mine. We are not thrown things we cannot handle in this life, and though the issues I had faced had tested me, they had also brought me strength.

I sipped coffee on my deck as I stared at the towering trees in the distance. It was six in the morning, and Octavia and Aleesa were inside sleeping. I was tired, but I could not stop my mind from racing.

We were back home now, and that meant facing reality. The judge's ruling would come in any day now, and I was terrified of the results.

Not only that, but there also were people popping into Element searching for me. They wanted to snap pictures and capture anything they could. Deke and I had to up the security so our members felt safe.

It was a shame how low people could go. Someone had found out that Aleesa had dance every Wednesday, and they'd waltzed right in and bombarded her instructor with questions. I'd apologized profusely for it, but that had not prevented the shame I felt.

This was why I hated the idea of fame. Average people put other average people on pedestals and expect them to be gods, but as soon as that person stumbles or falls, they are ready to eat them alive like wolves. They are ready to tear that person to shreds for not being perfect or living a perfect life.

This was also why I hated social media and had hired someone to handle it for me. There was nothing good for me there. I enjoyed living in the moment and worrying about my own life and issues. I did not have time to absorb other's problems and comment with sad or happy emojis.

My phone buzzed on the glass table next to me, and I gave it a glance.

Catalina.

I answered with a sigh. "Hello, sis."

"Hola, brother. Am I calling you too early?"

"No. You know I am usually up around this time anyway. You are not, though. Why are you awake?"

"I don't know." She sighed, sounding slightly defeated. "I'm working on this piece that I want to finish for an art show next week, but I feel creatively blocked."

"Hmm." I took a slow sip of coffee. "Because of my issues?"

"They are not just *your* issues, you know? She is my niece, and you are my only sibling. This matters to me and Mamá."

"I know."

"And I guess I just wanted to hear your voice. Make sure you were okay."

I smiled. My sister loved pretending to be tough, but inside she was as gooey as a roasted marshmallow. I suppose I was the same way. It was something we had in common, only because of our upbringing.

"I am okay, Cat," I told her.

"Good."

I placed my coffee mug down. "You know, I have never properly thanked you for always being there for me."

"Please," she muttered. "You don't have to thank me for anything."

"Yes, Catalina, I do." I sat forward, resting my elbows on my knees. "When I lost Eloise, I sort of lost myself. You know that. And at the time, I felt like I was just surviving with Aleesa until she was old enough to sort of do things on her own. I got lost in fatherhood, in trying to be the perfect dad. I took so many things for granted with you and Mamá. But I am thankful for you both. Because had it not been for you two, I know I would not have survived."

My sister was quiet for a while. Then I heard a sniffle. "Javier, you know it is too early for this sentimental shit, right?"

A laugh burst out of me. "Lo siento. I have a habit of being sentimental in the mornings."

"Don't apologize; that's a good thing," she murmured. "We were there because we love you so much. And you have sacrificed a lot just to make our lives easier. Do you remember how much Mamá had to work? We hated seeing her come home all worn down and exhausted. But she would still cook and clean and take care of us."

"Yes, I remember."

"And I will never forget this, but when we were kids, you said that one day you would make sure Mamá never worked again. You *promised* that you would give her the life she deserved. And look at her now? She lives beautifully in Argentina. She travels wherever she wants. She's finally shopping for outfits that aren't all from thrift stores."

I snorted a laugh. "You know it is serious when she stops thrift shopping."

"Exactly." Cat giggled. "Though I do think that vase she got me with all those weird faces on it was from a thrift store. She swore it was art, but that thing was ugly."

I chuckled.

"Regardless of all that, you kept your promise. If it weren't for you, I wouldn't have been able to go to art school. I wouldn't have been able to paint and sculpt for a living, but I can because *you* made a way for me to do that. You have been here for us since day one, so trust me when I tell you that we have no problem at all being there for you. Even if we didn't have all of this, we would still be here. We love you. *I* love you, hermano."

My eyes burned with tears. I blinked them away before more could accumulate.

"Thank you, Cat."

"Always. After the showing, I plan to come down for a bit. Your season starts soon, right?"

"Two more months."

"So soon. I'll let you know what day for sure. I'm gonna go now because I really need to finish this damn piece. Te quiero, Javi."

"Yo también te quiero, Catalina."

I placed my phone on my lap and took one more look at the trees.

Catalina always made me see the world a bit differently. She had always been the more optimistic one, and I appreciated her for it.

Though it was only a small shred, I could feel hope blooming inside me.

As long as there was a sliver of it, that was all I needed to get through each day.

# FORTY-SEVEN

## OCTAVIA

I was so thankful to have my best friend, Naomi, in town. She'd taken two vacation days and decided to drive from Raleigh to Atlanta to hang out with me.

"Don't get me wrong, I love babies, but watching them crown grosses me out every single time." Naomi snickered as the nail tech lifted her hand to evenly file her nails. "There's all that liquid, blood, and gushy stuff."

"So why do you still do it?" I laughed with her, examining my manicure.

"Because of the hefty paychecks, girl."

One of the things I loved about Atlanta was the *amazing* nail techs. When I'd realized I'd have to be living in Atlanta for a while, I'd been worried about where I'd get manicures and pedicures. But one quick search, and I'd been flooded with endless options.

Getting my locs retwisted was another bonus. There were so many loc stylists in the area, and many of them were holistic.

"So your boo let you have the day off, huh?" Naomi side-eyed me with a smirk. "How does that work, anyway? Are you still a nanny? Stepmom? Like, where does that put you with his daughter?"

"I'm still her nanny, and he insisted on still paying me for my time. He thinks I will feel like he's using me if he doesn't keep sending me deposits."

"I know that's right," Naomi said after a slight purse of her lips. "See, that's a good man. Smart too. And he clearly knows how to work that magic stick if he has you glowing like this."

"Listen. I don't like to brag, but he is *in-cred-i-ble*." I bit back a smile and shifted in my seat, remembering Javier telling me I was his *everything* right before slipping between my thighs and making the sweetest love to me.

I'd never felt so taken care of. He was so tender, sweet, and passionate, yet so dominating at the same time. He pleased me in so many ways—ways that my body couldn't keep up with but that it loved so much.

Luther couldn't even compare to him. Those were two different men, one fit for the streets while the other was fit for the throne.

"Don't you think me seeing Luther get arrested was too much of a coincidence?" I asked as my nail tech applied a clear coat of polish to my pinkie finger. "I don't know. It just felt way too easy. Like that was just a prank, and he'll pop up and harass me again."

"Octavia, you have to stop that."

"Stop what?"

"Thinking that every single win you receive is supposed to be through hardship. Last I checked, he's definitely locked up, and if you ask me, his ass needs to be in jail." She rolled her eyes, temporarily pursing her lips. "You see it as too easy. I see it as a blessing. Lord knows you don't need any more drama in your life."

I laughed at that. "That's true. There's so much going on. I just want it to level out a bit and go back to normal."

"And it will, now that he's out of the picture." She shot me a wink. "You have your man, your job; your family is thriving and healthy. This is your time to heal and bloom, my love, regardless of how easy it feels. You deserve more in life than heartache and pain."

"Aww, Naomi," I cooed, my eyes burning as emotion pumped through me. "Honestly, without you and Davina, I don't think I'd have my sanity."

"Wait . . . you've been sane this whole time?" she teased.

I busted out laughing, bumping her with my elbow.

"All done," Naomi's nail tech announced after applying the last of her cuticle oil.

"Thank you." Naomi examined her nails with a grateful smile. "Damn, girl. You were right. These nail techs don't play."

"I told you. You ready to go?"

"Yes, please. I'm starving."

After paying, we left the building and found Naomi's car on the curb. She drove us to one of my favorite restaurants in town. Venicio's had the best melt-in-your-mouth baked cod and cocktails. It was a bit on the pricier side, but neither Naomi nor I cared about splurging.

Truthfully, since I was living in Javier's guesthouse, and considering how much he paid me, I was able to save a lot of money. The main things I used money for were food, gas, groceries, and maybe a little online shopping.

A lot of it also went to Mama, to help her out with bills at our house in Maple Cove, or to cover Abe's therapy appointments. I couldn't wait until I could see them again. Maybe Javier wouldn't mind if Mama and Abe visited us. He'd probably enjoy it way too much.

Naomi and I walked into Venicio's, where a hostess greeted us and sat us down at a booth. As I scanned the menus, I heard a voice. A familiar, deep, conceited voice that made my stomach lurch.

"—thinks I have a fair shot at custody. I gotta say, this was way easier than I expected. I mean, it's right there. I can taste it."

I gasped, and Naomi's eyes swiveled up to mine. "What?" she asked.

"The guy in the booth behind me. I know who he is."

She frowned, then tilted to the side just a bit to see past me. "He's got nice hair."

"Yeah, I bet he does." I scowled as I plucked my phone out of my purse, ready to text Javier and let him know.

"I'd be so fucking embarrassed if I was that guy. Think about it. The whole world knows his wife fucked *me*?" Rafael snorted an obnoxious laugh. "Not saying I'm the hottest guy in the world, but imagine what kind of catch I'll be considered if a famous basketball player's wife feels the urge to go to bed with me. Imagine all the other women who will be ready to do the same."

"She was on your design team, right?" the man seated with him asked.

"She was. And the way it happened, bro. Oh, it was like a dream. I still remember it." Rafael paused, and when he released a wet gasp, I figured he'd taken a sip of his drink. "She was in my office, taking sips of my whiskey. Then she lets me put her on her hands and knees—"

I cleared my throat, resisting the urge to twist around and slap him on the back of his head. How could he talk about a dead woman like that? He was a horrible human being. I couldn't believe this was happening. Of all the odds in the world, I was here—right here in a seat behind the man trying to ruin Javier's life.

"It had to be fun if you ended up getting her pregnant," the other man commented.

"Well, see, that's the crazy thing." Rafael's voice became quieter as he said, "She told me about the baby—or at least that she suspected it. And she straight-up tells me she doesn't want me involved or raising it. At the time, I didn't give a fuck, you know. I had other shit to deal with, and a kid is the last thing I fucking want. Even now, I'll probably have to hire a few fucking nannies to keep an eye on her."

My heart thumped faster. I couldn't believe I was hearing this. He wasn't talking about Aleesa like that. Not my sweet girl.

"But it'll be worth it. The kid's face is already all over the place. People will see me with her, and I can get her started with the new line we have going for kids. It's going to be huge, just you watch. When they see her face, the dollars will start rolling in. The people love her already. I wish I would've thought about this before now."

Our waiter approached the table with two waters and set them down in front of us. I locked the screen of my phone and asked the waiter for five more minutes.

When the waiter took off, I looked at Naomi. "I need to do something."

"Hold on." She caught my wrist before I could climb out of my seat. "Don't tell me you're about to confront him, Tavia."

"Of course not." I put on a faux grin and gently tugged my wrist out of her hand. Then I slid out of my booth, tucked my phone into my back pocket, and picked up my cup of water. Then I turned toward Rafael's booth and pretended to trip, tipping my glass forcefully to the right so water could spill all over his food and run onto his lap.

"What the fuck!" Rafael shot out of his booth.

"Oh my goodness," I gasped. "I'm so sorry!"

Rafael flung the water off his hands as he grimaced at his wet trousers. I tried not to laugh, because he was wearing a gray suit and looked like he'd peed himself.

"Do you work here or something?" Rafael looked me up and down, grimacing.

I frowned back. "Do I look like I work here?"

"I don't fucking know, but if you do, I need to speak to the manager. What kind of unprofessional shit is this?"

"Well, I don't work here, and I told you I was sorry." I looked from him to his friend—a scrawny Caucasian guy with glasses, who was balding at the crown of his head. *Typical.* "I have to ask. What is it that you get off on more? Him telling you stories about using children for financial gain, or when he tells you about his affair with a deceased woman?"

Rafael's friend turned beet red.

"Who the hell are you?" Rafael hissed.

"Someone you're going to regret sitting next to."

I started to walk away, but Rafael grabbed my upper arm tightly—so tightly I nearly froze. Because the grip was familiar. It was angry and hard and ruthless.

"Um, you better get your hands off my girl before I cut 'em off." Naomi's voice rose behind me, and I looked in her direction. She stood a few steps away, holding a steak knife in one hand.

The crazy thing was, Naomi was the type to *definitely* cut or stab a man's hands if he got . . . well, *handsy*. She'd hurt men before, and she'd do it again. She grew up around horrible people, so this was nothing new to her. However, I would never let her do it here—not in Atlanta and not to a rich, petty man like Rafael.

"No, you know what? It's okay, Naomi. I've got this." I lowered my eyes to Rafael's grip. "I suggest you remove your hand before I make you remove it."

Rafael blinked rapidly as he snatched his hand away. "You spilled water on me on purpose. That's assault."

"Oh, please. It was an accident. Besides, a little water isn't going to kill you. You need a bath to wash away all the grimy shit you do."

Rafael stared at me, baffled.

"Is everything okay here?" A well-dressed man approached us, with eyes full of concern. I figured he was the manager.

"Oh, yes. Everything is fine," I told him. "Just a little misunderstanding. Right, Rafael?"

This time, Rafael blanched. "Wait . . . I know you . . ."

I simply smiled, refusing to stick around as he processed just who I was. "Enjoy the rest of your soggy lunch." I made my way back to Naomi, who was already collecting our purses and was ready to leave. When she'd looped her arm through mine, she rushed with me to the exit.

As soon as we were outside, she yelled, "Octavia, what the hell! You said you weren't going to confront him! I almost killed that man!"

"I know, I'm sorry! I couldn't help it!"

She busted out laughing. "Damn, girl. You had my heart pumping and everything! You can't just go off script without giving me a heads-up. You know I'll have your back no matter what, but damn."

I laughed. "I know you will." I grinned as we made our way to her car.

When we were seated inside, she looked at me and said, "Why are you still smiling?"

"Because I think I just spared Javier any more agony about this custody battle."

Her brows stitched together. "What do you mean?"

"I mean—" I unlocked my phone and turned the screen her way so she could see it. When she realized what she was looking at, her eyes expanded and an amused smile swept over her face. "I recorded every single thing he said."

"You smart-ass bitch." She squealed as she gripped the steering wheel. "This is why you're my best friend!"

I laughed as we threw our hands out at the same time to do our bestie handshake.

# FORTY-EIGHT

## OCTAVIA

As soon as Naomi dropped me off, I rushed into Javier's house. He and Aleesa were nowhere to be found in the living room, kitchen, or sunroom, but I heard giggling coming from outside.

I placed my purse down on the kitchen counter and headed for the back door. Javier had a tube of bubbles in hand and was blowing them while Aleesa ran around in circles, swatting at some of them and trying to catch others.

I walked down the stairs of the deck, and when he heard my footsteps shuffling through the grass, he gazed over his shoulder. One look at me, and the biggest smile spread across his face. It was so warm and genuine, making his eyes sparkle and his face appear softer.

"You are back sooner than I expected," he said, turning as I met up with him.

"Yeah, well, I sort of ruined lunch."

"You ruined lunch?" His brows drew together. He started to speak again, but Aleesa rushed his way and took the bubble tube and wand from him. She tried blowing, but spittle came out instead. "How do you mean?"

I unlocked my phone and showed him my screen. "I mean, I confronted Rafael."

This time, Javier put on a full-blown frown. "You *what*?"

"So Naomi and I were about to eat at Venicio's, and he was sitting at the table right behind me. I heard him talking about you, Eloise, and Aleesa."

Javier's eyes seemed to darken. "What was he saying?"

"I have it all right here." I pressed the play button, and Javier stepped closer to tune in. While giving a glance at Aleesa, who was still trying her hardest to blow bubbles, I increased the volume just enough for only us to hear.

As Javier listened, he seemed to zone out, but I didn't miss the way his jaw pulsed. The recording played Rafael's voice for about three minutes before it was just mine and Naomi's.

I paused the recording and looked into his eyes.

"Did he put his hands on you?" he asked in a low growl.

I studied the deep frown on his face, the angry lines forming between his eyebrows. Out of all the things he'd heard, that seemed to piss him off the most.

"He grabbed my arm, but—"

"I am going to kill him." He started to walk around me, ready to storm away, but I caught his hand.

"No, that's not what you're going to do," I said when he whirled around.

"He tried to *hurt you*, Octavia!" he shot back in a loud whisper. He looked at Aleesa, who, thankfully, wasn't paying any attention to either of us. Instead, she was now frustratedly dumping all the bubble solution onto the ground.

"Emphasis on *tried*," I murmured, guiding him a bit farther away from Aleesa. "But he didn't. If you go to him and incite violence, this recording will be for nothing. We have to play this smart. You understand?"

Javier was fuming, breaths coming out harshly through his flared nostrils.

"Javier." I cupped his face in my hands.

He squeezed his eyes shut, shaking his head.

"Baby, look at me."

Finally, he softened and slowly opened his eyes.

"Take a breath." I inhaled, hoping he'd follow suit. He dragged in a big breath through his nose and exhaled as I did. "Good. Again."

Reluctant, he did it again.

"Now listen to me," I urged. "Right now, you're not going to confront Rafael. What you're going to do is send this voice recording to your lawyer so she can have proof that Rafael does not have Aleesa's best interest in mind. After she has it and you speak to her, then you can go to Rafael and demand him to drop the request for custody. You'll give him an ultimatum: If he doesn't drop it, we can send the recording to the press and leak it, or have your lawyer play it for the judge in court. Either way, it'll destroy his chances. The last thing he'll want is news getting out to the press that he only wants Aleesa for financial gain. It'll destroy his brand and his business."

"I should've known," Javier grumbled. "I knew he wanted something from this. Damn, Octavia." He clutched my face in his hands and kissed me so hard, so passionately, I nearly stumbled. But he kept hold of me, and I laughed behind the kiss. "You are incredible. Do you know that?"

I could only smile . . . and blush.

"Seriously. I do not know why you fight so hard for us, but I am so thankful."

"I fight because I care about you both. And I'll be damned if anyone takes advantage of my Leesa."

He chuckled.

Aleesa walked toward us with pouty lips. "I hungry."

I scooped her up. "You know, I'm hungry too. Let's go make a sandwich while Daddy handles a few things."

"And strawbebbies," she said, grinning.

I couldn't help my smile. "With strawberries."

# FORTY-NINE

## JAVIER

I sat in my car for several minutes while parked in the lot of Rafael's building.

If I went in too worked up, I would probably punch him in his face as soon as I saw him.

So I sat behind the steering wheel, breathing as evenly as possible and staring at the lock screen wallpaper on my phone. It was a photo of me and Aleesa that Octavia had taken when we were at Disney World. Aleesa was on my shoulders, and I held her hands and smiled as she cheesed really hard for Octavia.

A smile tugged at my lips. My daughter had such a beautiful soul. And after dealing with Rafael, I was going to keep her. There was no doubt in my mind now. With that in mind, I climbed out of my car, slipped my phone into my pocket, and headed for the front door of the building.

After signing in, I rode the elevator up to floor fourteen and was immediately greeted with the secretary's desk. The sight of it made me pause. I'd never been to Eloise's job before, but knowing this was the place where she'd worked—where she'd encountered Rafael every single day—caused my stomach to twist.

"Can I help you?" the secretary asked. She was young, with big blue eyes and brunette hair. She forced a smile as she stood with wariness. Something told me she knew exactly who I was. After all, she did manage this man's schedule and handle his affairs.

"I am here to see Rafael."

"I'm afraid he's busy at the moment, but if you leave a message for him and your number, I can call back to arrange a meeting with you."

"Oh. A message?" I approached her desk, raising my chin. "Tell him he has two minutes to get his ass out here or I will start my countersuit right now."

The woman's eyes rounded. With a large step back, she said, "Uh . . . one moment."

She took off in a flash, rounded a corner, and disappeared. I folded my arms. It took a minute for her to return with Rafael trailing behind her.

"What the hell, Javier?" he snapped, marching toward me. "How dare you come to my workplace with this shit."

"Would you rather deal with your bullshit in court?"

His brows pulled together as he looked from me to his secretary. "Lidia, go get me some coffee or something."

"Yes, sir." Lidia collected her purse in a hurry and headed toward the elevator.

"I hope you did not talk to Eloise that way," I said when Lidia was gone and the doors had sealed shut.

"Follow me," he grumbled, ignoring my words.

I followed him to his office. He offered that I sit. I didn't.

"So I am going to get straight to the point, because, unlike you, I do not like my time wasted." I pulled my phone out and started playing the recording as Rafael lowered into his seat.

As each sentence of his played, his face whitened more and more. Where was that smug smile now?

I paused it, and he shot out of his chair. "You hired that woman to follow me, didn't you?"

"I did not hire anyone."

"So how did you get that? You set this up!"

"Rafael, I am not a schemer. I do not give enough fucks about you to have anyone waste their time following you around. We can just consider this my lucky break. So here is what will happen—" I walked closer to his desk, and he backed away. "You are going to drop this custody battle, you are going to leave me and my family the fuck alone, and if you do not do that, all it will take is one click from my lawyer to have this recording sent to Judge Dalton."

Rafael's throat bobbed.

"What do you think the judge will say when she finds out that you only wanted custody of a four-year-old so you could milk her for cash?"

"Oh, you are so full of shit," Rafael growled. "She came from *my* fucking balls, so you know I have the right!"

"No," I snapped, storming around the desk and gripping his collar. "You have no fucking right, and you are lucky I did not rip your balls off the moment Eloise told me about you." I shoved him backward until his back was against the wall. He tried acting like he wasn't afraid, but I saw it in his eyes. The fear swimming in them.

"If you do not drop it, the judge will know everything, and she will leave custody to me. And once that's finished, I will countersue you for *everything* your minuscule life is worth for trying to ruin mine. You know that I love her and that she is better off with me. Do not fight me on this."

"Fine, whatever," Rafael said. "Just get the fuck off of me."

I kept hold of his collar, still glaring down at him. Then, after counting to ten in my head and forcing myself to calm down, I shoved him away and stepped backward.

"Call your lawyer. Now."

Rafael blinked at me several times, almost as if he thought I was joking. But I was not, and he fucking knew I was not, so he sat down in his chair and picked up his cell phone.

His hands shook as he tapped the screen a few times, then pressed the phone to his ear.

"Put it on speakerphone," I ordered.

He released an irritated sigh but did as he was told.

The phone rang a few times before a male answered.

"Hey, Jim. It's Rafael."

"Hey, Rafael. What's up? Gotta make this quick—I'm on my way to a hearing."

"Yeah, listen. I need to drop the custody battle."

The line was quiet for a few seconds. "What are you talking about?"

"You heard me. I need to drop it. Today. Send a notice or a letter or whatever to the judge and let her know I no longer want custody."

"Uh . . . okay. What's going on, man? We had this bagged."

"He knows, all right?" Rafael pinched the bridge of his nose. "Javier has a fucking recording of me when I had lunch with Matt yesterday. Some . . . *woman* that he knew overheard me talking and got the whole thing."

"Shit. What did you say?"

"I was talking about the kids clothing line and about the girl, of course. And about how much money we could make with her as the face of the brand or whatever."

I hated when he called Aleesa *the girl*, like she was just some random kid he could pick out of a lineup.

"God damn it, Rafael! This is why I told you to keep your fucking mouth shut about it! Telling the media was one thing, but talking about it in public? It's the dumbest thing you could've done, even if it was with Matt."

"I know."

"Fine," his lawyer snapped. "I'll contact Judge Dalton today to cancel the battle. But you're still paying me for my time."

"Okay."

"I gotta go." His lawyer ended the call, and Rafael sat back in his chair.

"Happy?" he asked, throwing his hands up.

"No. But it will do."

"Yeah, yeah. Just get the fuck out of my office."

I made my way to the door but paused before walking out. "Did you even care about being a father?"

Rafael stared at me briefly before lowering his line of sight. "I . . . don't know. But I could have eventually cared. And I just . . . I wanted to see the kid in person. And whether you believe it or not," he said, rising to a stand, "I cared about Eloise. I fucking loved her. That sucks for you to hear, but it's true. I loved her . . . she just didn't love me back. And you were right before." He swallowed hard, as if he were swallowing a chunk of his pride. "She told me she was choosing you over me when she ended our affair. Even after I had promised her the world." He scoffed, head shaking. "To this day, I still don't understand why, if she claimed to be so unhappy at home."

"You do not understand it because Eloise did not care about worldly things," I said. "She did not care that you had money. She did not care that you were some semi-famous fashion designer. She took the job because she was bored, and sadly, she got caught up with you. What she really cared about was intimacy and love. She wanted someone to be able to give that to her *every single day*, but how could we, with careers like ours? We both failed her in those departments."

"No. *You* failed her. You chose basketball over her."

"I did not choose basketball over her," I countered. "I would have quit immediately if that was what she truly wanted me to do, but she made me promise not to quit. The thing with Eloise is that she struggled with making sacrifices. She wanted me to keep playing so that we could keep living out our dreams and have enough money to provide for her grandmother, but she also wanted me to be home more. She struggled with the sacrifices she had to make, while I failed to meet her needs."

"I would have done better if she'd given me the chance," he muttered.

"But she did not bother giving you one, did she?" I shot back. "Because she knew which one of us loved her most, no matter what she felt inside. She did not choose you, Rafael, and even if she were still alive, she would not choose you."

He said nothing to that, but I could tell my words hit him like a ton of bricks. His shoulders slumped, and the frown he wore melted away. Looking at him now, he looked like a sad little boy that had no one to love, and no one to love him back.

"Like I said before, I do not ever want to hear from you again." I gripped the doorknob and gave it a twist. "And if you *ever* put your hands on my girlfriend again, I will rip you to fucking pieces."

# FIFTY

## JAVIER

After dealing with Rafael, I went to the nearest grocery store to pick up a cake and took it home. After dealing with so much bullshit, we deserved to celebrate.

As Octavia cooked and Aleesa built a tower with magnetic tiles, I could not remember the last time I had felt so at peace. I kept thinking about my future, as well as Octavia's.

She had told me all about Luther being arrested, and I could tell that had brought her a lot of relief. There were times when I sometimes forgot to say I was coming toward her, but she would not get startled or panic. She would smile . . . perhaps because she knew this was a safe place for her now.

I sat on one of the barstools below the island counter, watching Octavia move from the stove to different countertops.

"—so I'll probably do brunch with Naomi tomorrow, and I can take Leesa so you aren't too worried about anything." Octavia paused on peeling a potato as she looked at me. "What?" she laughed.

"Nothing," I said, smiling. "I just can't stop staring at you. That's all."

She bit her bottom lip to fight a smile, returning to her potato.

"Enjoy your brunch with your friend. I can look after Aleesa."

"Are you sure?"

"Yes. Besides, you owe Naomi for ruining lunch with her."

She laughed as she started dicing one of the potatoes. "The crazy thing is she will never let me live that down. She was so proud of me but pissed because she really wanted to try the cod."

"Well, next time she is here, tell her lunch at Venicio's is on me."

Octavia grinned. "She'll love that. Oh—by the way. Davina and Deke are doing a wedding rehearsal soon, and Aleesa really needs to get that dress tailored. Javier, she is going to look so freaking cute."

"Oh, absolutely." I turned my gaze to Aleesa, who was now destroying her magnetic tower and making roaring noises. "She will be the cutest one there."

"How do you feel, being best man and all?"

"Oh, I don't know." I got off the stool and walked around the counter to wash my hands at the sink. "I am just happy for Deke. Happy that he's happy. He deserves it."

"Yeah, he does. And so does Davina. She's so nervous, and she swears after losing one marriage that she's some cursed wife."

I broke out in a laugh as I picked up a carrot and started peeling it.

"Javier, you don't have to do that," she said, watching as I went to work.

"I know. But I want to."

She looked up at me with bright brown eyes. "Can I tell you something?"

"Of course, amor."

"I'm really happy here. With you."

I paused on peeling the carrot to give her a careful look. "I am glad that you are happy. Hell, I'm glad that you are still here."

"Oh, trust me, baby," she said, picking up a cutting board full of diced potatoes, "I'm not going anywhere unless you fire me."

"Please stop saying that." I laughed. "You are not the nanny anymore."

"It'll take some getting used to this new *girlfriend* title."

I placed the peeler and carrot down before turning and standing behind her. After she dumped the potatoes into boiling water, I held her shoulders and brought my mouth down to her shoulder.

She sighed as I placed a kiss there, then tilted her head just a bit to expose her neck. I kissed my way up and didn't stop until I reached her jawline.

"Will this help you get used to it?" I whispered in her ear.

She twisted around, and I lowered my mouth to hers, kissing her slowly. Her tongue coaxed my mouth open wider. I could taste citrus on her tongue from the orange she'd eaten not too long ago.

It was so easy to lose track of time with her. We made out in the kitchen for several seconds before Aleesa yelled, "EW!"

I huffed a laugh as Octavia did, then glanced over my shoulder at my daughter. She was standing on the couch and looking at me now, cupping her mouth with hunched shoulders, as if me kissing her Tava was the grossest thing in the world.

I chuckled. "Looks like it will take some getting used to for her as well."

# FIFTY-ONE

## OCTAVIA

There is something so magical about weddings.

I realize that's a cliché thing to say, but it's true. When the wedding is your only *sister's* wedding, that makes it even more enchanting.

It's interesting seeing everything come together after so many months of stressing and planning. From the color scheme to the florals, the wedding dress, the bridesmaids and groomsmen, and even the flower girl.

No stone was left unturned. Davina's wedding planner had made sure of that and had done an incredible job.

We had twenty minutes to go before the wedding started, and I was working on the final touches for our flower girl. Her ponytail was drooping. I didn't have any curlers on me, so I decided to roll her pony into a bun and pin it with bobby pins.

"Am I pretty, Tava?" Aleesa asked when I finally rose from my squat.

I was surprised I had managed squatting in my dress. It was beautiful—burnt orange and silky—but it hugged me at *every* single curve, and it didn't help that the bra I wore had push-up support so powerful it made my breasts look like double D's. Don't get me wrong, the dress was sexy as hell and I loved dressing nicely, but even I had my limits.

"You are *so pretty*, my love. And smart, kind, and brave." I gave her chin a squeeze. "I'm going to take you to Auntie Cat so you can hang out with her, okay?"

"'Kay." She grinned and reached for my hand. I held her tiny hand in mine and left the preparation room.

Cat was already standing in the lobby, waiting, wearing an emerald green dress and gold heels. Her eye shadow was green, too, and her dark-brown hair was in tight coils.

"There's my little monster!" Cat said.

Aleesa squealed and ran to her aunt. While she did, I took a peek out the door to where the wedding would commence, and the area was packed. Nearly every seat was filled. I spotted Naomi in a pale-yellow dress, walking to one of the seats, with her sister trailing behind her.

"Good grief," I muttered. "So many people."

"Yep. It's filling up fast," Cat said. "Everyone's ready to see those two seal the deal."

"I know it's only one hundred and fifty people, but it looks like way more than that."

Cat laughed. "This vineyard was an amazing pick. Seriously, the view behind the altar? I'm not really into the whole massive wedding ceremony thing, but I can see why brides go crazy over stuff like this."

"Well, let's hope my sister is still not going crazy and is still in sound mind." I laughed. "I'm going to find her. Text me if you need me."

"Go ahead. Tía's got this." Cat winked before turning with Aleesa and asking about her flower basket.

I breezed through the hallways, spotting through the windows a few guests walking toward the entrance. For some reason, my nerves were just as heightened as I'm sure Davina's were. This was a big deal for my sister. This was her second wedding, and I knew she had a lot of emotions about it.

I reached the bride's quarters and gave the door a knock.

The sound of heels clicking on the floor moved closer, and then the door cracked open.

"Password," my mother said, one eyeball practically poking through the opening.

"Mama, please." I laughed. "We don't have time for this. The yard is filling up."

"It is?" I heard Davina ask in a high-pitched voice.

Mama opened the door just wide enough for me to slip through. She was being so extra about this, I swear. She refused to let anyone but us see Davina before the wedding. Especially the groom. Deke and his groomsmen were on the other side of the damn building.

The only other people in the bride's quarters were the photographer and Davina's best friend, Tisha.

"Tavia, my nerves are all over the place," Davina said, facing me.

"I told her she needs to try and relax." Tisha stood right next to my sister and adjusted one of the curly tendrils in front of her face.

I'd seen Davina in her dress before, but now she was in the full ensemble, and it took me a moment to drink it in. Her hair was styled in side bangs, with the remainder coifed at the back of her head and loose tendrils on the sides. Some of the tendrils draped in front of her face as well, and a maroon flower pendant was attached to the side. It was messy yet elegant, and I loved the hairstyle on her.

Her makeup was flawless, with gold tones, her lips painted a deep wine red. I had to blink a few times to adjust to her flawless state.

"Octavia?" Davina called, eyes widening.

"Sorry," I said, rushing to her. "I'm just transfixed, girl. You look so good!"

Her eyes grew misty as I took her hands and held them. "I'm so nervous, sis. What if something goes wrong? Or Deke gets cold feet?"

"Please. That man is not getting cold feet," Tisha said.

"Agreed," Mama chimed in.

I smiled. "I'm with them. Deke has always been ready for you. The question is, Are you ready to spend forever with him?"

Davina's mouth twitched as the photographer snapped another picture. Then she nodded and raised her chin. "I am. I'm just . . . *ugh*. I just can't believe today is the day."

I squeezed her hands. "It's your day."

"I'll be right back. Just want to capture some final touches of the groom," the photographer said, and she ducked off before we could get a word in.

"Oh, if your daddy could see you now." Mama clasped her hands together. "You're so beautiful, baby, and today is going to be a good day. You hear me?"

Davina nodded, and a tear slipped down.

"Okay, let's not do that, please." I wiped her tear away as carefully as I could. "You're going to ruin your makeup!"

"I know." Davina giggled. "And the artist already left."

"Come here. Let me fix it." I guided her to the bench in front of the vanity, then reached for my cosmetics bag. She closed her eyes, and I gave her a quick touch-up with a blender brush before saying "There. Just like new. Deke is going to lose it, Vina. I'm telling you."

"I bet he will." She looked at herself in the mirror, fingering her tendrils. "I'm . . . I'm so happy. Like, beyond it, really."

"Aww." I bent down to hug her but didn't smoosh my cheek against hers like I normally did.

"Well, let's get our happy asses out there so we can get in formation," Tish commanded.

"I swear you are always acting like the assistant, Tish!" I teased.

She thumped me on the arm, and I thumped her back. This went on and on until my mother finally cleared her throat and said, "Girls. *Really?*"

"She started it," Tish muttered.

I snorted a laugh.

"All right. Let's go." Mama opened the door, and because she was extra, she looked both ways down the hall before nodding and leading the way out, as if she were hired security.

The photographer hustled back our way, as well as the wedding planner, Justine. She was a beautiful biracial woman. Her hair was miraculously still in place, considering how much running around she was doing to make sure everything was in order.

"Ah, there you are. Yes, yes, yes! Beautiful bride. You look so amazing." Justine flipped her wrist to check her watch. "Just in time. The groom and his men are already lined up, so I'm going to have your gorgeous bridesmaids pair up with them while you stay here, until it's time for your grand walk." Justine squealed. Yes, she was a squealer. I suppose she had to be if she wanted to be in this line of work and keep the bride excited.

Deke's groomsmen were Javier (of course); EJ; another Ravens teammate, named Jacobi Bennet; and Deke's brother-in-law, Jack. All the men wore ivory suits with burgundy ties and pants.

Every single one of them looked crisp, clean, and handsome.

Especially my man.

Javier smiled at me as he hooked his arm through mine. I couldn't help smiling back or feeling those damn butterflies again. He looked delectable in a suit.

"Have I told you how sexy you are in that dress?" he asked, his mouth so close to my ear it made my skin hum.

"You have. Several times today, in fact." I pressed my lips, looking up so I could meet his eyes.

"I just want you to be aware so you can remember why I cannot take my eyes off of you."

"Don't be naughty."

"It is impossible not to be, amor."

My stomach fluttered again, and I bit back my smile. *No, Octavia. You cannot jump this man's bones at your sister's wedding.*

Music began to play, cutting our conversation short.

Deke and his mother stood before us and began their walk down the aisle. Everyone started quietly cheering for him, and Deke Bishop, being the man he was, soaked it all up with a big grin.

We followed shortly after. Javier held on to me, his chin up and a soft smile gracing his lips. The rest of the wedding party followed suit, lining up on their respective sides at the end of the aisle.

Then it was Aleesa's turn.

She walked with her flower basket and a bashful smile. She was so adorable in her burgundy dress. She smiled the whole way, tossing flowers in chunks and waving at her dad in between.

Javier waved back a few times, chuckling to himself.

Aleesa reached the end of the aisle, and Cat swooped in to grab her hand and lead her away from the main area. She propped Aleesa in the seat between her and Paola, who gave her granddaughter a squeeze and quick praise.

The ring bearer was Deke's nephew, Eli, a handsome kid with dimples, just like his uncle. He was going to be just as charming as his uncle, too, considering how well he absorbed all the attention he was getting from the guests.

And then, finally . . . there was my sister.

She approached the top of the aisle, with my mother on one arm and my brother, Abe, on the other. I held a hand over my mouth, wanting to smile and cry at the same time.

That was *my* family. My people.

Davina stood in the center like an angel. So much hope in her eyes after all the dark days she'd endured was truly a sight to behold. There was a point when I didn't think she'd ever wear a full smile again. I'd tried to bring it out, of course, but her light had faded, so it had been useless.

But now . . . *wow*. She was glowing. She was stunning. She was restored, and that alone was beautiful.

I looked at the groom. His jaw was locked, but his eyes were filled with tears. They shimmered in the sunlight, and he shook his head, trying his hardest to fight those tears, but the emotion eventually won. Javier clapped his shoulder and gave it a proud shake. Deke swiped at his tears, but not once did he take his eyes off his walking bride.

And yeah . . . I was pretty much sobbing now. He had so much love for her. Lewis was great for Davina, yes, but Deke was a perfect match as well.

My mother and Abe handed her off once they reached the altar, and my mother walked with Abe to their seats.

As the officiant spoke and I watched my sister and Deke hold hands and stare into each other's damp eyes, there was one thing I knew for certain: Life can truly be a wondrous thing.

Yes, it's hard, and some days are darker than others, but let me tell you something: When you have true love in your life, nothing can ruin you. Especially when the love runs deep and conquers all odds. Love like this should be cherished because it's so insanely rare.

As those thoughts ran through my mind, all I could do was look at Javier. The man who I knew for certain was my soulmate. The man who made me feel whole after so many years of emptiness.

The man who protected me.

Kept me safe.

Nurtured me and brought me back to life.

He was for me, and I was for him.

Javier's eyes connected with mine, and I wanted to throw my arms around him and hold on forever. I wanted to feel his arms wrap around me and for him to whisper in my ear how much he loved me and how he'd never let me go.

It amazed me how, when I first started working for Javier, falling in love had been comical and a thing of the past. The idea of it had literally made me scoff, because there was no way in hell falling for someone and investing all your time and energy into them was worth it.

But, you see, love was never the problem. It was *fear*.

Fear of the unknown.

Fear of being hurt again.

Fear of becoming so vulnerable that I also became breakable.

I had carried that same fear with me for *years*, thinking if I let another man into my heart, he would ruin me just as much as Luther had. Giving another man that kind of power over me had been petrifying.

But, without even realizing it, Javier had slowly brought me out of that depressing state of mind. He'd been there through it all, so patient with me, caring, considerate, and understanding. He'd never mocked me for my feelings and never made me feel like I was wrong for how I felt. He'd simply accepted me for the damaged, flawed woman I was and held my hand through it.

And being at my sister's wedding, witnessing the real, genuine love floating between them, reminded me how important it is to have this kind of love—especially when it's with someone who only ever wants to see you happy.

Sure, the love you give can be weaponized when you place it in the wrong hands; however, when it comes from someone who promises to never hurt you, defy you, or betray you . . . well, nothing can beat that. Not even fear.

Deke and Davina shared vows, and they were beautiful. Truly, truly beautiful.

And their kiss . . . well, of course Deke went over the top with it. He tipped her back just enough to angle her face, winked at her, and then kissed her passionately.

Everyone cheered, squealed, and rejoiced.

Because they did it.

They made it.

And, my goodness, how sweet it was to witness.

# FIFTY-TWO

## JAVIER

Deke and Davina's wedding was food for the soul for many of us. I had never seen my best friend smile so much, or seen him look at a woman with so much adoration in his eyes. Davina was perfect for him.

During the reception, I watched the bride and groom share a dance, holding hands and gazing into each other's eyes. Deke said something that made Davina throw her head back and laugh. I prayed they'd continue laughing like that together for the rest of their lives.

They swayed to "Saving All My Love for You," and as Whitney Houston belted out her lyrics, my eyes shifted to Octavia, who was sitting at one of the tables, with Aleesa on her lap. Both of them watched the newlyweds with stars in their eyes.

I smiled, and as if Octavia could feel someone looking at her, her eyes swiveled my way. Her lips quirked up, and she raised a hand to her lips to blow me a kiss. I caught it and tucked it into my pocket.

The dance came to an end, and everyone cheered for the couple. Then the DJ produced livelier music for everyone to join in.

Octavia placed Aleesa on her feet before grabbing her hand. "I'm going to run her to the restroom," she said.

"Okay."

She walked past me, but not without pushing up on her toes and laying a kiss on my cheek. I watched her walk away, her hips swaying in that orange dress. Seriously. She looked good. If Aleesa weren't here, I'd have run her back to the main house, found one of the empty rooms, and had my way with her.

"You're so smitten." Catalina stood at my side.

I glanced sideways at her as she sipped from a champagne flute.

"Who even says that?" I laughed. "Smitten."

"Um, you're dating a bookworm. You might want to embrace that word."

I couldn't help my smirk. "Sure."

"I'm going to take Aleesa to the hotel so you and your girlfriend can have some alone time."

"You do not have to do that, Cat." I waved a hand. "It is fine. Aleesa will probably not be tired for another hour or so."

My sister turned her head to pin her eyes on me, planting a hand on my shoulder. "I wasn't asking. Octavia deserves to enjoy her sister's reception, and you deserve to have fun with her and your best friend without worrying about Leesa. You'll thank me later."

"But don't you want to enjoy the reception?"

She scoffed. "I don't think I've ever told you this, but I'm not a wedding person. In fact, I don't even really like them. I just tolerate them. They're overrated."

"So why'd you come?" I laughed.

"Because only a fool would deny an invitation to one of the most famous basketball players' weddings."

"Understandable."

"I'll run to the ladies' room to let Octavia know I'll be taking Aleesa." She gave my cheek a squeeze. She knew I hated when she did that, and I started to say so, until she said, "I love you, hermano. Have fun, okay?"

My face softened. "Te quiero, Catalina."

She downed the rest of her champagne before placing the empty flute down on a nearby table. I watched her go until she rounded the corner for the restrooms.

I stopped by one of the open bars for a neat whiskey before making my way across the room to where Deke and Davina were speaking to a few of their guests.

Deke spotted me and excused himself from one of the people he was talking to, then he pressed a hand to Davina's back and led her my way.

"Big J." Deke greeted me with a dap and a brotherly hug. "You enjoying yourself?"

"I am. You did not have to stop your conversation for me, you know?"

"Oh, trust me, that was not for you," Deke said. "That couple would've talked our heads off all night."

"Really?" Davina asked, glancing over her shoulder at the older couple.

"Oh, yeah. They're friends of my mom's, and you know that woman can talk."

"I can't wait to tell your mom you said that." Davina pretended to walk off, but Deke caught her by the arm and reeled her back in.

"You're my wife now. You can't snitch on me."

She laughed as he hugged her around the waist and kissed her.

"I would never."

They kissed again.

"Should I give you two some space or . . ."

Davina giggled, playfully pushing Deke away so he'd stop trying to kiss her.

"Deke Bishop!" someone called, and Deke peered over his shoulder to see his manager, Arnold. "Congrats, big guy!"

Arnold made his way toward us.

Deke sighed. "Let me chat him up really quick." He dropped a kiss on Davina's forehead this time. "I'll be back for you, wifey."

When Deke took off, Davina let out a dreamy sigh and shook her head.

"Congratulations, Davina." I raised my glass her way.

"Thank you, Javier." She faced me, clinging to a half-empty glass of champagne. "I'm really glad you're here."

"Of course. I would not have missed it for the world."

She continued a smile, darting her gaze to Deke. "I just hope I can keep him happy, you know?"

"Why do you say that?"

"Oh, I don't know." She inhaled, then exhaled. "He's such an amazing man, but he has his battles, you know?"

"I do." I nodded. "But now that he has you, he will not face those battles alone."

"That's true." She turned her eyes to the ceiling. "It's just so crazy how life happens, you know? One minute you feel like the saddest, most hopeless person on the planet, and then it turns into *this*." She lifted a hand, gesturing to the entire venue.

"It is bittersweet at first," I admitted.

"Yes. And I will never say that to him, but I can confess this to you because you get it. It's not easy moving on."

"No," I agreed. "It is not. Some days I feel like I do not deserve to move on."

"Same," she murmured. "But we do deserve it. *You* deserve it." She grabbed my hand and gave it a friendly squeeze. "Octavia is head over heels for you, and she loves you so much. And one thing about my sister is that she'll be there no matter what. You can count on her for *anything*. So take care of her, okay?" Davina's eyes watered. "Because she deserves to be loved too."

"Yes. She does." As I said that, I looked to my right, and Octavia was making her way to us. Her face was calm, and she was so beautiful beneath the dim gold lighting. "Your sister will be taken care of, Davina."

"Promise?"

I looked into her eyes. "I promise that and more."

"Good." She released my hand and sniffled. "Let me blink these tears away before she starts acting like my mama."

I chuckled as she turned a fraction, and Octavia finally made it to my side.

"Cat has run off with your daughter," she informed me, hooking an arm through mine.

"Has she?" I pressed my lips. "I guess that just leaves you and me, then." I leaned down to kiss her cheek.

"Vina?" Octavia tilted her head to look at her sister.

"Hmm?" Davina was avoiding looking at her.

Octavia pulled away from me to step in front of her sister. "Were you crying?"

"No! What are you talking about? No one's crying."

"Yes, you were!"

She unleashed a laugh. "Okay, fine, but it's because today has been so amazing."

"Aww, sis. Was it everything you dreamed it would be?"

"Oh, it was more, Tavia. Definitely so much more."

Octavia hugged her sister.

"Oh, Lord." Davina looked past Octavia, and I noticed she had her attention on Deke, who was now surrounded by several people. All of them seemed to be asking questions at the same time. He looked at Davina with wide eyes that screamed *Help me*, and she covered her mouth to suppress a laugh.

"I'd better get over there and whisk him away." She was already walking away. "Enjoy yourselves! I'll catch up with you in a bit."

When she was a good distance away and Octavia had returned to my side, I said, "She looks very happy."

"She is. Deliriously so."

The music changed to a slower tempo, and Octavia squealed before snatching my drink out of my hand and placing it on a nearby table.

"I love this song." She grabbed one of my hands and tugged on it. "Dance with me—wait, you do know how to dance, right?"

"Absolutely not. But I will learn for you."

She grinned as she led the way to the dance floor. I placed one hand on her waist while holding the other, then brought her closer so we were chest to chest.

In my periphery, I saw other couples find their way to the dance floor, but I kept my focus on the woman in front of me. I leaned down just enough for my mouth to graze her earlobe.

"I am not sure what my life would be like right now if you were not in it." My voice was low and softer than usual.

I leaned back again, just in time to see she was blushing.

"You'd probably have some other woman on this dance floor with you."

"I doubt it."

"Yeah. I doubt it, too, actually. You're way too stubborn."

We laughed.

She reached up to hold one side of my face, caressing her thumb over the apple of my cheek. "I love seeing you like this."

"Like what?"

"So . . . free and happy."

"Is that really what you see?"

"Yes. When I first met you, your eyes were so cloudy, and I'm not kidding when I say I worried for you. I hardly knew you, but I did worry because I could only imagine how hard your life was."

I shrugged. "It has not all been so bad."

"No. But it hasn't been kind to you either."

"Well . . . life isn't very kind to anyone these days. But the beauty of it is that with the right people around, there is a balm to smooth out those rocky days."

"I love that. You know, sometimes I think . . ." she started, but clamped her mouth shut just as quickly and lowered her gaze to my chest. "Never mind."

I tipped her chin back up with my forefinger. "Tell me."

She stared into my eyes a moment, then sighed. "Sometimes I think I won't be able to live up to what you had with Eloise."

That shocked me to hear. "Octavia . . ."

She pursed her lips.

"I do not expect you to live up to anyone or anything. It does not matter what I had with her. What matters is what I have with you right now and in the future." I gripped her chin between my fingers and leaned down to place a soft kiss on her lips. "That is all I care about right now. *Us.* I am hopeful for what is ahead—excited, even. I am ready to spend the rest of my life with you."

Her mouth quivered as she held on to the hand I had on her cheek. "Please don't tell me this only to change your mind about me later."

"Would you stop?" I pleaded with a small laugh. "*I love you*, Octavia Klein. I love you, and I want only you. If I have to repeat those words to you every single day in order for you to believe me, I will."

A breath of relief left her while she nodded.

The song transitioned as she raised both her arms to hang them over my shoulders. Our mouths met at the same time. Her lips were so supple and sweet.

"Okay," she said between kisses. "Do it. Tell me you love me every day so I can repeat the same words to you."

# FIFTY-THREE

## OCTAVIA

***FOUR MONTHS LATER***

I never thought a day would come when a six-foot-five giant would be walking around my childhood home.

It was Christmas Eve, and Javier was currently reaching into one of the cabinets in my mother's kitchen to retrieve a glass bowl for her.

"Look at that. He makes it look so easy." She marveled over how effortlessly he could reach into a cabinet and grab things. Perks of being tall.

He handed the bowl to her with a smile.

"You have a good one, Tavia."

"Mama, really?" I laughed as Javier snorted.

"Do you think this needs more seasoning?" Davina asked, in front of the stove.

Mama walked her way and grabbed a spoon, dipped it inside, and gave the soup a taste. "Nope. That's perfect."

"Just like you, baby!" Deke called out from the living room.

I looked over my shoulder to see him still sitting on the floor with Aleesa. She had been allowed to open one gift for Christmas, and it had been a nail polish set . . . from me. Javier wasn't pleased about it, but Aleesa loved it. And I had a feeling the only reason he didn't like my gift to her was because he knew she'd beg to paint his nails. As a matter of fact, she was in the process of painting Deke's nails a lovely shade of blue.

"Okay, Deke. All done." Aleesa grinned, shoving the nail brush back into the bottle. I was still trying to accept that she was speaking more clearly by the day. My sweet girl was getting so big.

Deke raised a hand into the air to study his new manicure. "Dang, Aleesa. You're gonna have all my friends jealous of this bomb-ass set."

"Deke!" Javier and I called at the same time. We looked at each other, and I grinned. He wrapped an arm around me, giving his head a deliberate shake.

"You know we do not like using bad words around her," Javier said, and you'd think he was scolding a child.

"What are you going to do when ours comes?" Davina asked, meeting Deke in the living room. He stood as she approached, a warm smile sweeping across his face as he placed a hand on her belly.

I still couldn't believe my sister was pregnant. I mean, damn. They must've had one hell of a honeymoon. She was only four months along, so she wasn't showing much yet, but she was glowing. That couldn't be said in the very beginning, though. She had been vomiting left and right and had to reschedule so many meetings for work.

How did I know this? Because she'd call me to gripe about how she hated rescheduling things. Said it made her appear unprofessional. Like, hello. You have a whole baby growing inside you. Anyone who didn't understand that didn't deserve her time, in my opinion.

Twenty or so minutes later, I was helping Mama pour soup into bowls while Christmas jingles played from Abe's speaker. He left his bedroom just in time to snag a seat right beside his favorite player, Bishop.

"King Abe." Deke smiled at him. "Where you been hiding?"

"My room," Abe answered. "I was watching some of your highlights earlier. The game yesterday was a close one."

"Oh, yeah. It was. But we won, that's all that matters."

"It's good you have Christmas off and get to be with Davina. I can't believe she's pregnant now."

Deke huffed a laugh as Davina did. "Yep, she sure is. Ready to become an uncle?"

"Not really." Abe reached for a hunk of sourdough bread.

"Well, all right." Deke chortled just as Davina suppressed a laugh.

I took my seat beside Aleesa after getting her situated. It was really nice to have Javier and Deke home for Christmas. Both had joined us in Maple Cove for a quiet, cozy, mountainous holiday. Honestly, it was perfect.

The lights were dim and the kitchen illuminated with candlelight in each corner. String lights hung from the window above the sink and twinkled from the tree in the living room. I could still smell a hint of pine beneath the scent of turkey-meatball soup, because one thing my mother never skimped out on was a Christmas tree. She always had to have a real one, and that thing would live long enough to see Valentine's Day.

After dinner, Mama broke out a bottle of wine and poured some for me. Davina made a face when I took a sip, and I said, "You wish that was you, huh?"

She playfully shoved me. "Shut up!"

Javier had been roped in by Aleesa to have his nails painted blue. But he'd only agreed to having one hand painted, and only after quietly asking me if my mother had nail polish remover so he could take it off right after.

I sipped my wine, watching as he sighed and waited for her to finish. Once she was done, he stood and said, "Great. I need to run and get something from the car. I will be right back."

I watched him go, mildly confused. Aleesa made her way to me and grabbed my hand. "You want red, Tava?"

"Oh, no, baby. I already got my nails done. See?" I wiggled my fingers, and she observed each one carefully. Then she released my hand and made a *pfft* noise, as if to say *fine, but you're missing out.*

"So do you want a boy or girl?" I asked Deke. I knew Davina's answer. She didn't mind the idea of either.

"Honestly . . . whatever God gives me, I'll take it." Deke sat on the sofa, his back against the arm of the couch and one leg up. Davina sat between his legs, with her back resting on his chest, and held on to the arm he had wrapped around hers. "Whether it's a boy or girl, they're gonna have to know how to ball, though."

Davina laughed. "What if they don't want to be athletic?"

"Well, they better get into it." Deke placed a hand on her stomach. "You hear that, little Bishop? Get into it."

Everyone in the room broke out in laughter.

The front door opened, and Javier entered again. His cheeks, as well as the tip of his nose, were slightly pink from the cold. He walked into the living room and took a look at everyone.

"Is now okay?" he asked, focusing on Davina and Deke.

Confused, I looked from him to my sister and brother-in-law, who both nodded with warm smiles.

Javier drew in a breath, eyes turning to me. The fireplace was going, so his eyes seemed to sparkle as he approached me.

And then he did something I did not expect.

He dropped down on one knee and took one of my hands in his.

My heart started beating faster. "Javier, what are you doing?"

"I am asking you a very important question," he said with a boyish smile.

He squeezed my hand with one of his while his other dug into his front pocket. When he took out the ring box, my breath hitched. Aleesa started for her dad, but Mama swooped in and picked her up.

"Octavia, the time I have spent with you has been incredible. I wish I could put into words just how you make me feel, but . . . I am not a man who is very good with words." His mouth quirked. "As you know, English is not my first language."

My eyes began to water. "I know. It's okay."

"But what I am good at is providing facts. And I know for a fact that I love you—no, I am *in love* with you. I love that I get to come home to you, and I love that you are there for me and Aleesa. I also know that if I do not act on how I feel right now, there is a possibility that you will slip through my fingers, and I refuse to let that happen. So . . ."

He flipped open the ring box to reveal a princess-cut diamond ring that caught the light of the fire and glistened magnificently.

"If my plan is to hold on to you and our love, and to work on us every single day—if my plan is to make sure you are happy, *safe*, and loved, I do not want you to have any doubts." He pursed his lips as he shook his head. "Ay, I am no good at this."

A laugh bubbled out of me. "No, baby. You're doing great."

"Yeah?"

"Yes. I promise."

"You've got this, Valdez," Deke called.

A boyish smile took over him. "Octavia Klein, you are an amazing woman with a very beautiful heart. Not only do I want you in my life forever, but I want you to be in Aleesa's as well. So . . . will you marry me?"

"Hell, yes!" I breathed, throwing my arms around his neck.

A deep chuckle filled his throat as he hugged me below the ribs.

Deke whooped. "That's my boy!"

"Aww, my sweet baby girl!" Mama sang. "Let me get the champagne!"

"Yay, sis!" Davina cheered, clapping her hands.

I pulled away, and Javier did, too, but only so he could remove the engagement ring from the box and slide it onto my finger.

"My mother and Cat helped me pick it out," he said. "They are upset that they could not be here, but they want to FaceTime with us later."

I couldn't stop the big, goofy smile from spreading wider across my face. "We'll definitely FaceTime them." I studied the ring, almost going breathless. "Are you sure about this?" I asked, swooping my gaze up to his again.

Javier gave my chin a squeeze, his eyes softening and locking onto mine with intention. He then kissed me so deeply and passionately that I was left with no choice but to sigh.

"I have never been more certain about anything in my life," he murmured on my lips. "I want to marry you. I want you to be my wife. No one else. Okay?"

"Okay." I sniffled. "I love you. I love you so much." I pressed my lips to his, another tear skidding down my cheek.

"Te amo mucho, mi amor," he whispered in my ear.

# EPILOGUE

## JAVIER

***TWO AND A HALF YEARS LATER***

"Daddy." A hand gripped my arm and gave it a hard shake. "Daddy, get up! Ballet camp starts today!"

I groaned, peeling one eye open and spotting Aleesa's big green eyes. Her curly hair framed her face, and with a slight glance down, I noticed she was fully dressed in a black leotard and white tights.

"Where is Tava? I want a ponytail braid, and she does it really good."

Her question was a good one. I looked to my right, only to see Octavia wasn't in the bed. "Did you check the kitchen?" I asked. Most mornings my wife loved being in the kitchen.

"Yes. She's not there."

I sat up and rubbed my eyes. Footsteps thumped through the hallway, and before I knew it, Octavia appeared. But she wasn't alone. In her arms she had Remi, our six-month-old son and one of my three brightest lights.

"Good news is he slept through the night," my wife said, walking deeper into the room and placing Remi belly down on the center of the bed. "Bad news is he woke up, decided to poop, and pretty much had a bomb go off in his diaper. I'm talking baby poop *everywhere*."

"Ew." Aleesa scrunched her nose. "Good thing I didn't smell it."

Octavia laughed. "Good thing, indeed."

"Give me that big boy." I reached for my son and held him close. He looked at me with a slight scowl. "Okay, I am serious when I say this, Octavia. Our baby does not like me."

"Oh my goodness, stop it," she said. "Yes he does. He loves you."

"Well, why does he only frown at me when I hold him?"

"He just has to get used to you being around. That's all. Now that summer has started and you won't be on the road as much, you two can bond more."

"I guess so."

"Leesa, ready for camp?" Octavia asked.

"Yes! I can't wait to go! I've been practicing so much! Oh, and the paper thingy you had said they are giving us ice cream when we're finished today." Aleesa climbed onto the bed to sit beside Octavia. "Can you do my hair and put a ribbon like last time?"

"Of course I can, my love. What color ribbon?"

"Hmm . . . purple," she answered.

"Purple it is." She gave Aleesa a wink, then turned her attention to me. "I can drop her off. Will you be okay with Remi?"

"Of course I will be okay," I confirmed. "He is my son."

"Well, I'm just asking. I don't want him frowning you to death."

"Ha ha," I deadpanned. "Very funny."

She giggled, walking around the bed and placing a kiss on my lips. Then she dropped a kiss on Remi's forehead. When she did, Remi started bouncing, kicking his feet, and even reaching for her.

"You're Mama's sweet boy, aren't you?" she cooed to him, and I couldn't believe it, but he smiled for her. Just like that. She made it seem like such an easy thing to pull out of him.

"What about your daddy?" I asked, lifting Remi up so he could look at me too. Once again, Remi lost the smile and stared me down. "See, Aleesa was not like this. He is so . . . serious."

"Well . . . you are his father, GG."

Aleesa giggled. "Yeah, Grumpy Giant!"

Octavia kissed me on the cheek before making her way to the door. "Come on, Leesa. Don't want you to be late on your first day."

With a smile, I watched my girls go. I noticed that I was doing a lot more of that the last couple of years. Smiling. It felt good. My therapist said it was good. He said I was making true progress. That I was healing.

I watched Aleesa grab Octavia's hand and cling to it before they rounded the corner and disappeared. It pleased me to see Aleesa was so comfortable with her stepmom. She looked up to Octavia so much, and Octavia took care of and raised her like she'd birthed Aleesa herself.

I placed my son on my lap and cradled him in one arm, studying all his features—his light-brown skin and dark curls. His eyes were just as chocolaty brown as Octavia's, and he had my nose. His upper lip was slightly bigger than his bottom lip, just like his mother's. I know all parents say this, but he was a really cute baby. Too bad he hated me.

"You will learn to love me," I said as he continued glaring at me like a hawk. "Because whether you realize it or not, mi corazón, I will always love you."

I tickled him under his chin. His skin was warm and soft, which made me smile because it comforted me in a way. Having this delicate baby boy in my arms.

To my surprise, the corners of Remi's little mouth quirked up. He cooed and kicked his feet, peering up at me with bright eyes.

My heart swelled in my chest because this was perfect.

This moment. This life of mine. I had it all and could not have asked for anything better.

There was something Octavia had said on the day Remi was born that continuously ran through my mind. A few hours after his birth, she'd taken one look at our son, with tears in her eyes, then she'd looked at Aleesa, who sat on the bed right next to Remi because she was so excited to become a big sister.

Octavia sniffled before finding my eyes. She was so overcome with emotion that, for a second, she couldn't speak. Her mouth opened and closed, until finally she said, "We're so lucky to have sweet little hearts like theirs in our lives."

When she said that, I'd taken one look at my beautiful family sitting on that hospital bed and realized that I had survived.

Life had tried to wear me down and failed. The devil had aimed to trap me—to keep me low and defeated—but I was ripped out of his dirty clutches and provided heaven on earth. Right here. With my family.

And even now, there is one thing I know with absolute certainty . . .

No matter what comes my way, I will cherish all three of their *sweet little hearts* forever.

# ACKNOWLEDGMENTS

As always, I have to give thanks to God for allowing me to prosper with my career. I've gone through many obstacles and setbacks and shed lots of tears, and yet I'm still able to live my dream because of Him.

To my husband, Juan, who is always rooting for me and supporting me in every way. You helped me with so much for this story in particular, especially regarding Javier, his family, your beautiful culture and language, and the tidbits you knew about Argentinean culture. I'm so grateful to have you. Te amo mucho, mi amor!

To my darling agent Georgana, a.k.a. my *Georgie*—you never fail to amaze me. I would not be where I am without your constant support, love, and efforts. You've undoubtedly changed my life and my family's for the better. I'm beyond blessed to have you. Here's to many more books!

Thank you so much to Anh and Lindsey for once again believing in my book baby! It's always such a pleasure brainstorming and developing a better novel with you two, and I love that you care about my characters as much as I do.

To my entire family—there are way too many of y'all to list, but I love y'all and am so lucky to share blood with you, because without our family's strength and resilience, I wouldn't be the woman I am now.

And I'm almost positive that if you've read the acknowledgments from my previous books, you knew this one was coming. To my beautiful readers, I will say this until I no longer have breath in my lungs: I *cannot* be an author without you. I am here because of *you.* Even when it's hard—even when I feel like giving up—I push through because your continuous support gives me just enough confidence to keep going. You embrace me for who I am as a writer, and that's all I can ever ask for. I adore you all so much. Thank you for being on this journey with me.

# LET'S STAY CONNECTED

Sign up for my newsletter to stay updated and to receive exclusive information, graphics, teasers, and so much more!

For updates, teasers, and more fun exclusives:

**Follow me on Instagram:** @reallyshanora

**Follow me on TikTok:** @theshanorawilliams

**Join my Facebook Group:** Shanora's Shawties

Visit www.shanorawilliams.com for merch, info, and more details.

*Psssttt . . . I'm most active on Instagram, by the way!*

# ABOUT THE AUTHOR

*Photo © Alexis Beauford of A. Beauford Photography*

Shanora Williams is a *New York Times* and *USA Today* bestselling author known for her versatile voice, diverse characters, and high-stakes love stories. When she isn't writing, she's deep in family life, binge-watching her favorite shows, working out, or getting cozy with a book. She lives near Charlotte, North Carolina, with her husband and three sons.